REVELATIONS

Other publications by this author

Poems
Yakhal'inkomo
Tsetlo
No Baby Must Weep
Behold Mama, Flowers
The Night Keeps Winking
A Tough Tale, Kliptown Books
Third World Express
Come and Hope with Me
Freedom, Lament and Song
History is the Home Address

Essays
On the Horizon
Hyenas

Novels
To Every Birth its Blood
Gods of Our Time
Scatter the Ashes and Go

REVELATIONS

Mongane Wally Serote

First published by Jacana Media (Pty) Ltd in 2010

10 Orange Street
Sunnyside
Auckland Park 2092
South Africa
+2711 628 3200
www.jacana.co.za

© Mongane Wally Serote, 2010

All rights reserved.

ISBN 978-1-77009-808-4

Cover design by publicide
Set in Garamond 11/14
Job No. 001331
Printed by Ultra Litho (Pty) Ltd Johannesburg

See a complete list of Jacana titles at www.jacana.co.za

BOOK ONE

Let our lives be a revelation
as we pass on…

Chapter 1

BRA SHOPE TOLD ME that his ex-wife had left their home more than a dozen times before they parted forever. Tears welled in his eyes as he said this. If a person could give themselves to another, he said, he felt he'd done so: he'd given his body, his spirit and his mind, whatever their worth, to Tembile.

Sometime early in our friendship we were in Maputo when for some reason he decided to relate this to me. She too, he said, felt she'd given her everything. They'd given the best of themselves to their relationship. What had hurt him most, Bra Shope said, was when a sense of slipping away took over between them – hour by hour, day by day, week by week, he and Tembile drifted, slid apart, and he felt helpless as it happened. The more he tried to stop the trend, the more it escalated; the more he stood by and watched, the more apparent it became that he was helpless to reverse the situation.

These thoughts about his past life with his wife were pre-empted, I think, by our visit to the home of Dambuza, one of Africa's best painters and sculptors, with whom Bra Shope had grown extremely warm. I'd never witnessed him laughing so much as we relished prawns, beans, rice, pawpaws and pineapples, gradually becoming soaked in brandy. Dambuza's wife Olga was an extremely beautiful African woman, anchored in tradition but also steeped in the twenty-first century. She spoke fluently and with great ease in Tsonga, isiZulu, Portuguese and English, using the languages interchangeably depending on whom she was speaking to. With us were Vivian from South Africa, who'd arranged this Maputo visit and exhibition, and two other young painters, a woman and a man, the helpers Gebuza and Dulce. They came in and out bringing this or that, mingling, extricating themselves, watching, integrating here, whispering to Olga, smiling, pouring drinks and sitting down to eat, obviously listening and curious, yet also detached and polite. It was an intimate moment in a home that was firmly in Olga's grip, but where her husband presided and was obviously cherished.

When we returned to our hotel, Bra Shope found a way to stall me in the foyer.

"A most pleasant night," he said. "An unforgettable night."

We sat on the veranda, the sea hissing and roaring very close to us.

"No man or woman," he suddenly said, "human as they are, should ever think they can control another or tell them what to do. No! That's the stuff of the military, or of witches and wizards. No one on earth was born to be controlled, no one! Do you hear what I'm saying, Otsile?"

"Mmm, I do."

"Do you?"

"Are you going to give me an order now?"

He laughed and pointed at me, throwing his head back and flipping his hat.

"Yes, I'm going to give you an order. Because if you don't know what your grandfather or great grandfather have said and done, where they come from, the why and the how – and I'm their peer, so I can tell you – then, my son, how will you know which door not to open, or which to close?"

"Okay, I'm ready for your order," I said.

"Then let me tell you what the big problem was between

me and Tembile. She was a beautiful person, very loving. But we fought."

In a sense Bra Shope was talking about something I already knew, yet knew nothing of. There was a long silence.

"We were both masters at the same time," he said finally.

"How do you mean?"

"I mean there was no follower… Neither one could remain a follower forever."

"But why in a love relationship should one be a follower and the other master?"

"It's about how the one who turns out to be master handles their responsibility."

"Where is Aunt Tembile now?"

"Out in the world, somewhere far away. I don't know. Now and then I think about her and wonder whether she ever thinks of me. But don't let me speak of Tembile with you…"

Bra Shope was at ease, tipsy but not drunk, relaxed as a leopard on the sofa. He held his glass of whisky in his hand for a long time. Dambuza and Olga had touched something in him.

ଔ

We spent four days in the gallery in Maputo while Bra Shope was arranging the many small pieces he'd made with his hands – mating dogs, a peeing rhino, a one-eyed lion, a three-legged leopard chasing a springbok, a monkey searching her young for ticks as she dangled it by the tail. They were fashioned of wood, clay, stone, iron, beads, papier mâché, wire. Some were mere suggestions.

I stayed with him in the gallery. At times we had *mageu* for supper, at other times homemade ginger beer and buns or fruit. I shot many portraits of him during those four days and nights. I was less interested in the pieces; I felt he'd come here for other reasons and I was cynical. Somehow I felt myself rebelling against his lie; he hadn't come here to exhibit; he was merely curious about Maputo and had seized the opportunity when he was asked to exhibit.

Yet when I looked back before we left the gallery on the fourth day, the space had changed: the lighting, the use of space, the mountings, the colours reflected from myriad tiny forms – all seemed to call out quietly, to say, look! Bra Shope was sitting on the sofa in one corner, his hat tipped backwards. I shot a few pictures in black and white and in colour. For some reason you looked and looked again, as if called, or in disbelief or recognition. You couldn't be neutral when confronted with these small pieces from the hands of Bra Shope.

At the opening the gallery was full. People stayed for a long time, walking about, speaking in quiet tones. The media commented that this was an unusual exhibition. It captivated people; it kept them involved. Some of his pieces you had to pick up and examine to know what they were. Some you had to hold up to the light. People didn't know what to say or how to react; they were forced to interact because of the smallness of these artifacts that somehow demanded a closer look.

Bra Shope was saying something through this exhibition. He had told me before we went to Maputo that I should always watch people's hands. Hands are never indifferent, he'd often say. They shape the world, they shape life. The way people use their hands defines their relationships with others. Nations express their intentions through their hands; hands express a people's spirit.

He wanted me to take as many pictures as possible as people picked up the artifacts, held them to the light, smelled them, showed the artifacts to each other. I watched. I focused my lens on their hands: male and female, fingers, fingernails, arms; capturing them all.

This exhibition formed part of Mozambique's Independence Day celebrations, in this city whose people had once rocked southern Africa. Such ululation there had been throughout Africa and its diaspora when Maputo became Maputo. Since then the city had sunk and sunk, until one day there was a major plane crash in Mbuzini. What was that about, we wondered? How was it possible for a plane carrying a president to crash? But it had, and all these years later we were still asking why, and the silence was deafening. Bra Shope had discussed and pondered this with Dambuza and Olga, and raised many questions.

"South Africa must answer those questions," Bra Shope kept saying as we drove back to the hotel. Meanwhile the city of Maputo was unfolding before us – a township, a rural village, a town, signs of a city. Crowds at bus stops, on stoeps, at corners, walking, running, baggage in their hands, on their shoulders, on their heads. Cows and goats, poles, rubbish, broken vehicles and modern cars, scooters, bicycles and buses. Maputo with changed street names, long, wide streets that spoke Portuguese. A city abuzz with people selling every imaginable thing on corners and even in the middle of the street when the lights were red. Poor people on foot dwarfed by buildings that once sought to reflect Portugal, Spain, Italy, standing beneath the African sun by day and the African moon by night. Long streets aflame with fires and braziers and the flicker of faded street lights on tall steel poles casting long shadows in hasty flight; streets brimming with people and the blast of music. Maputo was no Portuguese city. It was a city on African soil, a city in lament, poor but culturally rich. It was a city of many languages, a Tsonga city that spoke to the Indian Ocean; a sweet and salty city that smelled of fruit and fish.

We broke away from the varied faces of Maputo and

drove up to the hotel. There we were saluted by the doorman, with his dark black skin, funny hat and badges more colourful than the rainbow on the lapels of his coat. He flashed a white but expressionless smile. Bra Shope was part of the tapestry here; he'd brought his contribution to this city, and since he'd been on TV, everyone everywhere seemed to recognise and greet him.

Chapter 2

CITIES, THESE THINGS WE call cities, are the same the world over. Cement, tar, brick, iron, electricity, lights of red, blue, pink, white, and a sprinkling of sun, wind, trees and flowers. Then streets, cars, people upon people and all the merchandise they want and don't want. At times they all seem to project the fragility of life; at other times they make life itself shrivel. Windowpanes by the hundreds, many storeys high, were twinkling against the morning light and the traffic lights; millions of eyes goggling at the city, staring in wonder, screaming with joy at the sight of it until I, too, felt gazed at.

I realised that I'd been walking awhile and had hardly met or seen a single black face. What had this city and its people done with their blacks? Yet I couldn't say that these people were whites – they were nothing like that.

Certainly some were so-called whites, but most were yellow or honey or brown. Yet there were no black people in this city. I became a bit apprehensive, I didn't know why. What would I do if I met a black person? I hadn't seen one, yet I hoped, I hoped I'd find one somewhere here among these millions of people. They didn't look at me directly, I noticed; here people looked at you by looking elsewhere, searching the empty space above your head. I looked them in the eye. Some smiled. Some were shy; some giving me a what-the-fuck look; I saw it in their eyes, their frowns. We strode past each other, propelled by the buzz and roar and rattle and hoot of the city. We were all busy going about our own chores, each of us together, those of us who'd woken up that morning and set out onto the streets of Santiago.

I'd never been here before. I'd always felt intrigued, suspicious, afraid and baffled about this country, this city. As a young African man, careful, watchful and curious, I'd heard of this country, this city, of Allende and Lumumba. I began to walk faster now; a bit angry, a bit fearful. I watched eyes, faces. And I remembered the woman who'd been shot in front of me...

Her face was so shocked, so afraid. Her eyes, staring and helpless, said no, no, no! Then her body took the impact as if beginning a terrible dance, a revelation. She threw her hands into the air, to the sky, her bag flew off her shoulder and her dress flew about, her body jerking and jerking as the bullets made little red holes in her, revealing her white panties before she hit the ground.

But that was far from Santiago.

Why had I walked into the cathedral? I hadn't been to church for centuries. But I was feeling sad, wanting to cry. I knelt on the hard wood beside a man who was now getting ready to stand up and go.

Our eyes met; even our pupils. Who the hell are you, I thought. I didn't know what he thought of me; his eyes were soft. He looked away quickly and stood up to go. Chile was a Catholic country, I'd been told. In my anger at this church I had once asked an old priest if they still mass-produced virgins. Now as I knelt here I thought, yes, the world needs thousands of virgins – a sure way to fight Aids.

Then I noticed all these elderly men entering the cathedral to kneel, make the sign of the cross, take a quick kiss at their thumb and leave. They were old men; they stood up, bowed, then walked out. Who were they? Where were they when Allende was besieged, bombed and shot, when there was a coup, when people began to disappear? Where were all these men and women then, who now come to pray? I didn't know why, but I felt contemptuous, angry, and also apprehensive. I stood up to go.

Outside, I was hit by the sunlight and the buzz of the city.

※

I don't know how to say this, but I must try. I saw a woman walk past me. Hell broke loose: she was dark, very dark, blue-black; she walked almost quickly, yet slowly, deliberately. I didn't see her face but only her legs, strong as if made of steel, but gentle as a cloud in the ease with which they carried her – then she disappeared. I was left with the image of her silky navy-blue jacket, striped blouse, short maroon skirt and high sandals. I should have called to her, said or done something. She must have seen me from behind, maybe snatched a glimpse as she passed me. Before I could do anything she was gone. Something told me she was very beautiful. But who was she? From where had she come?

Is she asking herself where I come from? From South Africa, I replied, alone on that long noisy street: I wanted to hold her, to embrace her; to look her in the eye and ask her to come and have coffee with me. She was so beautiful, I thought, strong, almost my own size, this lone black woman walking a Santiago street slowly, firmly, giraffe-like, so aware of the world around her, walking as if to a drumbeat. A line from a history class long ago came to mind: African people had developed the drum and its use to the fullest… But I hated this thought: I didn't want the world to connect Africans only with drums…

Where did this lone black woman come from? She'd walked as if fleeing her own vulnerability, watchful, aware, her step quick as a bird preparing for flight; except that she was already moving. Where was she going on a Santiago morning, walking down the street like that? Who was she here with, and for what? Asking that question made me suddenly heave deep in my gut. I felt I was going to vomit... I was lost at sea, feeling the waves, large and angry. Slaves: did Chile have slaves, like Brazil? Yes, the Mapuche. Where are they now?

Their spirits were in the skin, blood and marrow of the Chileans, who were not white at all! Here I was walking among them, Bra Shope and I as their guests, and they our hosts, the people of Chile... Had Bra Shope already realised this? He had the stealth of a cat, he seemed to sniff his way through his eyes; his frog-like eyes that could see a hundred and eighty degrees. He would have been studying our hosts like that.

Where had she gone, that black woman? Maybe, wherever she was, she was wondering to herself about that black man. I'd never know.

I was missing Teresa, and her brown eyes that stare back in surprise. That blue-black woman on the Santiago street had looked like Teresa, walked like Teresa. I would never tell Teresa about her. No, no, I must; I would. But what could I say of such a brief encounter with an unknown woman? Teresa liked to probe; and when she did, what would I say? That the damned cathedral was so overwhelming, that its pillars made me feel like an ant, like a thing; that on a Monday morning, the Chileans go there to pray?

Something here in Santiago reminded me of Maputo. What was it? The buildings, the people? There were no black people here. Perhaps it was the architecture or the language. Here also a president had died at the hands of his own citizens. The previous day I'd seen Mrs Allende: the frail frame, the old face, and what was it? A strength, a will, a spirit with a will to live: Mrs Allende was determined to live. I thought of Graça. Even now in the troubled times of the twentieth century, presidents get killed... Who had killed Allende? Like Lumumba and Machel, Allende was a dreamer. There were those who didn't like dreamers, who hated them.

I wasn't very far, I realised, from Guyana. At Chris Hani's funeral, it was a photographer who'd told me that Guyana's president, Walter Rodney, had been a dreamer, too: he'd wanted the ordinary people to govern Guyana.

"Press the red button on this walkie-talkie," they'd told him, "and it'll connect you with us in the army." So Rodney had pressed the red button. His family buried only his head and possibly his legs: the rest were blown away.

I didn't know why these broken pictures of history keep coming to mind. I was worried about Teresa. I must call her tonight... what time was it in South Africa? It was 8 am now in Santiago, I had to get back to the hotel to see if Shope had woken.

଼

I was drinking tea after my long morning walk. Santiago was like many cities I'd been to, I decided, although the only other Spanish-speaking cities I'd seen were Buenos Aires and Montevideo. Montevideo was multiracial; but Santiago was white, and Buenos Aires very white; yet neither was truly white. Why didn't they call themselves brown? The white here wasn't the white of London or Paris or Bonn; it was a browned white. Yet there was something in the features, in the blood, as the saying goes, that was neither white nor black, and since, for some reason, all white that is mixed is no longer white, in a sense I wasn't in a white city. Neither Santiago nor Buenos Aires nor Montevideo were white, but they weren't black either, even if they regarded themselves as white. Only Maputo saw itself as black.

I began pondering why the Europeans had decided

that the first people of America deserved to be hunted and killed. Why did the Americans decide that Africans should be hunted and enslaved? A white woman once told me that a man's desire for women was the same as the compulsion of Europeans to commit genocide in Africa, Europe and Asia.

It was still dangerous to be black in the world. So I kept wondering what on earth all these people, these Chileans, thought about us. I know, I know, we were saved by Mohammed Ali, Bill Cosby, Mandela and Oprah, and maybe that was why we now and then received a smile or some courtesy from managers and waiters. Besides, there were now black diplomats, which meant that there were black countries…

At times you feel someone looking at you. I felt so now. And there she was, that same black woman, seated at a table not far from me. Our eyes met and she smiled a most beautiful smile. Strange how a smile can reflect the inner being of a person. She continued eating.

The restaurant was crowded. In a busy hotel like this one, you were bound to ask yourself who all these people were. Where did they come from? Where were they going? Their languages, their accents, their style of kissing, the way they held hands, men and women, women and women, or men and men: all these were answers. I stood up and walked towards her. She expected this. She stood up, extended her hand, and we shook hands.

"Hi," she said. She sounded Afro-American.

"How are you?" I asked.

"Fine. Are you from South Africa? Yes? We've just come from there. A real fine country."

"Where in the US are you from?"

"Well, my folks come from Georgia."

"That's in the south, isn't it? What took you to South Africa?"

"I'm with the Avin Ikes Dance Theatre," she said. "And you, what do you do?"

"I'm a photographer," I said.

Just then, a tall man joined us. "Meet my colleague, Bill Boyant," she said.

Bill was very tall and strong, the colour of chocolate, and his brown eyes darting from their sockets seemed almost animal-like, were it not for his smile. But his smile cleared everything, and made him a lovable child with a happy, friendly face, a loving face that, like his eyes, told you something deep about him, something buried and glittering.

"I'm Otsile," I said, "how do you do."

We greeted, and he too recognised my accent as South African.

I turned back to the woman. "Please, before I forget," I said, "what's your name?"

"Melba," she said.

We settled down at her table with fruit juice and yoghurt.

"What brings you to Santiago?" Bill asked.

"I'm following a famous South African artist here," I said. "And you?"

"We've come to dance," Melba said.

"Following an artist?" Bill enquired.

"Yes sir," I said. "He's old, he travels a lot and he's been talking about Santiago for a long time. Chile, really, but I've discovered that he really means Santiago. Since we arrived here he's been offered many trips around the country, but keeps postponing them. He's busy, he says, but all I see him do is read, look at pictures and walk around Santiago, asking this and that. Now that I think about it, I suppose he *is* actually busy!" I grinned. "Have you been to any other African countries?" I asked them.

"Yes," Melba said, "to Senegal, Ghana, Mali and Zimbabwe."

"And to South Africa, Angola, Zimbabwe, Botswana and Mozambique," said Bill.

"I've been to the US, but mainly New York," I said.

Melba was struggling with my name, but I insisted on the correct pronunciation. Melba smiled and tried again.

"*Alright*!" Bill said. "I wish I had a French name, or something you couldn't pronounce: I'd also insist you get it right."

"Mine's a seTswana name," I said. Neither dared attempt the word seTswana.

"A friend of mine gave me the name Dimakatso," Melba said. She pronounced it *Dee-maa-ka-cho*, and scribbled it for me on a piece of paper.

"Bill," I said, "you must find a Motswana, Moswahili, Amharic or Kikuyu woman to give you your name."

In that moment of silence that followed, a terrible memory held me. Whose child was Bill? Whose child was Dimakatso? If the chain were reversed and we held its beads in our bare fingers, and began to move backwards to its origin, what would we find? Who said there was something called the middle passage? If we followed the chain back, it would lead us to the African continent, to the land and homesteads of lovers, children, fathers, wives and mothers, to the blue sky, the heat of the sun, and the fear, terror and insanity from what had befallen our people: the long, long chain of human beings hunted and chained and put on boats on that sheet of blue sea, where light and shadow and dark formed an endless mirror, at times concave, unable to carry anything on its surface, carrying the boat and cargo to nowhere, where people vanished as if into a deep hole, a hole that could never be filled.

"I don't know why all those people I met didn't give me an African name," Bill said.

"You met many people, though?"

"I did, I did," he said, his face blank. I became aware of his strong neck, his broad shoulders, his biceps and hands as large and powerful as weapons.

"He met them, alright," Dimakatso said. "He flashed his smile and charmed them... didn't you, Bill?"

"I was overwhelmed," he said, "I didn't really know what to do," he said.

"You smiled and smiled, Bill, didn't you?"

"What else could I do?"

Dimakatso coughed. Bill began to laugh, and we became aware of the music of the hotel filling the air, and of other people eating, whispering and gesturing to each other, engrossed eye to eye or looking lost in this Santiago hotel.

"So you're a photographer?" Dimakatso turned to look straight at me, searching my being.

"Yes."

"What kind of photography do you do?"

"I search out the barriers people put around themselves; I scale and violate them to enter their private space. And then I find the light and the shadow and the being of the person. And I click."

"That sounds real bad," she said.

"Rude," Bill said.

"Well I'm a photographer," I said. "And you?"

"What?"

"You dance?"

She nodded. "It has a short lifespan, so I dance each time as if it's the last, I can only hope that I do what I have to as a dancer," she said.

"What must a dancer do?"

"We dance from inside, through here," she said, gently placing the palm of her hand on her stomach. "We speak in silence through movement."

Bill was looking out at Santiago through the largest

window in the world. Beyond were the dappled colours of flowers, dead still, the green of the grass and trees, and the blue of the sky. Someone was laughing at another table, and now and then the cutlery rang out across the restaurant, among tables draped in red and white like altar boys, the Spanish sounding at times like people gargling.

"For those of us who are just a step out of the horror of being black," I said, "our problem is that our existence is far from our roots. We're like fish out of water."

"It's horrible," Bill said.

"But why should the world not be our stage?" Dimakatso asked.

"Because it's not where we come from, it's not real for us, it's irrelevant. It has rules that aren't our own." I said.

"I get you," Dimakatso said. "There's a lot wrong in this world."

"There is," I said. "But still, it created us."

"It did," she said. "We have to keep trying to get back in there," she said.

I nodded.

"And not be like dead fish," Bill said.

We fell quiet, and the whole hotel became alive again: waiters striding across the floor, clients drifting in and out; piped hotel music flooding the room. The sunshine spread across the room like a silver mat, climbing and descending the tables, running over chairs and people, tossing shadows that melted into funny shapes all over the room. The three of us were drawn together as if alone. Dancers and actors never really leave the stage, I thought, they stretch, aware of their next performance. Bill and Dimakatso were back there once more, having seized the silence. The voice of our silence grew loud and clear.

"I must be going now," Bill said.

"Don't leave me behind," said Dimakatso.

As they rose to leave, I wasn't able to tell from the rings on their fingers if they were married or not.

"Be seeing you." Bill said.

"You take it easy now," Dimakatso said. They strode out.

Chapter 3

PINOCHET WAS BEING held somewhere in England. He had gone there a sick man and now, it seemed, he was a prisoner. The English were saying many things, and the Chileans seemed about to reach for each other's throats. There were demonstrations: the left and right were both carrying posters, marching in the streets. I couldn't read Spanish, but I read the dictator's name on the posters of the left and the right. I wondered what the present held for these yellow-brown, honey-coloured people; what their past and future held. Their faces were sombre as they marched.

Bra Shope had left that morning for the flea market. Why had we come to Santiago? Oh yes, he'd been invited to talk at an exhibition. Shope was an old man now. I suspected he was afraid at times of where time, his lifetime, had brought him. But there were always people around him: they held his hand, showed him the way. Women, especially, fell into his arms. I was always concerned about him. He was afraid because he was aware of his vulnerability, yet also unaware.

When you lack something you're vulnerable, but what is it worth if you think you have something you don't? That's how he was always, ready to be received by women, young women. He stumbled into their arms, and when he did, I thought, they somehow became his mirror.

They had recently brought him round from a stroke and a heart attack. I thought he was dying then. So when he said we must come to Santiago, I came, although I was tired of travelling: tired of the flying, taxis, hotels, the people you don't know. But Bra Shope was a maestro at this. He hugged people; he kissed all these women and held their hands with joy on his face and in his eyes. I pictured his studio: unfinished paintings and sculptures on the floor, in the passageways, on the wall, on the spare bed. Sometimes I felt like covering them all with sheets. It was as if you were standing in a silent room full of naked people, unblinking, endlessly gesturing, wearing all kinds of expressions that remained unchanged until you looked again. They teased. When you looked away they changed their gestures; when you looked back they stopped and wouldn't look at you. They kept me so busy, I always left his place exhausted.

But the abstract paintings, for as long you looked at them, they danced. They changed colour, they wore different moods, they wouldn't leave you alone. And they were large, like the walls and pillars of old cathedrals. At times they talked to each other face to face: you could hear them. How did he sleep in a house like that? There was never any silence, always something moving. Even the eyes moved when you least expected it; it was disconcerting. How can you touch colour? You felt you did because it kept moving and yawning and being moody. Perhaps that's why in hotels they hang bland paintings that are dead still. People come to hotels to rest, not to struggle with paintings.

Bra Shope was my friend, but at times he drove me mad. He was just like his paintings: restless and opinionated. When he looked at you, especially when he was searching your being, you felt as if a big old frog was looking at you, rolling its eyes a hundred and eighty degrees, and listening carefully. For some reason I couldn't understand, this man attracted women. But it was always like that: I've never understood women and their strange tastes. I watched them: beautiful, intelligent, appearing on the arm of this strange creature, looking overwhelmed and submissive. Love, I'm told, is like God: it is everywhere, and has millions of people in its image who don't know it.

The tables were being cleared: I'd come for breakfast, and now lunch was already over. The tables were being undressed; they looked naked and exposed. The waiters were very determined, they wanted to go, I was sure. The waiters must have a bad time with the spoilt people who come to restaurants like these; they must be terrible brats.

Bra Shope told me this was a five-star hotel, yet I dreaded my room. It was nice, but sanitised. Millions of people had been in that Santiago hotel room; it was quite possible that I was sleeping where someone who'd disappeared had also slept, or maybe one of Pinochet's generals. Perhaps they'd held meetings here, plotting how to make Chileans, their own countrymen and women, "disappear". This republic stood on bloodied earth, filled with the bones of its indigenous people, and into this same earth had vanished those who the generals bound and "eliminated".

The previous evening, I'd said to Bra Shope that in the same manner that Africa survived the industrial revolution of the West, Africa must find its way into the twenty-first century – in leaps and bounds, to rescue the wretched, the poor and the mute.

"Yes, but have we learned," he demanded. "Have we come to terms with the fact that evil has the strength to overcome good? Africans don't seem to know this. They're so humane they border on naïve."

"I don't think we're that naïve."

"You're a fool! What do you know? Here come strange men by boat, without wives, women or children; from where we don't know. What they want, why they've left their place of origin, we don't know. Yet we give them land and food, and soon they take our women and wives and make them their own. They start fighting us for our food and our land, and they defeat us..."

That was the note on which we'd left our discussion the previous night. Then he'd complained that he couldn't keep up with my late nights; he wanted to sleep. I went to my room. This morning he had been in the arms of a young Chilean woman who guided him out of the hotel to Santiago.

Hotels are strange places. Every day of the year people of all types and colours, men and women, lovers, families, killers, generals from different places – all with their own plans in their heads – leave bits of themselves and move on. Thinking about it can be curious, even frightening. Shope had been thinking and speaking about these things. He thought out loud: maybe it was old age. His mind had lots of thoughts that sometimes came out all at once, as if from the barrel of a machine gun.

Shope appeared just then, gliding through the throngs milling in the lobby, listening to the young Chilean woman on his arm. They were walking slowly, oblivious of anyone else. I walked towards them, feeling how impersonal hotels were as I tugged on his bright shirt sleeve.

"Otsile!" he said. "How are you? Meet Sarah." We shook hands.

"Let's sit," Shope said, "and have a drink." We walked into a lounge where a very tall man in a dark suit and bowtie was playing jazz on a piano. How terrible that all of us who are not American think most music is American. You listen to America everywhere – why? Around us were couples young and old, business people and lovers, who all seemed to have been here so long they'd grown roots. As it was a Saturday, perhaps they were all relaxed amid the gleaming gold, the red carpets and black-and-white tiles, the ceiling white as a cloud and the terrible paintings casting shadows from the high walls onto the sofas, tables and people.

"I was just saying," said Bra Shope, "that in the old days when Africans fought for their survival, an apprentice, called an *udidi* in isiZulu, accompanied a warrior to all his battles, carrying his weapons. Tshaka's *udidi* was Cetywayo, who defeated the British at Isandlwane. As an *udidi* you styled your life around your master. It was like life talking to your genes – the way your master sat, stood, walked, gestured, spoke, laughed, cried, hid, went to the toilet, spoke to women – it was your whole life."

We were about to sit down when I spotted Bill and Dimakatso, and hurried over.

"Hi," I said.

"Hey you!" Bill said. He looked tired.

"Hey!" Dimakatso said.

"Come and meet Bra Shope," I said. We crossed the black-and-white tiles. Bra Shope had already pulled two extra chairs to our table, and as we walked up the short flight of stairs I saw him studying us.

"Bra Shope," I said, "this is Dimakatso…"

"My pleasure, my great pleasure," he said, hugging her.

"… and Bill," I said. Bra Shope held his hand awhile, shaking it, looking him in the eye. "Please sit down, have some drinks with us," he said in a manner that would have been difficult to refuse.

"It's a really great pleasure," Bra Shope said. "Please meet Sarah." Sarah smiled and they shook hands. Something about women when they first meet and there are men with them reminds me of dogs sniffing each other. Sarah was silent and watchful; Dimakatso eyed Sarah briefly. Bra Shope, I could see, was very happy. Dimakatso and Bill spoke to each other in soft voices. The waiter came and we ordered drinks.

Dimakatso was so bright, dark, clean, so present in the world! Her short black hair, bright smile and big watchful eyes struck a note in me. I rose and raised my camera to try to capture the moment.

Bra Shope was saying something to Bill; now Bill was replying. The women were quiet, listening. Then Sarah spoke.

I clicked and clicked. But I wasn't getting the shot I thought I would. I watched, felt the light and the shadow, really watched and waited. But I knew that somehow I'd missed it: in the words of the song, I'd spoken too soon. For in looking for the moment to get the right picture, the light and the shadow must be correct. Human beings have millions, maybe billions or trillions, of moods that make a difference to a photograph. People are multidimensional in so many ways. Dimakatso moved slightly, then leaned forward, glass in one hand and chin in the other, to listen to Sarah; Sarah shifted, facing me, and leaned slightly towards Dimakatso; Bra Shope looked up, raising his hands over his head in surprise as Bill laughed. I had the light, the shadows, the colours, the large round room with its pillars and curtains and the piano in the background. I clicked quickly, and got it.

"Mapuche..." I heard Sarah saying as I sat down.

"So when did you come back?"

"Yesterday," Sarah said, "to meet with Bra Shope, as Otsile calls him."

"A dictionary?" Dimakatso asked

"Yes, I'm almost finished," Sarah said.

"I've just come back from Africa," Dimakatso said. "At times I had a deep sense of belonging, but at other times I felt like crying. I'd suddenly lose focus and ask myself who am I, where I really come from..."

"It's like that with the dictionary. Although I say I'm almost through, I often ask myself what makes me so sure I'm really done. I have to search for some of the words – on the rocks, in the air, the light in the sky, the shimmering trees.

A language is a people, it smells like them, feels like them; but very, very few people are left who speak this language." She went quiet then. They faced each other, then looked away, and discovered that we were still there with them.

"Did you violate us?" Dimakatso asked, wearing a sad face.

"No, I didn't," I said. Then Sarah, Bill and Bra Shope looked at me too – it looked like the greatest photo in the world, but I couldn't shoot it: I'd already sat down.

"Have something to drink," Bra Shope said, looking tired himself.

"We waited to toast with you," Dimakatso said, looking at me. "We must; Bra Shope has brought us all together." We raised our drinks and toasted.

Then Bill said, "Bra Shope, I'm ready now for my name."

"The problem," Bra Shope told him, "is that if you're not careful, and you choose the wrong name, you may curse the person you're naming. Names are very important. But I feel to give you an isiZulu name: Musa, Mercy. I've never talked to a dancer of your calibre so close."

"How do you know my calibre of dancing? You've never seen me dance."

"I know, I just know," Bra Shope said. "I can see, I can feel it…"

"Musa?"

"Yes," Bra Shope said. "Musa."

We all drank to Musa

"Musa means mercy?" Bill asked.

"Yes, you know, we have to make a conscious effort not to always wail about what happened to us," Bra Shope said. "It's a rare chance to be sitting here, and we must try to see where we want to go. That's why I named you Musa. Sarah and Dimakatso are talking about a foundation for the way forward. We need mercy from our ancestors for this, to be looked after, loved, given wisdom, counselled! You know, on one level Africa can be thoroughly hearty; it can also be merciful. On all levels it's pregnant with hope. How do we develop that? How do we build a better world with Sarah's people? How can we co-operate to start the movement going forward?"

I don't know why they all listened so intently to what Bra Shope was saying, or why he spoke about such serious subjects and in such a solemn voice. It felt as if he was instructing us in what needed to be done; how we should link up with Sarah's people. I don't know why these words so disturbed me. Africans linking with Mapuche, what did that mean? At this point I looked at Sarah, really looked, reviewed her, stripped her naked – I saw her long black flowing hair, her deep, dark, honey-yellow skin, her pores thick as if to pour something out; her large eyes and long nose, her height and broad shoulders.

I remembered Bra Shope saying on the flight over that Sarah's people, like the Khoisan in Africa, had had to take sanctuary in the blood and marrow of others to escape genocide. How did that work? How did people achieve that? Did Sarah know who or what she was, what blood was in her veins? I felt a deep sorrow, but I was also afraid. I saw Bra Shope's lips moving slowly as he gestured. His eyes were solemn; Musa, Sarah and Dimakatso were listening, and I heard the piano, the intercom, and the many, many tongues of the hotel.

The waiter returned. Something about him: his face, hair or skin colour, was like Sarah. "Could you bring us a rum and Coke," I asked, "and a red wine, a screwdriver and a whisky on the rocks? I'll have whiskey and soda." He scribbled and left. Sarah hardly looked at him.

"I think the southern countries must come together, they must talk politics and policies, economy and social upliftment..."

"I'm amazed by your dreams, Bra Shope," I said, and I really was. Not that I disagreed with what he was saying. Nor fully understood. The shared possibility of linking our histories – the Khoisan, the Africans, the Mapuche and the Afro-Americans, the long-gone past arcing over into the here and now – it was staggering.

I felt something mysterious about Sarah's claim to have just returned from home. I felt it couldn't be home as I knew home. She smiled and said it was in a jungle. She was compiling a dictionary, she said, but felt she hadn't yet fully reached the depth of the language of her people. She spoke of herbs as something to be treated with great care.

Why had civilisation not prepared me to understand Sarah's language, which was English yet not English? It was the same with Musa. At times, his English was foreign to me. He told of how in the US the young black men around the age of fourteen, fifteen or sixteen would disappear from the radar screen of life, as he put it. One would get caught stealing sweets from a supermarket; another might hold up a petrol attendant, someone else would hijack a white woman or shoot and kill someone his own age, and the law would snatch them away. Maybe ten or fifteen years later you might hear of them again. They were very different by then; they'd have to be. They weren't fifteen anymore; they'd never slept in a bedroom, sat in a lounge, or had a meal with their families. They'd lived among men only. Some, like George Jackson, never made it out of jail; they were trapped and killed.

I kept seeing the chandeliers, the piano man at the piano, the gleaming black-and-white floors and the grand pillars, and the smiling staff behind the reception desk.

"I really don't know why we're discussing this," Bra Shope said. He looked away like a bird drinking, tasting, listening more carefully by looking sideways towards a sound, and I knew he was getting drunk. Dimakatso was cupping her wine glass and pondering it. The waiter glued his eyes on Sarah, and she looked back solemnly.

"I love your necklace," I told Sarah. It was an unusual necklace, and not just for adornment to offset her dress, by the looks of it. Having worked with traditional healers, I suspected something more.

"You do?" she asked, holding it up, trying to look at it. "It comes from my great grandmother," she said.

"It's extremely beautiful," Dimakatso said, touching it with delicate fingers.

"She was a traditional healer," Sarah said.

"Oh!" Dimakatso said.

"Please, don't start on voodoo now," Musa said, "you've all been so heavy this evening; give us a break. I'm just a young guy trying to make sense of the world as a dancer!"

"A young black dancer," Dimakatso said.

"Okay, okay..." said Musa.

Sarah looked from Dimakatso to Musa, trying to comprehend what was being said, but from her look, I thought she could sense it.

Hundreds of people were moving about the hotel, all reflected in the large chandelier overhead. There is genius in the founding of a hotel, but they're also sterile creations, and very lonely. Sometimes they unnerve me: I imagine I hear hundreds of toilets all flushing at the same time, sending huge loads of shit rushing through the pipes all at once. Still, hotels are ingenious: all these people meeting and interacting, their footsteps, gestures, stares, blinks and kisses, and the piano man gently kneading us all together.

"I'm starving," Musa said.

"I must be off," Sarah said.

"No, you must come and eat with us!" Bra Shope said. "I insist..."

There was no refusing, and soon Bra Shope was shepherding us towards the dining room.

Bra Shope... the man from Boschkop, outside of Pretoria, with its scattered houses, hills and lakes and pristine veld, and an almost eerie quietness. What do those skies, the wind, the heat hovering over Boschkop, what do they know, I wondered, what would they say to us, thousands of kilometres away in Santiago?

As we entered the dining room, the song *Farewell Argentina* was audible over the ringing of the cutlery. When I'd heard this song many years ago, for some reason I'd thought of it as a liberation song. Perhaps it was because of its depth of spirit and hope; its ability to fathom in tone, form, word and range the essence of people. At the time I'd related this song to the struggle in Africa, and also to what I'd heard about the struggles in Latin America – Chile, Cuba, Nicaragua, Bolivia – those countries where the multitudes were seizing their freedom. Yet communism had failed, the Eastern bloc had fallen. Why were we all seduced by the glitter of capitalism?

We settled down at a table.

"Black people shouldn't feel they're being stereotyped when people say they're the world's dancers, runners, or singers," Dimakatso said. "The challenge, as the world races on, is to build on that."

"Mandela's added another role," said Bra Shope. "That of reconciler."

"A black dancer, why not a black reconciler?" Musa asked.

"Or a black artist," I said.

"Or a black photographer," Dimakatso responded.

"Personally, I prefer to be called an *African* dancer," Musa said. "That anchors me somewhere in the world: on a continent, within a system."

"You must seek your true self," Sarah said. "I often look for myself in the genocide and in Chile," she said. "That's why I'm working on the dictionary. In my language Mapuche means the people of the land, and we're landless. So Musa's right, he's an African because Africa is the land where his culture, his economy, his people are anchored. We, the Mapuche, are caught in a vicious circle. The Chilean political system discriminates against us, whether Allende's or Pinochet's. It subjugates us. So our young people have taken sanctuary away from who we are, and it's only the old who hold onto the idea of being Mapuche. When they die, the people of the land may disappear. What use are we without the wisdom of our own language?"

"Ah, but the world's shrinking," Bra Shope interjected. "It will make us all closer neighbours than humanity's ever known. We need to come to grips with this."

"How strange indeed that we're all sitting here together in Santiago," I said, "a South African man from Alexandra, an elder from Boschkop, a young lady from Georgia, a young man from Carolina and a lady from Valparaiso. It makes no sense, yet in a strange way it does. The whole day I've been trying to make sense of this – and I began the day wondering if there were any black people in Chile."

"There are very few," Sarah said.

"But do you know what I mean?" I asked.

"I know what you mean by strange, Otsile," Bra Shope said, "but listen, consider something much bigger, that the world is going to become one neighbourhood: we're going to live flesh to flesh with each other. Do we know each other well enough to live so close? How are we going to live cheek by jowl in this shrunken world, poor and rich; black, white and yellow, different ethnic groups, some the victims of genocide, some who refuse to leave ethnicity behind, others who know the fullness of the world?"

"It comes back to the age-old question," Sarah said. "How can anyone want to own the trees of the earth or fence in the air and the sunshine, or claim the buffalo, the deer, the snake for themselves? How can you want to live well, breathe the air, drink the water, and exclude others?"

There was silence among us.

A sudden strange noise came from somewhere. All of us at the table – perhaps everyone in the hotel – began looking around for the source of the noise and its meaning. Meanwhile the sparkling chandeliers danced on the high ceiling and the floor, on our faces and in our eyes, and the knives and forks chinked against the dishes while the music of the singer and his piano floated above the muted voices.

"Otsile," Bra Shope said suddenly, out of the blue. "We're so far from home…"

"And so are we," Dimakatso said, as I was trying to imagine why Bra Shope had said that.

"Me too," said Sarah. "Although Chile is our country, to reach my people I have to cross so much time, so much distance, so much…"

Hearing this, here in this hotel in Santiago, tasting the fish, potatoes and gravy, and noticing that I was a bit drunk, I realised that all of us at this table had been devastated by history, by time, by the West, by the whites. Here we all were, far apart in so many respects, yet bound now by a common, a terrible reality.

"It's a demonstration, that noise," Sarah said.

"Who's demonstrating?" Bra Shope asked. "The left or the right?"

"What?" said Musa.

"What demonstration?" Dimakatso asked. But Sarah and Bra Shope didn't hear; they were heading for the doors. We rose to follow.

"It's the right," Sarah said.

"Are they still strong, then?" Bra Shope asked.

"If the army joins them," she said.

"Pinochet! Pinochet! Pinochet...!" The voices were gradually fading. From another continent, from a five-star clinic in London, Pinochet had traversed the mighty ocean, crossed in spirit into Chile, entered right into our hotel. Now we were all returning to our dinner tables; men and women from all corners of the world.

"Pinochet! Pinochet! Pinochet...!" the chandeliers seemed to sparkle. He became the subject of spirited talk in the hotel dining room for the rest of that night. The man was imprisoned in England; in Santiago the right was demonstrating and the left was in a panic, for the right owned the army and the economy, even though they were few.

Sarah gave us a long history of Chile now, which embraced Europe, Spain, and England, and returned to Santiago.

"We must be very careful," she finished, breathless from her long monologue. "The minority right in the global village won't allow justice, democracy or prosperity for the human race at the expense of its murderers, dictators, exploiters or the ultra rich. This is where the whole world has arrived," she said. "All humanity must ponder this."

There were tears in her eyes now. "A man I know brought me my lover's hands in a plastic bag, and he asked me, 'Where are your other comrades?' He put the plastic bag on the table with Kbio's hands inside. I knew them, even though they weren't on him, I knew them..."

Twenty years, a hundred years, centuries settled over our dinner table. Perhaps we too – Musa, Dimakatso, Bra Shope and I, if we thought a bit, traversed space and time, nightmares and devastation, if we asked our ancestors – could bring more severed hands to the dinner table. Instead, a great silence overwhelmed us.

"It's astonishing that the human race has globalised finances," Sarah said at last, "but is unable to globalise justice."

"Justice is a commodity," Bra Shope said. "Just as a prostitute is devastated in body and mind, but is still a human being; so justice, in the hands of human beings at this time, is devastated, but waiting to be made a reality. Without it, nothing can be whole."

He sipped his drink, then gulped it. He broke off a chunk of bread, wiped his plate with it and swallowed, and then endlessly wiped his hands on the floral serviette.

"What is justice?" he asked. "Is it punishment? Is it truth and reconciliation, truth and forgiving, or truth and compromise?" His face was stern, his eyes unblinking. "And what is punishment? Is it humiliation? The instilling of fear? Is it to teach? To warn? To set an example? Which of these does man fear and try to avoid?"

"I think human beings want honour," Dimakatso said. "To be punished is to lose honour."

She leaned back in her chair looking resigned, her arms folded across her bosom and her head slightly tilted. Sarah was fiddling with her fork while Musa sipped his drink and Bra Shope twisted his bread. We'd finished eating, and it was now early in the morning.

☙

Throughout our last two days in Chile, my mind kept pondering: how could honour render the truth relative? And why? If truth is relative, then what is real? Hadn't humans founded justice to make truth reality? Had we failed? I thought so.

I was having these thoughts at the opening of Bra Shope's exhibition entitled *In Truth We Reconcile*. Lots of people had come. Bra Shope walked in, holding hands with Sarah. I got that picture. He was looking very old and tired, and someone introduced him to Mrs. Allende. If she was here, I thought, if she was real, how could truth be relative? I also shot a picture of him hugging Mrs. Allende, and then another as he gave Dimakatso a long kiss, while Musa stood amazed, with comprehension on his face. I don't know why it always felt like vinegar to me to think about all these women in Bra Shope's life.

There were introductions, then a toast followed by a song and poem. Bra Shope walked forward. For a long while he looked at us quietly.

"My friend Otsile and I will be leaving your country in two days' time," Bra Shope began. "I mention him because he is my friend, a dearly beloved comrade who is young and has had many lives. Today he's a photographer, a great photographer. I hope when you see his pictures you'll also think so. Yesterday, Otsile was a freedom fighter, a soldier in my country, which is now in the process of reconciliation. Both he, the freedom fighter, and the apartheid fighters, will seek amnesty from our people and nation."

"They will stand before the nation, each of them, and say 'I killed, and therefore I seek forgiveness from you, and the reconciliation of my people.'" He paused and looked about, and found Dimakatso and Musa. "I say these things because I carry them in my heart, and because when I arrived here, I found these things here too. They weigh heavily on me. Since I've been here, General Pinochet has dominated my very being. When I left South Africa I thought President Salvador Allende would rescue me and give me sanctuary. No doubt he would, though at this moment not overtly, I think. How will the things he stood for become reality? But I must not make a speech. I have brought fourteen paintings that have really challenged me. Let them speak if they can."

He moved back. He walked towards Sarah, held her shoulder and almost sighed loudly.

There was applause, a song, a poem and another speech; then people began to walk around. Dimakatso hugged me very strangely; I had never been hugged by a woman in that way. With her arm around my neck she gently, with great care, led me to Bra Shope's painting called *Way of the Cross*. Something about the painting suggested a crucifix, except that here Jesus on the cross was also carrying a woman on his shoulders. Both were muscular and their faces were in great pain. At their feet, which touched the ground in dance flight, were children, helping to cover Jesus' genitals while covering their eyes.

"What on earth is this?" asked Dimakatso in a strange voice, gesturing towards the painting.

"Bra Shope told me in private that this is the time for the future..."

"You know, our dance troupe has a piece called "Revelations". This suggests it in a mysterious way that I can't explain..."

Our eyes met in that moment, really met. Much later she was to say that she knew in that moment that we'd meet again, that we had to. The following day many of the people who were at the exhibition, including Mrs Allende, went to the theatre to watch "Revelations". The next day Bra Shope and I flew back to South Africa.

Santiago stayed with us for days after we got back. Bra Shope and I spoke endlessly between ourselves and with our friends about that great city. We spoke because we didn't understand what we'd understood.

Teresa fetched us from Oliver Tambo Airport. Whenever I was with Bra Shope she was very conscientious towards me. She'd come to me first, hug me and kiss me, looking me straight in the eye. Then she'd go to Bra Shope. Her voice, tone, body language, smile and laughter were all her, Teresa. At times I was happy she could be like that, so free.

At other times it hurt me. We'd tried to talk about it, but we couldn't. We fought. We fought, I knew, because there were some things that were private to her, and there were also things private to me. I wished I could let go, accept that she was and must be a free being. I accepted this, but I felt threatened – I didn't know why. When I told her so she snapped at me. She once tried to explain why she loved Bra Shope, and I snapped at her. I hoped that one day we would laugh at ourselves about this. Bra Shope seemed oblivious to all of this. That was also what made me so angry about it all. I knew he knew that this caused problems between Teresa and me, but he seemed not to care; he was oblivious. He'd never once referred to it with me, and I didn't know if he'd done so with Teresa. This was the problem: I got suspicious.

One of us was on heat when we got home. Teresa never took the initiative overtly; I did. I'd move and then she'd descend like bricks from a falling building. Perhaps it had to do with chemistry. As we got home – and I hadn't known until then how much I'd missed home – we didn't waste any time: we were soon in the shower, and then we were biting each other on the floor like reptiles.

"I missed you," I said.

"I know, I could feel it. I missed you too!" she said.

"I know!"

"How do you know?"

"Well you surrendered so!"

"You made me feel as if I was totally, totally portable," she said.

"I love you," I said.

"I love you too," she said. "How was your trip?"

"Good, very good!"

"I don't like it when you answer so quickly, as if you're about to say, 'Ask no questions and I'll tell you no lies...'"

"Well, sweetheart, allow me to organise myself," I said.

"Then say so. Don't 'very good' me. Say 'I need to organise my thoughts so I can tell you how the trip was,'" she said.

"Yes ma'am," I said. "You're quite right. But you're a philosopher, so let me share this with you… A judge in Spain, Judge Gazone, brought charges against the tyrant General Pinochet, and Britain then arrested him on these charges. Chile was pulled apart at the seams into left and right by this faraway yet very intimate event, and for the first time since Hitler, perhaps, the world, and all humanity, has had to examine very closely the issue of justice: what to do with national tyrants, and how to protect national rights at an international level."

"But that could be construed as foreign interference in national events."

"Yes, but what I'm saying is, shouldn't we look at it this way and examine its possibilities?"

"We can," she said, "but of what consequence is that exercise? You underestimate the power of the right. You know the right controls the economy, therefore the armies and the media. It's formidable; it can reduce the important issues you raise to a mental exercise, nothing more. Nothing will happen to Pinochet, as nothing will happen to PW Botha: anyone who touches them will suffer. Justice or no justice, it's not the choice of victims that matters now, it's the dictatorship of the right to keep the peace."

"Isn't that a cynical view?" I asked her.

"What may seem like cynicism may actually be an understanding of reality, a search for the solution to an impasse – that's all…"

"If the balance is tilted, things fall apart…"

"Exactly," she said.

"But why is justice always seduced by evil? Why is the left always susceptible to defeat by the right? Where in the world today can we say the downtrodden are building a new order? You well know, Teresa, that I come from a rich political culture. We mean it when we say we're going to build a nonracial, nonsexist, democratic and prosperous South Africa."

"Tsile, you and I both share that culture," she said. "And because of that we must be realistic. We're still on that journey; we still have to build that South Africa. It can and must be built on reality, not illusion. Like it or not, the truth is that the left in this country is not, at this point, anywhere near being toppled by the right…"

"You're right," I conceded. "And it's very important to keep a perspective. There's no political power without military and economic power, or without cultural and intellectual power."

"On one hand, we've reached an impasse. We have no power, no motive force powerful enough to defeat the right any further than we already have – politically, that is. On the other hand, the right has lost its political power. It can no longer rule. Thanks to the freedom struggle, it's reached the moment in history where the oppressed refuse to be ruled under apartheid any more."

"And in Chile, the left and the oppressed are no longer prepared to be ruled by the junta."

"That's the general relationship between the left and the right, as we enter the new century – the new politics and economics of the global village," Teresa said. "But between the two is a vast grey area of illiteracy, poverty and disease."

I didn't know why we always ended up in this small space, this *lesaka* as Teresa called it. I thought of it as *lekgotla*. We usually ended up there when we were very happy. The room was elegant and the carpet soft to lie on, but if I stretched my arms I felt I could touch the walls on either side. Whatever the previous owner may have built this room for, to Teresa and me it was *lesaka* and *lekgotla,* respectively: *lesaka* in the sense that all home matters got settled here; *lekgotla* in the sense that broader world issues were dealt with here. It had to do with the fact that once Teresa had thrown off her shoes, put on her beads and wrapped her colourful cloth around her, she ceased to operate from tabletops, stoves and beds, but had this great urge to be as near to the earth as possible.

We'd ended up in the *lesaka* after our shower. I didn't know how we'd got there or why we were talking about these things. We'd dragged General Pinochet to the *lekgotla* with us; we were dragging him all over, examining him.

"... then we went to see an Afro-American dance performance called 'Revelations'," I said.

"'Revelations'? Sounds interesting."

"Lots of energy, beautiful music, beautiful attire: hats, umbrellas, long, colourful skirts. Strong men and women, professionals. But, oh God, Teresa, I learned about the whip, the deaths, the ships; about the fields, the pain; then the revolt, the joy, the conspiracy. I know a lot about the slave trade now. It started in the fifteenth century and went on into the nineteenth century. Now I also know the trauma, the pain and the burden on the descendants of those slaves, what they have to bear; I know from two hours sitting there listening, seeing, feeling the music and the bodies of those men and women..."

She touched me gently on my forehead.

"When you sink into these depths I know you so well, Tsile," she said. "You're such a sweet innocent child; you're a revelation to me. At these moments I really wish I could be robust, as large as the sky, the ocean; to let you go, Tsile, let you know that you're a free spirit. But I love you so..."

I knew what Teresa was saying. She was a woman, she knew me the way a woman knows her man. I too wished

I could be robust; large, deep, understand her womanhood better. Sometimes I did know her; at other times I didn't. When I didn't I became fearful, I succumbed to anger. There are many things I could say about Teresa, but they're so intimate, so private. If I could, I'd have taken photographs. But I couldn't, for it would have felt like violating her. And if I couldn't take a picture of something, how else could I express it? I'd have liked to talk to Bra Shope about Teresa, but I felt he was the last person I should talk to, especially about her, in that way. She was so strong, agile as a leopard stalking its prey. Teresa, with her deep black skin, her tallness, her large hands and arms and thighs, this African woman from the Vhavenda, her soft thick hair, full lips and broad face. I didn't know why she was a lawyer instead of a dancer; I wished she were both. There were times when I'd heard her cry and cry and cry... if that's what you could call it. Then this big four-bedroom house would suddenly become very quiet.

ఴ

Mantwa and Seabe would be coming the next day. Then the house would be full.

I woke up; Teresa had cooked *ditloo, leraka, dinoto* and *kgogo*. We ate. At the end she served pawpaw and bananas. After we ended with tea, she began reading the newspaper on the lounge floor, far away somewhere. I went to the darkroom.

Teresa came from a large family. She was the third of four sisters and three brothers. They had a large house, first at Evaton and now in Temba, near Pretoria. In that home lived her parents, her grandmother who was her mother's mother, and her great grandmother who was her father's grandmother, and sometimes the children of her brothers and sisters. Everything was negotiated there, and there was respect and politeness. Now and then, when I felt arrogant,

I felt I was fighting a deaf mute who didn't know why I was fighting. I even said *ausi* to Teresa's younger sisters, because everyone seemed to add the prefix to everyone else's name. I used to think that being polite took a lot of energy, and because I didn't know why one had to always be polite, I often tried to take shortcuts. But if you're used to being treated politely, you notice when others take shortcuts with you. I never knew the significance of this way of relating, which seemed such an old-fashioned set of manners. I dealt with it directly or indirectly as I related to Teresa or her family.

Teresa had settled smoothly into my home. There were only my mother, father, brother and sister for her to deal with. My sister Mamollo was younger than me and grew up with two brothers. She'd lost her husband at an early age, and made her way alone in Soweto and Johannesburg. She was a mixture of tomboy, city girl, and spoiled brat who felt the world owed her. My brother was mostly aloof, and my sister was not only negative but talkative. These things almost kept me away from home, but when Teresa occasionally visited my home, I had to go there to pick her up. I listened to her manoeuvring her way around the pitfalls and landmines of my family. They laughed; she laughed. And although Mamollo was usually aggressive to everyone, with Teresa she seemed to know when to stop. But because she didn't always get her way with Teresa, I always felt Mamollo held a grudge against her. My brother Matime always wanted Teresa to himself. He was aloof to others, but spoke softly to her. He came to our house only if I wasn't there; he'd been to see Teresa several times while I was away.

Teresa was very careful in the way she related to my family. Our parents had not really accepted her, especially my mother. Who was it who sang *Mother-in-law Blues*? That's what held Teresa by the scruff – the mother-in-law blues.

"KwaZulu-Natal could become a big problem for South Africa," Teresa said, tossing her newspaper aside to look at the photos I passed her.

"The whites could also become a big problem. They don't think it's right that they be ruled by blacks," I said.

"And the poor could become a problem too, because they don't think they should live in poverty in a free South Africa," Teresa said.

"A lot of challenges for Mandela," I said.

"Twenty-seven years in prison, and this is what he inherits when he gets out," Teresa said.

"But the poor who suffered under apartheid have also inherited the white intolerance of crime in this new South Africa."

"Is it all just a power struggle?" Teresa asked.

"This is the black woman I met, Dimakatso, Melba…"

"Who?"

"Dimakatso," I said. "In Santiago, at the hotel."

"Are there black people in Chile, then?"

"She's not from Chile. Remember I told you about the Afro-American dance group?"

"Mmm." She looked at a photograph for a while, then put it down and looked at the others.

"Is there anything like empathy in human experience?" Teresa asked.

"Why?"

"If you jail people today, and they jail you tomorrow, do you gain understanding? Do you come closer to their own experience because you're going through it yourself?"

"Is this just a general question or is it specific to something?"

"Well, my mind's on Chile and Pinochet, but it's general as well," she said.

"That's a complex question," I said. "Who says I should

have been jailed? If they'd come across me when I was in MK, they'd have arrested me, but I didn't think it was right that they should. Our agents were sometimes caught, and they expected to be arrested when that happened, but I don't think they accepted it."

"So, what's in the way of empathy in human affairs? Is it a blind spot, a deaf spot? Not seeing the other in the same position, if the other's perceived as being on the other side?" Teresa asked.

"Does it matter?"

"It must, because in these affairs, where does the cycle get broken? When?"

"The other side has its rules and objectives. Doesn't that justify action?"

"Does disagreeing with the others' rules and objectives justify such actions?"

"There's no such a thing as objectivity," I said. "Apartheid is wrong, democracy is right."

"How can you say that?" Teresa asked.

"Objectivity is relative."

"Relative to what? To what we stand for? To what makes us the other, on the other side?" she asked.

"We negotiate because we know objectivity's relative – whatever we do, in the end we must sit around a table and talk," I said.

"To seek a common understanding?" she said.

"Yes," I had to agree.

"So while Pinochet was in detention in that five-star hotel in London, was there no way for him to come to terms with the fact that those he'd detained for supporting Allende may have suffered?"

"Teresa, please, you're the lawyer, I'm a freedom fighter who's now a photographer."

"And I'm a freedom fighter who's a lawyer. But, Tsile,

please take me seriously. I'm trying to understand something about people – is it possible to understand suffering from the other's perspective? This may sound like just a legal issue, but I mean it in a broader sense!"

"Doesn't law prepare you to identify facts, put them in context and examine their content to make an objective decision?"

"You've seen me cry, haven't you?"

I nodded.

"And I may not have actually seen you cry, but I've sensed it," she said.

"Well, maybe…"

"When you're overwhelmed," Teresa said. "That story you just told me, you were also telling me something about yourself; you were empathising, remember?"

"What story?"

"Was his name Joe? He confessed to you that he'd been responsible for letting ten young boys and girls be captured and tortured, and some were killed. And later that day your structures decided to execute him. You were trying to explain that as a freedom fighter you dealt with life and death, bloody deaths. That must have had an impact on you as a human being. But then immediately you said you'd shared this in confidence." She looked me straight in the eye. "Was that empathy?"

"*No one* must betray the revolution…!"

"I know, I know. And I agree. But there's cowardice, fear, greed, ambition and poverty. All of these are a basis for betrayal. Can we stand aside and understand that?"

"I really thought, Teresa, that your question was broader than that…"

"Maybe it is, maybe not. My issue here is empathy."

"Yes there's empathy; no there isn't. So what? What are you getting at here?"

"Tsile, empathy is the ability to shift from where you stand to the other side, with the other's rules and objectives, and say, she or he did this or that because of seeing things this way. Is there such a thing...?"

"But to what purpose?"

"So you understand the other."

"I understand white people and their racism; I understand that they're afraid, they've become privileged, they believe their role is to preside, be superior, that they should be followed and keep the status quo forever..."

"But there's a choice. You could say that they're racist, so we'll also be racist. Or that they're racist, so we won't tolerate racism, no matter which side it comes from; in other words, that no matter what the rules or objectives, racism against anyone won't be tolerated!"

"Teresa..."

"Does that also arise from empathy? Is there such a thing as empathy?"

"Well..."

"Well, Tsile? Can we repent?"

"Repent? I'm not a Christian, so I wouldn't know."

"No? So you and I are freedom fighters, and there's no such thing as repentance in our life, our vocabulary, our revolution?"

"There must be..."

"Could Pinochet repent, or is there is no such thing?"

"Well..." I said.

"Tsile, you and I may be freedom fighters, but we also come from a culture that says *motho ke motho ka batho*, not so?"

"Teresa, there's history, you know. Its lessons can't be ignored. But you're right, our culture has a bearing on history."

Chapter 4

TERESA'S DAUGHTER MANTWA looked like her father, who was tall, dark skinned and handsome, with strong bones. And he was very sharp. Now and then I sensed things he and Teresa had done and said together, when Teresa became quietly stubborn and pursued an issue relentlessly.

Mantwa was a very pretty girl. She was lighter, had piercing eyes and a disarming smile with a gold tooth. At times she sounded just like Teresa, especially when she said "I was with Joel" instead of "with my father". Her father now had a new wife, Lulama. I'd once seen them at a supermarket in Sandton. He had an aloofness that kept other people at a distance. But Mantwa overcame his aloofness as if slipping under a fence; she had this way with her father. I wondered how she related to her new mother.

Seabe was like me. I got told this over and over, and I'd begun to believe it myself. I'd watched them, Mantwa and Seabe, in the house. At times I'd really have liked to talk to them about things, if only I could, to ask if there was a way we could do things better. They could be so sweet to each other. It was to do with Teresa and Nomazwi, Seabe's mother. Both Teresa and Nomazwi came from large families. Nomazwi was from somewhere in the middle of twelve brothers and sisters, and anchored among her mother, father, grandmother, and many uncles and children of her uncles and sisters. She was hard as a wire, and held her strength very quietly. Now as a head of department in the government, I could see how systematic, firm and precise she would be. But Seabe hadn't inherited all that. It was always so funny to sense myself as I stood with Seabe, as if I were looking into a mirror, even right inside myself. Seabe was sixteen, an age that could create big problems in a household. But Teresa somehow managed, and at times I had to use coercion. It was when I saw Mantwa's tail go up, stop wagging and stiffen in the air that I would stop in my tracks and seek a man to negotiate. Everyone needed empathy, if such a thing existed. But I also had to lay down the law.

They had arrived two days earlier, each from their other home. They quickly occupied their space and began to explore Teresa's space and mine. Men become the odd ones out in such a situation. I moved around on the margins, and consistently fought to enter the circle. Seabe sulked at times. Mantwa closed her bedroom door for hours at a stretch. Teresa negotiated while I kept watch; or perhaps guarded was the word.

It was the festive season. Although Bra Shope and I had seen each other occasionally, we really hadn't spent much time together. I could see that soon I'd be moving in his direction. Teresa was now in command. She took charge when the family was in crisis, especially when the children and their parents became involved and interacted with us. Teresa approached them, fended them off, and then you saw the fighter in her, the lawyer in her. I manoeuvred around this. I'd learned that there was such a thing as observation, and that I needed to know how to handle it. I'd also learned that now and then there was another side to marriage between parents in the home. As wives and husbands and the children and sisters and brothers of others, we must learn to wait, be patient, negotiate. With our past marriages and divorces and regroupings, together the four of us belonged to eight households, about sixty people, who multiplied through uncles and friends and the children of siblings, uncles and aunts. Under such circumstances, sailing through and around different generations, you grew quickly, you learned to look after your own and to negotiate to survive. Teresa saw it this way, and said that the lesson she learned from all this, besides divorce being a disaster, was that there was no such thing as a complete divorce. At the end of the day we were all the keepers of our brothers and sisters.

We were weaving around each other now. At a game reserve recently I'd seen how an old springbok, having perhaps lost the power to smell which bitch was on heat, had learned to look after the young. The females flaunted their colours and beauty at the males that hovered around them. It was Mantwa who drew my attention to this from the back seat beside her mother, while Seabe sat in front with me.

For some reason, this stuck in my mind. It seemed to teach me something. Perhaps my ancestors, too, had learned from this when they laid the ground rules for maintaining extended families. The old people managed large networks of people, ran their lives like that and their interactions with nature and the wider world. They insisted on procreation by all means necessary. They made rules for everyone. They sought the best for the human being from everything else, and sought to maintain human, plant and animal life through a system of totems. They created a lifecycle from birth to beyond death through the system of ancestors, and they commented on everything through proverbs and idioms. They observed; they learned and they applied what they learned. At times they failed and paid dearly, but they got on with life.

Teresa's great grandmother, Nkoko as everyone called her, was straining at the seams of life. At times you sensed her impatience with life, at other times despair, but also her joy in her grandchildren, great grandchildren and great great grandchildren. She said each child gave her so much and made her the youngest in the family. She sat on her chair in the kitchen or on the stoep, seldom in her room. At times, she walked around the yard to plant or clean. Yet she'd take you by surprise by asking who Michael Jackson was, what he did, why young people knew so much about him. Why did Mandela and De Klerk fall out? Why was everyone so interested that Bill Clinton had a mistress; didn't they know they were allowed more than one wife by nature? Nkoko had definite views and wasn't afraid to express them. She always asked after me, and at times she called me Joel. I heard that Joel came to see her from time to time.

When she recognised my name, or my face or voice, she'd ask me about Nomazwi. But Fana, Nomazwi's new man, thought those who'd been in MK had an inflated view of themselves, and he had no time for me. News travels far and wide, making secrets non-existent, so I heard what he thought of me. Fana had been at school when I was in the war and was now a CEO; and I was a photographer in the free South Africa who considered himself a freedom fighter, so that's where I belonged.

The free South Africa was a strange place to live in. Now we were all responsible for the apartheid legacy, we were all responsible for our country. Nkoko and Bra Shope understood this; but we, the young, failed to grasp it, and what we were supposed to do. Nkoko had been a young woman during the Anglo-Boer War, a *spijuni* for the Boers. She spoke impeccable Afrikaans, impeccable seTswana and impeccable isiNdebele. She saw, heard and remembered, and she asked a lot about people. She still had most of her teeth, but I'd heard from Teresa that a doctor suspected she had a cancerous growth. She refused to travel or visit, however, and wouldn't get into a car.

She would wait. If you came when everyone else was away, you'd find her cooking, talking to the children, sweeping the house or yard, or watering her kitchen garden. She hummed and sang, talked to herself. She liked watching TV because she didn't want to miss Mandela if he came on – I always asked her if she'd seen him. She wanted to know who Thabo Mbeki was, where he came from, why everyone thought he should take over from Mandela; then she wanted to see him if he came on TV.

"Is this Joel?"

"No, Otsile."

"I mean no harm, my child, when I mistake you for Joel. Where are my photographs?"

"I gave them to you."

"Two, only two. But you took a lot," she said.

"I selected the best for you," I reassured her.

"You people must look after Mandela. He's looking after us all so well. If he wasn't here now, this whole country would burn to ashes."

"So you've said, and I think about it a lot," I said.

"The *badimo* have given us Mandela, he is the child of the *badimo*. Hear me, listen well. The warriors of this land have given us him to lead us, to lay a foundation for Africa, to build a nation that must contribute to humanity. Do you understand me?"

"I hear you. I must think about it!"

"And are you one of those who went far away to learn how to fight?"

"Yes, I'm a member of MK," I said.

"Mandela's soldiers?"

"Yes."

"You must be very careful, I warn you again. There's another war coming. A great and destructive war. But the *badimo*, having helped in the transition that has now happened under Mandela, have left wisdom for you, for Thabo. The final war that must be fought is an African and European war. We have the wisdom to limit its effect, we have that. We also have the means to choose if it's a war of words or weapons. But it's a war. Mark my words. A war of resources, that's what it will be. Thabo will take over. He must know that it's the *badimo* who allow him to take over." She paused.

"When I was a little girl, growing up close to my father, the Boers and the British used to deliver the heads of our leaders to their followers in bloody sacks, to show us we'd been defeated. Did you know that? I chose the side of the Boers during the Anglo-Boer War. My father used to say they were the white Africans, they would make white ancestors for us. So I joined them. The only thing I never did was lift my dress for them, though they tried me many times. A woman who lifts her dress gives away the last of her womanhood; it shouldn't happen easily. I would have died next to them, you understand, but none deserved that I lift my dress for them. Only one man made me do so."

She sighed. "Ngwenyama. I had the reigns of my father's ox wagon. We were going to the river, then to the mill, then to drop some elders at a gathering. He appeared on a bicycle. He came straight to me. He said, 'When can I see you?' And I asked, 'Who are you?' He told me his name, and I knew who he was. There was no woman who didn't know him; his name wasn't Ngwenyama for nothing."

Nkoko's face was beaming with youthful joy and beauty. Something in her spoke to me of Teresa, which was also one of Nkoko's names.

"My father was a traditional healer and advisor to the chief. Ngwenyama was their messenger, and also what you'd call a scout. He knew a lot about herbs, animals and nature. And he wanted to see me! From his look I knew he meant more than that. *Ditaba dimatlhong,* as the elders say: the news is in the eyes. You must understand that I'd been brought up by the elder women in every respect. They'd taught me about myself, about them, about my grandfathers, fathers, uncles and brothers. They'd taught me about the moon, the sun, the dances and songs; about cooking and surrendering myself to the rule that they would examine me every evening, and that I would pass my virginity test. Ngwenyama wasn't going to make me fail it just like that, nor any other man."

Like Teresa, Nkoko was a very pretty woman. She was dark and must have been tall and strong; her large eyes beneath a thicket of eyebrows were bright even in her old age. More importantly, Nkoko was a fighter. I think that was why she was still alive now: she'd fought for it. Maybe she wanted to see the Mandela era. In her simplicity, she sometimes left one with the most profound ideas to ponder.

Bra Shope and I would visit Nkoko again soon. It was one of the wonders of the world to see Bra Shope attempt politeness and respect; to listen. I saw that only when he spoke to Nkoko. It was a great struggle to eventually take a photo of Nkoko, and I envied Bra Shope, who could sketch Nkoko without having to face her questioning and probing.

She always reminded me that she was a princess of royal blood. She'd tell me that the only reason she let me take photos of her was because I would use them responsibly. I had to. I had no choice after she'd said that! She checked now and then. Whenever I saw her she asked where her photographs were. At the moment some were being used by Bra Shope; others were still just negatives while I decided what to do with them. If ever I forgot what I'd told her the last time and said something different, she'd take me to task. *Kgomo e tshwarwa ka dinaka, motho ka loleme,* she'd say. You catch a cow by its horns; you catch people by their tongues.

Teresa's grandmother Mmemogolo, who later became Nkgono, meaning great great grandmother, was quieter; more preoccupied with what she produced with her hands. She and Nkoko came from different parts of the country. Nkoko eventually married a Vhavenda after Ngwenyama died while travelling the land looking for medicinal plants. He was killed by a leopard. He fought it, Nkoko related, so that the cat staggered away fatally wounded, and collapsed not far from him. Two leopards had met, fought and fallen. Nkoko mourned for a full year. In the fifth year she was married to Takalane, also a Vhavenda, with whom she had eleven children. When Takalane died in Leboa from lung disease, Teresa's father then took Nkoko into his house, with Nkoko's lastborn, Madiphororo, who was named after Nkoko's mother.

Tonko, Teresa's father, began a chain of shops in Temba, where they all still lived. Nkoko was the one who followed people's histories. She took great interest in Teresa's grandmother, Nkgono, who came from Marapyane. Nkgono had five sons and two daughters, one of whom was Nomsa, Teresa's mother. Nomsa spoke seTswana, isiZulu and English fluently, and she was a priest's wife, which may have been the reason Nomsa was subdued. Nkoko was very vocal about her traditions, customs and beliefs, which were not Christian. Nomsa was a staunch Christian, so although they talked and discussed things, there was an area both sides knew not to touch on.

Teresa was fascinated by this, and was now able to mention the matter. She used her great negotiating skills to do so. Throughout South Africa, among the Amazulu, Amaxhosa, Vhavenda, Amaswati, Amandebele, Basotho, Bapedi, Batswana and Mashangaana, lay a deep and dangerous conflict that was known but never mentioned. It emanated, as the Basotho said, from the division into *bakgoloa* and *bahedene*. The *bahedeng*, or heathens, practised and believed in African traditions and customs; the *bakgoloa* were the converted, who according to Western standards were Christian. And then there were the African traditional churches that came in all hues, sprawling across the African landscape. Teresa had been able to enter this arena with Nkoko and Nomsa, only because she always said before posing questions: "I am young and lost, I want to find my way, and I think everyone has the right to their own belief, as long as it doesn't undermine anyone else."

"Whatever we do," Nkoko told her, "in the end what's important is to salvage our humanity and give it all to the brevity of life. If we can do that, what's the problem?"

"As the elders say, *motho ke motho ka batho*," Nomsa agreed.

"Then there's no conflict between your beliefs; you both believe in the wellbeing of humanity," Teresa said.

"Yes, but how do we achieve that wellbeing?" Nkoko asked.

"I was brought up in the Christian tradition," Nomsa said.

"I have no problem with Jesus," Nkoko said. "I think he's a *badimo* of the human race."

"I hope the *badimo* you pray through also speak to Jesus. If they do, fine."

"I speak to Jesus when I speak to my *bokhokho*. He's also my *khokho*, and I think he knows I'm his child."

"The problem is all the witchcraft associated with *badimo*," Nomsa said.

"Yes, but there's also plenty of evil associated with the church. In the name of Christ the church has killed, created misery and poverty, seized our land and left us destitute," Nkoko said.

"But in general the church brings good to people," Nomsa said.

"In general the *badimo* bring good to people," Nkoko said.

"But which people?" Nomsa asked.//
"Well, my people."
"Who exactly?"
"Black people, African people."
"Not to me," Nomsa said.
"That's your choice. But just try, try them," Nkoko said.
"Nkoko, Nkgono, can I speak please? I beg to say something," Teresa said.
"Yes, my child," Nomsa said.
"This one's just using us to practise being a lawyer," Nkoko said.
"That's alright," Nomsa said, "*e bethwa e sa le metsi*, a stick is shaped when it's wet. She's giving us the opportunity to help her."
"*E bethwa e sale metsi*, how true!" Nkoko agreed.
"I wanted to say that we all agree that both the *badimo* and the church bring good to the human race, but on the other hand, that there's evil in the constitution of the *badimo*, and also in the church. Am I right?" Teresa asked.

There was silence.

It's strange how often, without our noticing, we quickly get lost in familiarity. And so we take many things for granted. Why is this always so? Then things degenerate. Perhaps this is how nature manifests its dynamism, at times violently. The spirit lives on faith, the body on indulgence, the mind on thought, and each thrives on the others. None benefits from neglect. All things fade in life, even love, friendship, passion and compassion; all fade to become just memories, which themselves are unreliable.

Perhaps this is how a cruel unspoken rule crept in between Seabe and me: that neither of us would ever mention his mother, Nomazwi, in our new home. But just as the rule became established without ever being mentioned, planned or agreed, that was also how it was suddenly broken.

"Mama wasn't home that day," he said.

Our eyes met, and for a moment there was a shocked silence between us. It was the mind taking over from the spirit and the body. At that moment Teresa walked in, and as if we were both holding something very, very hot, both Seabe and I dropped the subject. But something like that always shows. Teresa looked at me.

"Are you okay?" she said to Seabe, the way only Teresa can ask that question.

"Seabe was telling me about the difference between a house and a home," I said.

She looked at Seabe, then back at me.

"He was saying that when he and I were living in Lombardy with his mother, he learned that home was where you always looked forward to returning. He says he gets confused now, because wherever he is, he looks forward to returning somewhere else."

Teresa stopped in her tracks then. She hugged him. He smiled, shy, inhibited, uneasy. "How did the old people handle this? Remember how we belonged to everyone: grandmother, grandfather, uncle, aunty, mother, father, elder, brother, sister? Remember?"

"That was different, we didn't always have to pack a suitcase like they do."

Seabe looked at me sharply, acknowledging my words as if they'd pierced him in the ribcage.

"I have two homes, Mantwa has two homes, sometimes..." he trailed off.

"Mantwa gets upset about it too," Teresa said. "She never talks about it, but I know she mopes about it. Eventually she gets over it."

The fridge was purring, and there was the smell of chicken cooking. In the background we heard the voice of a Zimbabwean musician backed by marimba, guitar and percussion. Teresa sighed and sat down, resting her chin in her hand. Seabe leaned against the wall.

"Where's Mantwa?" I asked.

"In her room," Teresa said.

"Seabe, will you make tea?" I asked.

"Okay," he said. I joined Teresa at the table.

"It's a heavy Saturday morning," I said. "When Seabe raised this home thing, I was thinking of Nkoko, Nkgono and Bra Shope. Are they the same generation?"

"Bra Shope's much younger, but they're the same generation."

"They had the full experience of African traditions and customs. We grandchildren were socialised under the apartheid system, but we also had the full experience of liberation culture. Seabe and Mantwa are starting afresh."

"No, Tsile, not quite. You and I aren't really the same generation: you're twenty three years older than me."

"My age group is the one that earned the results and benefits of the struggle, so we're the ones beginning afresh. Seabe and Mantwa are just drifting. The only thing they have is a memory of two homes."

I could hear Seabe's footsteps; I could almost hear Teresa's eyes blinking. I still didn't know why Nomazwi and I had ended the way we did. And Teresa was right. She was the product of June 16th, 1976. I wasn't, I was the product of March 21st, 1961. I wasn't *Siyanyomfa*, I was *Mayibuye iAfrika*. Seabe and Mantwa were Mandela's children. They would be an experiment in reconciliation.

We had built a home, Seabe was right. It was significant that Nomazwi and I had built a home. As adults we'd never had a home. When we came together we had to love each other in snatches. She, like me, was a member of MK. That was the only time I really learned to love someone. She and I had hurt from that love; we'd fought, really fought; and she and I had come to know each other. Is it then that familiarity sets in and love diminishes; when lovers without knowing it drift apart? Or does love nurtured in heat soon shrivel and disintegrate? Perhaps it was meant that we should meet and then part. We watched as we both hurt, and instinctively, like animals, sensed, smelled the distance growing between us. But we were helpless, it seemed, we could do nothing but drift. And somewhere between us was Seabe. Nomazwi snatched him and they went off to huddle. I hit the street then, and met Bra Shope.

It seemed so long ago, but at times it felt like yesterday. Memory is so unreliable, yet so obstinate. I knew from being with Teresa that there was a wildness about me. Now and then she felt she was on a knife-edge, faced with my silences, my pondering of the past. I knew I must sometimes feel like a rough stone. Nomazwi's tomboyishness had been very attractive to me; and was still. I won't describe the things she used to do, especially when she became intimate. But she also liked big trucks, and drove them like cars; she jumped fences, wearing high heels, but never forgot to be feminine about women's things. I missed that.

Teresa felt something was amiss, sensed a distance bordering on alienation. I wished I could talk to her about it. But I knew it was no-go area. Yet temptation forever tempts, and she pleaded with me to speak. My instincts warned me never to say a word, and so the tension pressed between us. Sometimes Nomazwi had really made me laugh. Then at times she'd come home and say, "Why do women have small hands?" She'd really disliked it when I teased her, saying "Who's the man here, why are you hugging me as I should hug you?"

How does fondness like that just fall away, drop like a tired petal? This is what created Seabe, and then twisted him, gave him this look; the silent stare, the watchfulness.

Nomazwi and I had tried then for his sake, for the sake of our child, to save things. But it didn't work. It was as if a great weight was resting on something fragile, pressing, crushing it. Fearfully the three of us watched it happen. And one day it broke down irreparably. Nomazwi disappeared; Seabe disappeared. I longed and ached and cried for them, but they were gone.

The streets of Johannesburg are rough like the cutting edge of a saw on flesh: Berea, Hillbrow, Yeoville, Alexandra, Ivory Park, Tembisa, Kempton Park, Lower Houghton, Midrand, Saxonwold. It was somewhere there that I met Bra Shope. I think now that my attention was caught by his ability to listen.

He listened and listened. Bra Shope was older than my parents, who'd been my good friends, but I told him things I'd never told them. When he saw Nomazwi for the first time, once I'd found out where she and Seabe were and dragged him there, he said, "You've burnt your bridges here!" I was afraid. I felt so angry, so helpless. Nomazwi walked heavily, like an elephant with a baby. My whiskers told me I was in danger. Why did she stride like that, I wondered. She seemed to be living out our being in the same house without talking to one another; sleeping on the same bed but keeping our distance; loving each other and not saying so; knowing the other was hurting but not being able to soothe the other or say sorry.

I've said too much; Teresa must never hear all this. It was Teresa who urged me to make contact with Seabe. But she used to look at me strangely when I came back from seeing him – there was a question she never dared ask. She feared for herself, I knew. I knew because of the question I never asked whenever she went to see Mantwa.

Today Seabe had broken this silence.

I wished Mantwa had been with us at that moment.

I knew from the tips of the hairs on my skin whenever Mantwa talked to her mother about her father. I didn't know how to handle the pain it caused me. I knew it was fear; I knew the fear was from uncertainty and jealousy, from knowing about loss and wanting love. I knew that. Children also know these things, just as kittens know when they catch a mouse that they must play with it first. Children likewise play with their parents. That's how Teresa knew that Mantwa sulked and wanted a home that at times was neither here nor there for her.

We drank our tea in silence. From the large window in the kitchen the sun flooded in, spread over the floor, climbed the furniture and danced on every moving thing. As I watched Teresa sip her tea, like a bird drinking water, her ex-husband Joel flashed through my mind. I'd seen him on many occasions, and he and I had an unspoken rule. We were polite, we acknowledged each other quietly. On my side it had to do with the politics I'd learned in my movement: that my right was also an obligation to the rights of others.

This was difficult, as difficult as the politics of MK. In MK we had no right to harm civilians, black or white, because our country had to be nonracial. Also, we were largely a sabotage liberation army, and always selective about what we sabotaged. But the world, the human race, was not always so innocent. There was also an arrogance about us. Joel and I had a polite, quiet arrogance. I suppose it had to do with territory. Hyenas have a bad smell that defines their territory, and strong jaws to enforce it: even leopards fear hyenas. In a similar situation women flash peacock feathers and strut and charm. I sometimes wished things could be better for Mantwa and for Seabe, but Teresa and I tried; I hoped that we all tried.

What did Seabe and Mantwa talk about when they were with Bra Shope? I was curious. Because whenever they saw him, they flashed the happiest smiles, they giggled even before either said anything. They hugged him. Mantwa would hold his hand, and Seabe would act the big man.

I think that when Nomazwi and I were in the bush, we hoped and believed we'd build a good home for ourselves in South Africa. But now that I say this, what did that really mean? Freedom; the liberation of our people. A nonracial, nonsexist, democratic – and as the president recently added – prosperous South Africa. I'd never really thought about parliament, or government. I might have thought about the state, and I certainly thought about the future army. But I didn't think about how a nonracial, nonsexist democracy would walk the streets of a racist South Africa. I'd thought a lot about the economy of the country, about the institutions to be created to run the politics and the economy. But as I saw them emerge, I realised I'd never imagined them in the forms in which they now appeared as they were being created through the constitution. The more I heard people using those words at public rallies and on the radio, on TV, in Parliament, the more I became afraid. I felt these people had never known these words before then. There's a way I can call your name, and you would just know I meant no good. There was a new kind of person in this country and on this globe. Everybody in my country now spoke about nonracialism, nonsexism and democracy. But that was what MK had been fighting for as its strategic objective, and not everybody had been MK. It was dangerous to be MK.

"But, sweetheart, what did victory mean for you?" Teresa asked as I revealed this fear of mine to her.

Like a cat, in that stealthy, stalking manner, Mantwa had joined us. She looked quickly at all of us and then asked; "Why are you having tea like that?"

The three of us looked at her, as she searched our faces. She sensed she'd walked into a moment.

"Like what?" Teresa asked.

"Uh," she said, lost for words. "It doesn't matter." She sat down next to her mother, leaning slightly on her. I didn't know if Seabe would lean on me like that. He'd never done it, and I thought it was because he didn't really know me. That made me sad. I loved Seabe. From outside I could hear the birds, traffic, dogs barking, voices. People who speak isiZulu, Sesotho and other African languages speak loudly at times, they talk to each other across streets.

"When are we going to eat?" Mantwa asked.

"Soon, soon…" Teresa said.

"When?"

"Let me surprise you…"

"Have we invited Remogolo Shope?" Mantwa asked.

"No."

"I wish we had," she said. "The last time he was here, he showed me how to draw a woman and a man as stick figures. My teacher loved it. At first she didn't believe I drew it, then I drew them both on the board. The class laughed…"

"You know what he drew for me?" Seabe said. "Stick figures of a bully, a happy person and wise person. When I get enough money I'm going to frame them. I didn't know he was a famous artist. My teacher told me when I wrote an essay about him."

"He's so funny," Mantwa laughed.

"He is," Seabe said. "He told me he speaks to Jesus. Then he acted like he really was. Only, I don't know if I believe in Jesus, but I love the story, not the lesson of the story," Seabe said.

"He once told me God tells the best jokes in the world," Mantwa said. "He says the reason dogs sniff each other's bums is because God created the first two dogs…" She giggled. "And he told them the other's bum would sharpen their sense of smell to help them survive. So they try to sharpen their smell on each dog they meet, like this..." Mantwa got down on all fours, as Bra Shope had, "and they're sniffing and sniffing, and because the dog being met sniffs the bum of the one it meets, the next one that meets it wants to sniff the other one it smells, who wants to sniff the other one... He went on and on and I had to shout at him to stop because my ribs were so sore from laughing."

We were all laughing now.

"I didn't know what to say when he asked me why there are black people and white people. He said it's because one likes the sunlight and the other likes shadows. Like different sides of the same coin, he said. Then he asked me how we can make sure the coin doesn't fall flat. Sometimes I think that's easy, then other times I think it's very hard, and then I think it doesn't matter anyway, and I get tired trying to work it out. I wish he hadn't told me this." Seabe said. "Sometimes I get so angry!"

"Angry at what?" Mantwa asked.

"I don't know. Anyway, it doesn't matter."

Teresa and I caught each other's eye, and pondered what we'd heard in silence. Happily we didn't take the parental role of questioning, correcting or commenting on what Bra Shope had said. We just laughed and kept our peace.

Is it a human right for children to live with their mother and father? Seabe was friendly but cautious with Teresa; Mantwa was friendly but careful with me. And really, Teresa and I gave them no choice. We could do nothing about their caution, so there was peace. Or was there?

Teresa went to the stove. Seabe was doodling. I went to relax. Mantwa was humming a song and swinging her legs back and forth unconsciously, watching us. She had a way of watching that made her look like there was something she only knew.

We'd been able to pull together. It was really Teresa who had done it. She'd say things to each of us privately, and at times to us all, that made us rethink what we'd said, done, or even thought. She had a way of making us see both sides of the coin. I didn't know what would happen now that Seabe had broken the rule meant to protect Nomazwi – or really to protect the nest Seabe knew I'd found for myself. He obviously thought it was fragile, and now the rule had disintegrated.

Which really meant that we needed to examine ourselves, and what had made us afraid. Our routine was now interrupted. I knew that a new chapter was being written. I didn't regret it, though I was uneasy. But I was also very happy for Seabe. He was the one who had kept quiet and so created the rule. Now he had broken it. Nomazwi could now feature in our lives: in Teresa's, mine and Mantwa's, as well as in Seabe's. And so now would Joel, Lulama and Fana. It could get confusing, but it mustn't.

The Bible speaks of being our brother's keeper. It's about the blood that flows in us all, linking us, defying denial. You can't know love if you don't know hurt, fear and uncertainty. To see the young ones pack their bags and go back to where they came from, their other home, always left a brief silence among us after the loud goodbyes. But then, Mantwa also had to find a relationship with Lulama, and Seabe with Fana.

Chapter 5

BRA SHOPE AND I were due to leave for Cape Town the following day, to open an exhibition at the National Gallery. The gallery's kombi driver, Nel, loved trucks, comedies and cowboy movies. Teresa was very suspicious of him. She couldn't say why; she just disliked him. But Nel never forgot to ask after Teresa.

Seabe and Mantwa had left not long ago. Whenever they left, a vacuum seemed to enter the house. This and the fact that I was leaving the next day pulled Teresa and I together. It was Sunday, early evening. It was a lonely moment: a moment when life got thrown into what it couldn't handle, and the pressure put us on trial.

We sat in the lounge. Papers were scattered on the floor; teacups and plates on the table. Teresa looked tired. She switched off the television. I sat down next to her. I don't know how it happened, but we fell on the floor. When we awoke we were semi-naked. It was dark, the curtains weren't closed and things seemed unfinished.

"What's your programme like tomorrow?" I asked her.
"I need to put the public hearing together."
"About the traditional healers' institution?"
"Ja," she said.
"We must talk about that."
"How long are you in Cape Town for?"
"Till Thursday," I said. "What must I say to Nel?"
"Nel? You like him, don't you?"

"You don't, right?"

"Something's not right about him!"

"Because he's white?"

"Tsile! Stop your nonsense now. Because he's white! What's that supposed to mean?"

"Because he's Afrikaans?"

She looked at me, then looked away in silence.

"What shall I say to him?"

"Whatever."

"He always asks after you; he's very fond of you."

"I'm fond of him too, very fond." We dragged each other into bed then, in silence.

ଓ

Nel was leaning against the wall, tall, bubbly, broad shouldered, with a handsome smile, waving as we entered the arrivals terminal. We shook hands and entered the kombi.

"Good flight?" he asked, and began speaking about the mountain fire. He seemed to know a lot about the helicopters, the fire and the cost of the mission.

Nel wasn't well educated, Bra Shope had once said, yet he knew so many things.

"Did you see the headlines?" Nel asked me now.

"About Mugabe? Yes. I have a funny feeling about it."

"That's no funny feeling," Bra Shope said. "It's the knowledge of something looming."

"Looming...?"

"My gut feeling is that we're still in the fourteenth century," he said. "The slave masters and the slaves are still in dialogue. I really hope I'm wrong..."

Soon we were nearing the hotel. We could see the fire on the mountain, smell the smoke. The army helicopters were busy, to-ing and fro-ing between the sea and the fire, splashing water over the burning veld.

Bra Shope was concerned about his speech. He rarely was, but when he was, he'd be very irritable. I think his concern had to do with Cape Town. It was odd to be in this city. Cape Town was like a pretty woman. It brought out all shades of reaction from people. I found it emasculating. An African in Cape Town was an outcast, a lost species. Cape Town was a very white city; also a coloured city. It felt like apartheid. Cape Town in its prettiness was very ugly: it had distorted the human spirit, twisted and broken it. It was here where the first African Renaissance battle was fought, when the Khoi and the San fought and defeated the Portuguese who'd tried to land. They met them with a hail of arrows and spears. But it was also here where the slave trade made South Africa one of the few countries on the continent to import African slaves. This trade in human flesh and spirit had lasted over hundred and eighty years and extended to the interior of the country, where it raged. I'd been here with Bra Shope before, and I believed it was this that irritated him.

I sat him down; sorted him out. And together we began to write him a speech. He called it "The Evidence".

Nel took us to the gallery, where we walked about it in the quiet of the green-and-yellow passage and the white interior. The lighting splashed silence over the breath of the paintings, over their vitality, and also confined each painting to its space. There was peace here, but it was vulnerable, fragile. I sensed it from the way Bra Shope was walking.

"Did you know that a San child prevented a hyena from approaching it by holding a tree branch overhead to appear taller? I'm utterly fascinated…"

"Where did Nel say he saw that?"

"Nel isn't the issue for me," Bra Shope said, chewing on one arm of his spectacles, thoughtful as an old schoolmaster. "The San child is the bloody issue. I'm wondering how a primitive pagan child, uneducated, uncivilised, would know to do this?"

"Yes, astonishing…"

"The child was one with the environment. The hyena, hungry and tenacious, followed with relentless determination for forty kilometres. The child was lost and tracking its elders' footprints in the sand, exhausted, running, carrying a large bush over its head. When the child dropped to rest, the hyena came closer, ready to take its prey. Then the child would raise the branch, and the hyena with its steel jaws would back off, watch and wait, and then follow as the child began to run again."

Bra Shope was breathless now. "I want to paint that! The speed, the strength, the breath, the fear. The utter suspense. The victory of the spirit and flesh over life. Do you know what I'm saying? I would call it *The Spirit of Primitive Man*. Heh, you see, Nel doesn't know what he's done. He's taken my hand without knowing or intending to, and revealed the indestructible spirit of the human race. Nel's badly brought up; he wouldn't understand what I'm saying, but at least he had the sense to be curious and relate the story to others."

"But where did he see this?"

"Namibia, I think he said."

"Perhaps in a documentary," I said.

"What does it matter where?"

"I'm still a soldier at heart," I said.

Cape Town is a city where you can smell the ocean – well, in some areas, that is. Most of Cape Town is like Europe. Well, no, some parts are like Africa, and parts reflect Malaysia. It's also a very Afrikaner city, but also Xhosa. In all respects it reflects South Africa, a country of two nations: one white, and the other black; one rich, and the other poor. Both nations think the other is strange. Both are aloof from the other, yet aware instinctively that this cannot remain so forever.

As in the restaurants, the gyms, the places of pleasure, of learning, of heritage, in the national parks, museums and monuments, so here in the National Gallery too, the majority of people were white. They had come in large numbers to this exhibition of one of South Africa's – no, Africa's, perhaps humanity's – outstanding artists.

"Good evening, ladies and gentlemen," Bra Shope began. "I really should not speak tonight. I won't say anything about what hangs now on the wall. The only reason I speak is to share the new ideas that came to me not long ago." He paused.

"We are in a city that will determine the future of our country. We're in a city that belonged to people whom we have killed, obliterated. We're in a hostile city, depending on who you are, how dark-skinned you are. The evidence and the memory of this are related. My evidence is in the wreckage at the bottom of the sea; and in the fine sand of this city. It lies also in the blood of some of us, who have skins of different shades of brown, and sometimes kinky hair, flat noses and large bottoms. This is the evidence of the past that we must deal with now. I hope I can help us to enter into this process, to begin the journey to find the evidence..."

Bra Shope looked over his spectacles and searched the audience. He lifted his hat slightly, cleared his throat and looked this way and that.

"If we do not attend to the evidence of these issues as part of our national agenda, then where is the future of anything we do?" He looked again searchingly over his spectacles, beneath the brim of his hat, his eyes probing. There was a long pause in the hall after his question.

I clicked the shutter as his eyes roamed the audience, as he removed his spectacles and peered beneath the brim of his hat. I used natural light, and even in the photograph – which turned out to be one of his best portraits – the silence of the moment was palpable. Perhaps it was the silhouettes of those behind him that emphasised the dead silence that hung there, punctuated only by an isolated laugh or a lone throat being cleared.

Then he said, "I thank you." It was the cue for the packed hall to jump back to life.

As I hung around Bra Shope afterwards, I picked up that he was irritable. He was rude as he spoke to people. Soon I'd have to drag him out of there. There were two nations in South Africa that were speaking past each other. One wanted to preside, the other wouldn't allow it. We shall never again allow white domination in this land, it kept saying.

☙

In the white areas where we were, Cape Town flaunted its homeless like dirty petticoats peeping out. Bra Shope said it was like filthy underwear flung into your face. It did the same with its teenage prostitutes, who now lifted their dresses beneath the streetlights to show off their thighs and genitals to passing cars. On street corners children – little girls and boys like week-old puppies – knocked on your car window, plucked at your clothing, asking for bread. Other homeless people hung words on cardboard boxes in the still night of this pretty city, in the silence beneath Table Mountain where the whispering wind smells of the sea. We walked the quiet streets then because Bra Shope didn't want to talk to Nel. He was tired of speaking English, he said, and attempting to speak Afrikaans; he wanted to talk with himself. So we walked. All the way to the hotel Bra Shope was quiet, sullen. It's strange how the child remains inside us and occasionally peeps out. He sulked with me. He brushed past the homeless women, men and children who came at us saying all sorts of things. One beggar appealed to me after he'd failed to stop Bra Shope.

"Tell your stingy friend," he said, "soon he'll join us, the homeless. Tell him I'm waiting!"

I fled this man, these children and women now gathering around. I needed to think, in the soft night of this pretty city and its winking streetlights. My mind kept asking, is this the Third World? Stubbornly I kept saying yes. The sea was shimmering in the distance, reflecting the lights of streets and cars. The twigs of ships and boats kept dancing, pounding against the sky. The traffic roared, the traffic lights purred; the young night hung out its gentle shadows, its thousands of winking stars, and the moon dangled above the line between sky and sea. Bra Shope was walking ahead, a silhouette with a hat, his hands deep in his jacket pockets, transformed into shadows by the lights that fell upon him. I took another photograph, one he would cherish for the rest of his life. Then he went to his room and I to mine, besieged with thoughts and images.

ଔ

Nel drove us to the airport at midday. He told us that once, when a traditional healer had disappeared in the bush, they knew what had happened when they found human hair in the dried white hyena droppings. He also said that when he wasn't driving the kombi, he was cutting up bodies and chopping heads open for postmortems. Bra Shope didn't look at Nel, although he was sitting in the passenger seat. He kept his face turned away, glued to the window as the kombi wove along the winding road against the slope of the mountain, with the city below us.

"That fucking Nel," Bra Shope said as we stepped into the plane. "What's he on about? Why's he so gory? His head's full of shit that keeps spilling out!"

I couldn't understand why we'd come to Cape Town. For Bra Shope's short speech? Anyway, we'd finished our job, and Bra Shope wanted to leave immediately. He hadn't seen Jean, whom he always listened to as if he were a child. She was young, coloured and sharp, a one-time political activist. I wouldn't have been surprised if she'd said she was in MK. I didn't know how or when she and Bra Shope had met, but whenever we came to Cape Town he would meet her privately and spend a lot of time with her. Bra Shope was discreet in such matters, which dignified what he did, because unless you were very close to him you wouldn't really have known. Even when you were, what did you know if you never actually saw it?. But you saw it in his eyes, in his face. You heard the body whisper. But Jean didn't come. We took off from Cape Town barely twenty four hours after we'd arrived, back to Johannesburg.

"Nel knows strange things," Bra Shope said once we'd settled down and the plane had reached cruising altitude.

"Teresa resents him," I said, "but she's never been able to explain why."

"Trust women in that regard. They have sharp instincts. They have to, because to some extent, they're the hunted," he said.

"Hunted?"

"Yes they are!"

"What do you mean?"

"Don't be over sensitive with me" he said. "I dislike that nonsense. You know, for me respecting women is not an issue. I was born and raised with that knowledge. You and your feminists react to the truth of nature in a very superficial manner. The truth is that their physical build is defensive; you know that, heh?" He looked at me.

"Defensive?"

"Yes. It needs extra protection; it's vulnerable and defensive. That's why they have a strong sense of instinct," he said. "To survive. So if Teresa feels uneasy about Nel, I would too."

I felt a little lost on the subject, so we fell quiet for a moment.

He ordered a double whisky and almost gulped it down.

"You ask as if you don't know! What are you talking about? Haven't you hunted women? Haven't women run from you at a party, have they never kept an appointment with you? A man your age must know these things. You handle matters differently when you know these things. The human rights issue we must address through the constitution is correct in law. We must address that. But that doesn't remove our responsibility as men to behave with an understanding of their vulnerability," he said.

"Women don't want to be vulnerable," I said.

"But they are!" he insisted.

"Vulnerable?"

"Yes, they are. And they relate to life in a defensive manner."

"I want to ask Teresa about that," I said.

"And ask your mother too," he said. I didn't know whether to be offended by that; there was something derogatory in his voice. But I couldn't say so, although I was tempted, because he was older than me. So I said nothing.

"I hope that as they talk among themselves in their numerous caucuses," he said, "the women discover this. They must accept it but still fight for their rights, for equality. Then there'll be no confusion or contradiction."

It was quiet in the plane, except for the roar as it winged across the sky. The plane was full, but after lunch most people began to fall asleep. The wintery sunrays hitting the small thick windowpane were weak. Bra Shope ordered another whisky. Soon he was peering into the empty glass. I could see that his two shots were hitting him. He burped.

"Otsile, listen to me, please. Why do you think all of Africa, where the human race began, believes in initiation?"

"To teach us about life, to make good community citizens, to teach tradition, custom, culture…" I said.

"You know, at times I ask myself what I like about you, why I love you. Moments like this make it clear why I do. You're a child of Africa," he said.

"Am I supposed to thank you for a compliment?"

"I don't know what you're supposed to say. All I know is, you deserve my saying so. You know, not many people would even catch me pondering this about them."

"I'm humbled you'd say that about me," I said.

"But tell me something. What do you think of Nel?"

"Jokes aside, he's a funny man. He's been to Namibia, Angola, Mozambique… What's unsettling is that he seems only to have been in the bush in all these countries," I said.

"He's not funny, he's peculiar. He's a different species of human. But you're the soldier; you should know. Or is it that because you're both soldiers, you'll always be comrades, irrespective of which side you were on?"

"I'm curious," I said.

"About?"

"What you just said," I said.

"Curious? What nonsense. You're not sniffing at his naked behind, you're comprehending who he is."

"I'm curious precisely because I'm comprehending who he is."

"What's there to be curious about? If you comprehend him, you also know what he's capable of."

"If I know what he's done, do I stop regarding him as a soldier? Okay, so he was on the other side, but our business was similar, even if our aims were different."

"Now I'm curious. Isn't the aim the determining factor?"

"Sure, but you're forgetting what you originally asked me," I said.

"No I'm not. I asked whether you regard him as a comrade, irrespective of his aim as a soldier."

"Bra Shope, there's the Truth and Reconciliation Commission. I ask myself, if he is what you and I think, and he gets amnesty, how do I regard him then? Or if he serves a sentence and comes out, how do I relate to him? Naturally, he and I would talk about being soldiers."

"Talking doesn't mean you're comrades," he said.

"I know. But I also know that if it comes out that he was a brave, honest soldier, I'll respect him. I won't regard him as a comrade, but I will respect him."

"So, respect and comradeship, there's a difference, heh? I must think about that."

"To me comradeship means I'd protect you with my life, because we believe in the same principles and we're prepared to die for them," I said.

"I can't quarrel with that. But you've made my point; you've answered my question after all your roundabouts. Anyway, why shouldn't Nel share his experiences with us? We're one country now, and if we voice our opinions, why shouldn't he?"

"He's sharing what he thinks were interesting experiences," I said.

"And indeed they are. The shit thing is that in a sense he makes us his accomplices. It's been infuriating me. But I didn't have the guts to say, hey, tell me what exactly you were doing in the bush you've been talking about?"

"It's not about guts. I don't want to carry his ghosts: I've got my own. And if he shows me his, I'll tell him exactly what I think," I said.

"You're right, you're right," Bra Shope said. He began to fidget with his ears. Then he asked for a last shot, charming the young air hostess until she reluctantly gave it to him.

"Strange as it may sound," I said, "soldiers are some of

the most honest beings on earth."

He looked away through the window, then began to pour his drink. Finally he looked at me.

"Sometimes speaking isn't so different from farting," he said. "Both make a noise that's natural and tolerable at times, but at worst it can be insulting."

"I have been and will always be a soldier," I said.

"I'm not trying to snatch that from you, so you don't need to cling onto it," he said.

"You're ridiculing me!"

"No," he said. "You're being ridiculous."

"Why?"

"Why tell me you've been a soldier, as if I didn't know?"

"Because I know certain things about being a soldier."

"Look, we were talking about women. Let's stick to that."

"Well, I'll ask Teresa," I said.

"And your mother, as I said."

"I learn from what you say, so I'd like to discuss this issue about soldiers with you."

"You're avoiding something."

"No. I think both you and Teresa have drawn conclusions about Nel. I haven't."

"Because you're a soldier?"

"And because I don't like concluding before I've thought things through…"

"All I said, which seems to make you uncomfortable, is to trust Teresa," he said. "She has instincts you don't have."

"She may, but I don't have to think like her just because she has these instincts."

"Why are we going on about this. Nel's forgotten he was ever with us."

"It's not Nel we're talking about."

"You're such a stubborn person!"

"I hope so, when it comes to a principle…"

"Okay, fine," he said. "Still, ask Teresa before you make this principle."

"Can I ask you something else?"

"Since when do you ask me if you can ask me something?"

"Why did we leave Cape Town as if we were running away?"

"Cape Town hits me on a nerve."

"Why?"

"I'll have to think about that…" He leaned back and peered through the window.

They were clearing the plane. We'd forgotten we were in the air, that there were others around us. The plane began to descend. I felt tired; I longed to lie down and rest. Nel had touched something in us. He liked Bra Shope, I reflected, and Teresa. Yet the people he liked reacted badly at the thought of him. He made both Teresa and Bra Shope uncomfortable.

I wasn't ready to drop our argument. Bra Shope can be abusive now and then, and I was feeling pissed off. "You and Teresa need to remember that this country's on a path of reconciliation," I said.

"You're right," He clicked his fingers. "Your lady and I must think about that."

"If you don't, you'll become racists, and not only that…"

"Isn't Nel a racist?" he interrupted.

"Suppose he is. Are you going to be a racist because he is?"

"Not at all. But you see, if he's a racist and I'm not, how can we reconcile? Isn't reconciliation a cycle from me to him and him to me, a give-and-take compromise, an acknowledgement of truth, a way of reaching consensus and finding how we can move forward from the past? Isn't that the basis of reconciliation?"

"If…"

"If he's a racist," he interrupted again, "how do we start

that cycle? You see my problem?"

"Okay, but why do we think he's a racist?"

"You can't be a white South African and not be a racist. Otherwise there would have been no apartheid…"

"Another sweeping statement. So all blacks are righteous because they were oppressed by apartheid?"

"No. All I'm saying is that apartheid empowered whites but disempowered blacks socially."

"So we're righteous?"

"No. We were socially powerless to deal with white citizens," he said.

"So for reconciliation to take place, blacks must first be empowered?"

"Yes. We already have judicial and social power now, but not economic power, one of the most crucial forms. Without economic power we can't even begin to deracialise our society. Government must find ways to empower us economically through specifically aimed projects, programmes and processes."

I laughed.

"Why are you laughing? I wasn't joking."

"You're so earnest!"

"We're dealing with serious issues! You raised them, I'm responding."

"Okay, okay…"

"It's not enough to say, well now Nel works for the democratic government, so we're reconciled. Please! Let's look around – what was the South African Defence Force? Why was it created, how, by whom? What did it do, where? And who were its members? Nel and the rest of them!"

"Yes, but they were both black and white! So are the blacks who were in the SADF also racists?"

"They supported racism…"

"And so?"

"What do you mean by 'and so'? And so, what?"
"They supported racism, and so they're racist?"
"Don't be so funny, man!"
"I'm not being funny…"
"If you're black and you support racism, you're an accomplice…" Bra Shope said.
"I see…"

Chapter 6

WE ARRIVED HOME exhausted, but earlier than we were expected. Teresa, without saying so, was maintaining the space she'd created for herself in our absence. And since Bra Shope and I could no longer talk, I took him home. Then I went into my darkroom.

In the dark, with music on the radio, I stayed under the red light when it was on and in darkness when it was off. I watched the moments, forever frozen, emerging from the photo paper. There's temptation, there's evil in the darkroom. Voices cling and pull and push; they ask you to be dishonest, to be vain; they try your courage. But you must go on and not succumb. Beauty emerges from reality; skill must find and facilitate it to make it happen. Beauty and ugliness mustn't be manipulated: each is of its own. They reveal things long after we're gone, and those who experience them then do so because reality speaks to them. Then, only then, will these people be saved.

I heard the voices. I fought them. I swam in the dark, in the red light, absorbing the music and the radio voices, drinking in the solitude. All this was really about me. To be a photographer you must have courage. You have to be brave; it's like fighting. Their eyes emerge, drawing you back to their reality. To extract the images you must cross the line between yourself and the image.

You have to make choices. What will you capture forever, what will you leave behind? This defines whether you're a photographer or not. You either speak forever or remain forever silent. What do you want to say? When things depend on you to say them, you must speak up the best you can. Sometimes the eyes resist seeing. Even light and shadow conspire at times. The subject speaks in so many ways; you have to choose the best way to say what has to be said.

I had just four photographs when I returned and slipped under the blankets beside Teresa. You have to be brave even to persuade your partner to make love. I touched Teresa. She didn't respond. I tossed and turned. She ignored me. Time and sleep took me, saved me.

ଓ

In the morning we lay together in bed, talking. I was wondering about religion and tradition, why there was such tension between them. Why wasn't it possible to see that science, religion and tradition were connected?

Teresa said it was because I was only dealing with the concepts, while she was dealing with both the concepts and the human beings who make the concepts. Human beings are dynamic, she said, and so are their concepts.

I knew what she meant, but I wasn't asking *why* these concepts were contradictory. I expected them to conflict. I was asking why we didn't *accept* that they conflicted. It's not like they conflict for the sake of being antagonistic, and then clash. They clash only if the antagonism is left too long. This happens even at a personal or social level. How strange that one could become philosophical while lying in bed, next to, well…

"Science is logical; religion and tradition are spiritual," she said.

"Science is also spiritual. Who decides who will become a scientist? And religion and tradition are also rule bound and logical, so they're sciences too."

"Then where's the contradiction?" she asked. "Perhaps in our interpretation."

"That's right," I said. "So is contradiction between them the issue, or is it the way the spirit and mind interact with reality?"

"Then what of logic? Our interpretation is faulty, not them themselves."

"Then we're at fault, not them."

"They are too if we misapply them."

"No, then we are."

"No they are, by their application."

"Okay," I said, feeling that this was futile.

"Don't just say 'okay'. Look, wars have been fought over this! You're the soldier, you should know."

"You're a soldier too."

"Okay, we're both soldiers, can we explore this?"

Do we confront each other for the sake of it? What thrusts all this stuff into our lives? It was a brief discussion. I couldn't help thinking that instead of continuing last night's hostility, we should have told each other that we loved each other, made love and kept our peace. But life just isn't that simple.

ଔ

It was that time, early on a Friday evening. It had me slowing to a halt in front of Nomazwi's gate. And there she was, hosepipe in hand, wearing a navy-and-white tracksuit. My mind flashed back to Angola, where the trees danced in the air hot as an oven, baobabs and others, so green beside the wide river, the blood vessel of the camp where we washed ourselves and our clothes, and from which we sometimes drank, although it wasn't allowed. That's where Nomazwi and I come from. Whenever I took her by surprise and appeared at the river she'd smile a beautiful smile. But now a different picture flashed through my mind: her sorrow and pain, her face distorted with anger and bitterness in the days when we were at war with each other.

I pulled up the handbrake and switched off the engine. Briefly we glanced at each other. I wondered if she'd timed it so that she'd be outside when I arrived, to keep her distance. I wasn't sure whether to get out of the car or to wait.

"Seabe, Seabe!" she called.

He appeared at the front door, then hurried back in, emerging again shortly, bag in hand. Nomazwi waved at me and I waved back. I was feeling very sad, I didn't know why; or maybe I knew but didn't want to accept it. Seabe got into the car, banged the door, buckled his seatbelt.

"How's your week been?" he asked without looking at me.

"Fine," I said, starting the car and rolling it. I took a last look at Nomazwi and waved; she waved again. I wanted to ask Seabe where his other father was, but I didn't. What did he talk about with Fana? What did Fana talk about with him? We drove off in silence.

Teresa was at the stove when we arrived. Mantwa wasn't coming. Seabe wasn't supposed to come this weekend but Nomazwi had asked if I'd fetch him, as she was going on a trip.

After supper the three of us went to visit Teresa's grandmother and great grandmother, Nkgono and Nkoko. Teresa's parents, Tonko and Nomsa, were rarely home because of their business. Seabe kissed both old ladies as we arrived, and sat down between them. They were watching the Sesotho news.

"Where's Mantwa?" Nkoko asked.

"With her father," Teresa replied. "It's her weekend with him," she added.

Nkoko laughed. "The things we live to see!" she said.

"What do you mean?" asked Teresa sharply.

"Don't you ask me that," said Nkoko. Teresa vanished into the kitchen, appearing angry. Anger is a state of helplessness, I thought as I watched her.

"How are you, Nkoko and Nkgono?" I asked.

"Fine my son," Nkgono said.

"The things we live to see," Nkoko said again. Seabe looked at her.

As I looked at Nkoko and Nkgono, I saw how deeply my seTswana had been injured by time. I had to try to look to them too. It's no longer important to keep saying that this or that is African culture, I thought. Indigenous knowledge, Christianity, colonial culture, apartheid culture, struggle and liberation culture, and whatever we called Western culture – these were all a part of African culture. We'd been through the inferno, our people, and now our challenge was to find what we'd learned from that experience. How would we use what we'd learned to contribute to humanity, so we could put out other infernos as we learned to collectively contemplate who we were as a nation? We mustn't be afraid to learn from the totality of human experience. I needed to discuss this with Bra Shope and with Teresa.

Teresa returned carrying a tray of cups and biscuits. For a while we sat there while the pictures flashed on the TV screen.

"I'd like to know why traditional people and religious people don't talk to each other," Teresa said.

"I agree that they should talk to each other," Nkoko said.

"They are one people, people of God," Nkgono said. "They must talk to each other."

"But they don't," Teresa said.

"It's the white man. He owns God, he's the problem," Nkoko said.

"But why would you believe that? You know he doesn't own God," Teresa said.

"He doesn't. But it's common in villages for Christian people on one side of the river not to talk to those of the same surname on the other side, because they consider them barbarians," Nkoko said.

"She's right. It's not about witchcraft or worshipping idols rather than God," Nkgono said.

"What about witchcraft and idols?" Nkoko asked.

"It's true, these divisions are not right, something must be done," Nkgono continued. "God doesn't belong to white people. He's God of us all."

"I have no problem with God," Nkoko said. "I reach God through my ancestors."

"Ancestors were people, some of them as evil as you and me," said Nkgono. "How can they help you reach God?"

"As angels do. Or as Jesus or the saints did, according to the church."

Seabe had dozed off, and Nkoko took him to another room to lay him down.

"There's really no issue here," Teresa said, looking at me. "It's belief, fear, a refusal to go forward into the unknown."

"It sounds so simple, but in reality it's hard," I said.

"No, what I'm saying is, the old man in the Northern Province was right," Teresa said. "What would we lose if Christians and traditionalists talked to each other about these things?"

"So how could it happen? Maybe the politicians must bring both sides together and mediate."

"Something like that. This country has a culture of negotiation. We must start small and find a way to broaden it," Teresa said.

"But why do that?" Nkgono asked.

"To explore each others' knowledge," Teresa told her.

"And then?"

"It would enrich our lives. Especially for us, the young,"

Teresa said earnestly. "When we came in, Nkoko said 'the things we live to see'. She's right, there's something wrong in our lives: the soul of our being is in agony."

"Poor baby," Nkgono said.

"I shudder when I try to visualise Mantwa and Seabe's future," Teresa said, "what they'll believe in, and at times what I should believe in: in the God of white people? In witchcraft? What? I don't know at times; I despair, I get depressed."

"And where does science fit in?" I asked.

"First the traditionalists, then Christians, then scientists, and everyone else..." Nkoko said.

"Some scientists are Christians, and some are traditionalists."

"That's hopeful," Nkoko said, "but there's chauvinism there too."

"None of these categories has all the answers," I said.

"But we would learn new things if all of them were part of our consciousness, with no grey areas in between," Teresa said.

"The politician must accept the traditional leader, and the traditional leader must also accept the politician," I said. "That's the starting point. You can't start by saying democracy is superior to traditional systems."

"But it is..." Teresa said.

"It may be, but what does that matter if it leads to war?"

"Not just war. It's also about resources."

"It's over resources that there will be war. To avoid war, it won't help for politicians to say that since resources are threatened, we're sending in the army.

"No army wins a war," she said.

"You should know."

"So this is what you were discussing all day?" asked Nkgono.

"Yes, since morning," I said.

"I don't think we should despair," Nkoko said. "We must explore the unexplored. School and initiation, what's the difference? We should talk about how each one can improve the other. So too traditional healing and medicine, or *kgotla* and court and parliament, traditional food and other foods. I could go on and on."

"That would bring out what's unique to this country, to this continent," I agreed. "And more people would cease to be ignorant and illiterate. They could move to centre stage and become active."

"It would also help us to discard what we don't need, and keep what's still useful. We could retain what works." Teresa said.

"Yes," Nkoko said. "It is your turn, you young ones. We did what we could. And I'm proud of you all."

She paused, and then continued. "You know, Nkgono and I brought cattle to our fathers. Our husbands married our whole families, not just us. She's Christian and I'm not, but it was the same for us both. We're bound, according to tradition, by the fact that we were taken from where we came from through cattle. That act gave us a certain status in the families we married into, and in our communities. The man's side of the family had to earn the woman."

"Otsile, did you and your people earn me?" Teresa asked.

I couldn't answer this question frankly and honestly, so I didn't reply.

◈

When we got home I began to consider *lobola*. This took me back in time. I didn't know where my uncle was. I hadn't seen my mother and father in a long time, nor my brother and sister. Two years earlier we'd buried the oldest person on my mother's side, my great grandfather, who was her father's father.

I began to feel afraid, almost desperate. What if I heard now that my father or mother had died? But there was a problem. My father had never agreed with my divorce, my mother even less, and so they had a problem with Teresa. I realised then that I'd in fact run away from home. Not deliberately and consciously. Maybe I was searching. I didn't know if I was really obliged to hold to the rules my parents had laid down. It took courage to fight, to assert oneself, but what was I asserting? That I wasn't traditional? What was I then? I wasn't Christian, so what *did* I believe in? MK? The ANC? What? What did it mean that I was an adult and therefore responsible for my decisions? On what were my decisions based? Belief? What was my belief? Who would my ancestors be then?

These were very personal thoughts. The ancestors wanted us to pay *lobola*; they didn't recognise anyone who hadn't paid or been paid for by *lobola*. The problem deepened. I couldn't share it with Teresa. Seabe would also be affected by this. He'd rarely been to my parents' house since Nomazwi and I parted. The Bible professed that the guilt of the first generation would be visited upon the second and third generations – you were either blessed or cursed! God said so, and so did the ancestors. The Bible was the word of prophets who had a written culture. The word of the ancestors was an oral culture. Deep inside I didn't believe in the cruelty of the ancestors or of God. That was why I didn't belong to the church. But I belonged to my people, some of whom belonged to the church, others to the ancestors only, and some to both the church and the ancestors. I belonged to all of that.

CR

That night I fell asleep with a heavy heart, and slept as if alone in the bed. My mind reeled as I tossed and turned. The serene countryside began to unfold in my mind: the mountains, the rivers, the lush green veld, the large acacia trees.

"Nothing," I said when Teresa asked what the matter was. I couldn't tell her. She stared at me, and turned to cover her head. Soon she was deep asleep.

I felt afraid. I wanted to pray; I longed to talk to my ancestors, but I hadn't done so for so long, I didn't know how to begin, nor how to pray. I thought about exile, about MK, the camps, the front line. The ghosts had come back to haunt me. That night I dreamed – it started in the countryside and ended in a nightmare. I was a dead man walking, working in a field where there were large trees. I heard or thought that the trees would bear mealies, yet I knew there was no such thing. As I was walking I realised that the rake I was using had no teeth. Because I was barefoot, my feet were swollen. I was concerned about the trees, the rake and my feet, and suddenly I was in the river trying to catch a large bird. At first the bird seemed scared, but I made eye contact with it, and it spoke Afrikaans and became menacing. I realised I'd walked into a trap. I knew soldiers were waiting somewhere and that guns would soon go off, and when I looked back there were ocean waves rolling towards me. I thought I should drown myself, but when I turned back to the waves my feet were stuck in mud. I faced the soldiers, who were now huge menacing birds flying over me trying to peck at my head. I began to run, I tried to go underwater but something kept me afloat. One of the birds landed on my head with its huge claws and I felt its incredibly weight. As I ran, Teresa shook me.

"Are you having a nightmare?" she asked. I was wet with sweat and I knew I'd been crying.

She put her arm around me and fell asleep. I was too upset to sleep. I felt a deep sadness that I couldn't shake off, as if I knew something awful.

Chapter 7

"Did you know men can be raped too, Papa?" Seabe asked out of the blue as we sat at the breakfast table.

Teresa and I looked at each other.

"Yes, why?" I asked.

"My friend's father was raped."

"How do you know?"

"He was there when it happened. Now he goes for counselling."

"Where did it happen?"

"He was about to drive into the yard. They held him at gun point. They said he must get out of his car and take off his trousers. And open his legs and lean on the boot. And three thugs raped him. My friend and his mother and sister and his friend were still in the car."

Silence fell at the table.

"I didn't know a man could be raped," he said.

"Yes," I said, lost for words.

I was lost in thought now. It all began to link, without meaning to, to my nightmare. Teresa kicked me under the table. I looked up at her. Seabe was looking at me. In silence we went on eating.

"Men and women can be raped," Teresa said. "Did your teacher talk to you about this?"

"Yes. And my friend had to leave the class."

For some reason, I began thinking about our jails. I'd read somewhere that they were bursting at the seams, and that most inmates were blacks. HIV was rife in prison, rife in male jails. There were gangs in jail. Gangs survived on victims.

Teresa was saying something to Seabe. Our eyes met. Her face was calm. She was talking to Seabe about prison life. It dawned on me then that the young in the most civilised century faced the greatest odds, life's worst horrors, and would have to do more to stay alive as human beings than an endangered animal species. Seabe's face was grave. His eyes were glued on Teresa's.

"I'm telling you all this so that you know," Teresa said. "It's a waste of time to be afraid. You must keep yourself informed, and have adults you trust and can talk to about anything and everything. And also learn to talk to yourself." She stood up and hugged and kissed him.

"Hug your dad," she said.

Seabe looked at me and sort of smiled. I stood up and we hugged.

"What do you want to say to Seabe?" Teresa asked me.

"I'm very proud of him," I said. "I'm moved by the fact that he's shared this with us."

"Yes indeed," she said. "Shall I give you some more to eat?"

"Yes," Seabe said.

"Sex for the young is now linked to death," I said. "The young fear being abused; they have to be wary of adults. Boys and girls can both be raped. We must be strong."

I wasn't sure I knew what those words meant. How does one become strong? Knowledge is strength. It's courageous to want to be informed. I said so to Seabe. I didn't want him to just be afraid.

"It's normal to be afraid," I said.

"Will the thugs be arrested?" he asked, looking at me. He was wringing his hands, his shoulders drooping. I saw then that it must have taken courage to talk to us about it. He must have been thinking about it while we were at Nkoko's.

He probably hadn't slept well.

"Were you afraid last night?" I asked. He kept quiet awhile, looked down, then up at me.

"Yes," he said.

"It's normal. I get afraid myself," I said. "But then I ask myself why I'm afraid. The police will do their work to arrest the thugs. What's your friend's name?"

"Puso."

"Puso and his sister and mother will have to help the police," I told him.

"How?"

"They'll have to remember everything that happened that night," I said, "and tell it to the police. Puso's father will also have to think of everything he noticed and tell the police."

"What sort of things?"

"The height of the thugs, the colour of their clothes, their voices, their faces, everything," I said.

"But it was dark, it was at night," Seabe said.

"That makes it harder, but anything any of them can remember may help the police. The police will also look for other clues, like hair, blood, pieces of thread, shoe prints, the type of gun. All these will help," I said.

"So do men get Aids from being raped?" he asked.

"If the attacker was infected they can, from the sperm that enter the body."

"Where do the sperm go in?"

"In the asshole," I said.

He suppressed a giggle. But he was also thoughtful. Teresa was leaning back in her chair, arms folded, her eyes moving between Seabe and myself. I wondered if she'd already gone through this with Mantwa.

Seabe sighed deeply, and sat back, thoughtful. He was still wringing his hands and swinging his knees.

"Does poverty cause Aids?" he asked.

"No, poverty doesn't cause it. But poor people can easily get infected, because their lives aren't well protected. Poverty makes people more likely to become prostitutes. Not knowing about it because of a lack of education also contributes. And poor people who get infected can die more quickly because they lack nutritious food and money for medicine, and they may fear to get treatment. And because there are so many poor people, it contributes indirectly to infection and death from HIV/Aids."

I hoped I'd made the point. But I was worried about overloading him.

Teresa began to clear the table. "Do you want to put on a CD for us?" she asked Seabe.

He put on Bob Marley. One of these days Nkoko will ask us about Bob Marley, I thought. None of us talked about going out today. I listened to the music, and Teresa did some paperwork while Seabe watched TV.

Something had happened at the breakfast table between Seabe and me. I didn't know exactly what. But the menacing terrain that lay ahead for Seabe had opened up before me: his challenges, the world that awaited him. My eyes could catch only a glimpse. My gut, the fibre of my instinctive being that had been insulated until now, lay bare, absorbing this illogical, unintelligible message of fate, spoken in various tongues. I knew then that I was the one who had to find a way, without offending him, to help Seabe find his third eye, which he'd need to watch his back. Nothing, nothing must strike him on the head from behind where he was most vulnerable, nor must he injure himself so in any way, for there we are most fragile; the damage is irreparable.

Through this feeling I realised that I would always be aware of him from now on, wherever he was, whether with me or not. I was developing a scent for him; I was growing antennae for him, for my boy. And therefore, somehow,

Revelations

even as I feared for him, I wasn't angry. I had no energy to be angry.

My energy was concentrated in a gut instinct for my boy. I rejoiced that I'd spent my youth, all of it, in the liberation movement. I felt anchored, although I also knew that something else besides the consciousness the liberation movement had so generously given me, must also reside in my gut. Nkoko and Nkgono had let me into that space. I had to be mindful that my father and mother came from a long line of people. I was lucky indeed that both memory and experience allowed me to embrace my great grandmother, which meant I could reach back into the millions of years that were mine. You are an African, all this was saying, whispering to me from ages past. The liberation struggle had given me something else: not only Tshaka, Sekhukhune, Nyabelo, Hintsa, Sobhuza, Moshoeshoe, Montshioa, Adam Kok, Tshibase and Ngungunyane. Knowing about these fighters had also given me a spirit of no surrender, that would live in me to the end of my days.

I had to find a way to share this with Seabe. It was okay for him to be afraid. He was an evolved version of the animals, and animals had developed ferocity, speed or camouflage precisely because they knew danger and fear so well. It was okay for Seabe to be afraid. But because he was human, and a gatekeeper of life, he had to be more than just afraid. He had to have some knowledge that resided in his gut.

Miriam Makeba was singing away from the CD player; I was alone at the breakfast table. I could sense Teresa somewhere, and Seabe shuttling between the TV and the CD player. All was well. The whole of Africa was free, and now we had a job to do. *"Homeland..."* Miriam Makeba was singing. The tone of that song from the seventies combined with buried memories and transported me back in time...

I was in Swaziland, not long after my military training in the Soviet Union. My recollections of Swaziland were vague, but the Swazi language had sounded at times just like isiZulu spoken backwards. Somehow siSwati and isiZulu were the same, yet different. SiSwati was unusual to a sePedi ear. It became a preoccupation with me because it was a matter of tribalism. Tribalism had cost lives on the African continent, yet it had nothing to do with us Africans; it had been engineered by the Europeans. So why, then, did Africans follow its rules and play it out in spilt blood, in death and destruction?

I remembered the mountains of Swaziland, the lush green hills, the pines at Piggs Peak – why would anyone call a town that? I remembered the pine needles spread thick and deep like a slippery carpet throughout the yard where I'd stayed.

Nkosi, the old man who received me when I arrived there, told me the pines were an abomination: they used up the water and were foreign to the area. Nkosi carried himself in silent dignity, with integrity and calm. He seldom spoke, yet his silence spoke volumes, told you there were things he alone knew. His silence was deep, almost threatening. I understood that if I knew what he knew, I too would be silent. I wanted to be like him, to know what he knew. He held the only secret left in Africa. It showed in his eyes and face. It hung on his broad shoulders, clung to his gait. I watched, listened, sensed him. I felt it wasn't important for us to keep on talking. We talked through silence. Silence demands discipline, courage. It seeks understanding and embrace; and rewards with self-knowledge and fulfilment. I sensed his approval, and therefore I knew he and I were comrades. It wasn't spoken or planned. It was a conscious communication emanating from somewhere other than the tongue; maybe the eyes, the face, the sigh, and from being present, just sensing the other.

I discovered that baba Nkosi woke early in the mornings. I would hear movements, then silence. Then one morning I caught up with him. He was facing east, seated on a grass mat with his legs folded, murmuring. I sat down next to him; folded my legs as he had. I listened. I heard the birds in the great, great silence of the early dawn. I saw the clear sky, felt the silent breeze sweep over us. His voice was part of the whispering breeze. He was calling the names of the iNkosi of old, traversing the great plains of southern Africa. In anguish, in ecstasy, in doubt, anger, confidence and pleading, he called their names and asked them to intervene.

"Give this young man strength, wisdom and counsel," I heard him say, "to know that he carries the spear you have carried, fights the war you have fought, seeks the freedom, peace and independence you have sought. I remain your humble servant, sent by you to carry out errands and do my duty, as I listen also to our time and circumstance. Guide us. We are willing."

I never joined him again at his shrine. But each morning at three I woke, faced east, folded my feet, and spoke to the ancestors about the war we were fighting, against colonialism, against white domination, against apartheid. I asked for guidance for the mission I'd been given.

At that time I was preparing to enter what is now KwaZulu-Natal. I'd crossed Swaziland in a short time, being moved from one place to another. At Piggs Peak I settled a bit, and then received my mission. I ended up on the border of KwaZulu-Natal and the Free State, in a small town called Villiers, where people spoke Sesotho and isiZulu.

My host, Mma Lerato, an old lady of eighty two, met me at the post office inside a shopping complex. She seemed able to sense everything without looking. As described in my brief, she was wearing a red-and-white blanket and a navy-blue *doek*, with a reed basket on her head. We spotted each other; I was to follow her. I followed for a kilometre, and on the way she kept stopping to talk to people. When we'd gone down a steep bridge, she stopped to wait for me. We'd ensured that I wasn't being followed.

"How are you?" she greeted me.

"Well," I said. "How are you?"

"I'm happy you've come. I hope you like this place. It's small and people are expecting you; I've already mentioned that you're coming. You're from Gauteng. I'm told you speak sePedi and a bit of Sesotho. You're my nephew, my sister married your father who is a Mopedi, but since you're from Jo'burg, you really have no language." She laughed at me. "You've had a lot of trouble in Gauteng: not finishing school properly, not finding work, not being married. You've come to see Ngaka to guide you. I've briefed Ngaka about who you are. He suggested you attend a meeting today. It's to resolve a big issue in this small town, which seems to have political problems. We need to stop this and find a solution. Any questions?"

"No," I said, as we were approaching a young woman. She was tall and bare headed, large boned and large bosomed, wearing sandals and a knee-high brown skirt with a slash. "Dikeledi is a good woman," Mma Lerato said. "She works at a place where she'll be able to help us."

Dikeledi's dark expressive eyes were shy and polite, but she was clearly examining me; she'd heard about me.

"Dikeledi, this is Abuti Tshepo," she said.

"It makes me happy to meet you," Dikeledi said. A dimple on her cheek gave a pleasant touch to her smile, and her hand felt large and firm as I shook it. I was a bit confused, unable to read what her warmth meant. She said she had to get to the shops, and we parted.

The hilly landscape was harsh, dry and very cold. Villiers was a poor town, and the coloured and African areas were poverty stricken beyond description. The houses in the township were old, and new shacks were springing up rapidly, sprawling like weeds. Mma Lerato's house was two-roomed with a kitchen garden, peach trees, and a clean-swept yard with a shack in it. She let me into the shack and showed me my narrow bed, chair, makeshift table and homemade paraffin lamp. It was neat and spacious, with an improvised carpet on the gravel floor, and zinc walls carefully papered in coloured adverts, black-and-white news photographs and headlines screaming of South African life. Later I learned that Dikeledi had done the finishing touches. It was a modest home, but warm and cared for. Mma Lerato left me alone, and I fell asleep on the bed.

"Abuti Tshepo, I have to take you to the meeting." Dikeledi was shaking me to wake me up.

I followed her into the yard, where people were sitting in a circle. Some of the women were on the ground. I found a chair among the men, while Dikeledi joined the other women on the ground, next to Mma Lerato.

"... Let us first welcome Mma Lerato's visitor." Everyone looked at me; some nodded, others waved and smiled. There was a pause. Then the man said: "As I was saying, Thuso will explain his actions to all of us."

All eyes turned towards the figure of a young man seated right beside me, who seemed to be the accused. By sitting next to him, I realised, I had chosen a focal point of the meeting. I was most uncomfortable. I felt I should have been advised; but since no one had done so, I couldn't now correct this, as it would attract attention if I moved. I stuck to my position, telling myself I'd done no wrong.

Thuso began to speak. "It was at night. I went into the room where the mothers were sitting on the mattress where the coffin was. I asked if I could interrupt. When they allowed me, I showed them the bottle and asked if I could put it in the coffin."

As I looked at Thuso there was a strangeness about his shoulders, his face, the manner in which he held his hands and legs and perched on the edge of his chair. He was most uncomfortable, shaking and wringing his hands.

"What was in the bottle?" Ngaka asked.

"*Moriane*," Thuso said.

There were grunts and whispers from the men and women.

"*Moriane*? Are you a wizard?"

"No I'm not," Thuso said. "I loved my mother very much. I only wanted her to rest in peace. *Moriane* is a calming herb."

He was shaking terribly.

"Then what happened?" Ngaka asked.

A middle-aged woman spoke. "I asked him what he was doing. He told me he wanted to strengthen his mother. I was shocked by his uncivilised manner. I am his aunt, his mother's sister, and we were never raised in this tradition, we were raised as Christians. I asked him, as you have, if he was a wizard, where he learned to do these things, what right he had to do this."

"Did he answer?"

"No. He just stood there, like a wizard caught in action…"

"Do you have an answer?" Ngaka asked Thuso.

"Humbly, I say yes. I have an answer," he said. "But my answer enrages my aunt, whom I also love very much. And now, because of all this, there's a lot of anger between us."

There was a deep silence. Everyone but Ngaka had their eyes on the ground. Thuso's aunt was sobbing.

Thoughts raced through my mind. Why was I brought to this meeting? Didn't Mma Lerato and Dikeledi realise they were compromising me? What was "political" about this meeting? Who was this *ngaka*? Who were these people?

"Mma Matshidiso, could you ask for strength from our God?" Ngaka asked. "Please pray for us."

There was silence. Then groaning, grunting.

And then spontaneously another woman began to pray: "God, you have made the sky, the earth, the great waters, the rivers, the mountains; you have made the animals and the plants; you have made us; you have also known that we would come here to deliberate as we do. Please help us. We need you. We need your presence among us. You have given us this mission to understand your ways. Let us in humility and humaneness understand what we have to do, and learn from this pain and heartache. Guide us, preside, and give us wisdom."

Silence again. Someone cleared her throat. Another coughed. Someone grunted.

I felt angry, betrayed. I had nothing to do with coffins or bottles of *moriane*. I didn't belong here among their witchcraft and prayers and humility. It was these things that had no logic that had made us lose our land and freedom, made us into slaves. Why did I have to be I here?

"Thank you," Ngaka said. Can someone give us a hymn?"

Dikeledi started a hymn, her voice leading, towering over the other voices, amazing in its power and tone.

We have walked about

We were lost

We have struggled

We have been in excruciating pain

We were looking for Jesus.

The tune was very familiar to me, but I knew it with different words, coined by the young pioneers who were not a lost generation:

We left our mothers and fathers behind

We entered countries we did not know

We are seeking freedom

We are fighting for freedom.

"I just want to add a few words," Ngaka said, "to the powerful prayer and that most beautiful hymn. We need to remember that we are one people, and that each one of us has the capacity to err."

Yes, I thought, I have erred. I should never have sat next to this frightened man. I should never have come to this meeting.

"Please, can you help me?" Thuso asked, looking at me.

I felt like swearing at him; slapping him. But I held still.

"I need to go to the small house," he said.

"Small house?" I said.

"Yes, please." He extended his hand in such a manner that I had to take it. It was twisted like a bent twig. He shook like a tree in a storm as he tried to stand. He was straining terribly; his hands quivering.

What was all this? What was going on? His weight fell onto me, and I had no choice but to hold him firm.

When I tried to move, he said, "My brother, please steady me. I'm crippled."

"Crippled?" I said. I know now that the way I said it sounded contemptuous. All eyes were watching us. Thuso limped so badly, it was as if I was holding jelly in my arms. His hands felt soft in mine. He laughed. I laughed. We began to walk to the small house. It was a pit latrine.

"Take it out, please, take it out," he said urgently, "or I will mess myself." I opened the zip. I touched something warm and mushy. My God! I had never in my life touched another man's penis. It was large as a tree trunk. Who takes it out for him?

It spurted, and the unending stream of urine hit the bottom of the pit, bringing up the smell that engulfed us.

"My wife helps me sometimes," Thuso said. I pushed it back, zipped him up, and almost carried him out of the small house. Then we were back again, face to face with the circle. Who was his wife, I wondered. Was she here in this terrible circle? I cast my eye around, but I could decipher nothing from the eyes of the many women. What if it turned out to be Dikeledi? I looked at her and she looked back at me across the circle. I thought about his marshmallow. I'm mad, I thought, I'll fail in my mission if I go on like this.

With the accused back, the proceedings continued.

"Who gave you the *moriane* in the bottle?" Ngaka asked as if nothing had interrupted the proceedings.

"I've been taught *moriane*. It was the sickness that interrupted my *gothwasa*," Thuso said.

Silence. For the first time Ngaka cast his eyes to the earth. "Before Thuso goes on, let me say this. I want everyone to listen carefully."

"This brother has gone mad," Mma Matshidiso interrupted. "He's a wizard. He's evil. He has a room down there." She pointed somewhere in the distance. "In that room the most evil things go on. He and his wife are evil. Otherwise why is she still with him, allowing him to do these things? He talks to himself and burns witch things in that rondavel. There is shit in there; there is *bojoala*, there are skins of dead animals, and sticks. The smell in that rondavel knocks your brains out. Why is he doing all this? Who taught him? He's spoiling our good name in this community. His mother was a woman of prayer, as you know, so where does he get all these things he does? When he came with that bottle to the coffin, I called his uncle. He was also shocked, and asked him to go outside. Thuso refused; he insisted on putting the bottle in the coffin – in the coffin of a woman of prayer! Why?" She was breathless with anger. "To protect her from what? Whose permission had he sought?"

A man spoke now. "Mma Matshidiso is right. She called me to witness this evil. I asked him, my nephew, what the matter was. Why was he doing this, who told him to, and why?" The man coughed as he spoke. "Thuso looked at me, and asked if I knew he'd been to *thwasa*. I didn't answer him, because it would make me his accomplice: he would have splashed bedbug blood on me. I said to him, how can you answer my question with another question? He said he meant well and loved his mother. But I told him she was my sister, and she would never have allowed this.

"He said that my grandfather, his great grandfather, wanted him to be a *ngaka*, so I should understand what he was doing. He was staring at me with his crazy eyes. I asked him to go outside, and when he didn't I pulled him out by the hand. Fortunately he didn't resist. Outside he kept making sounds as if he would vomit. I asked what he was doing, but he said he meant no evil to the community. But I was right. Look where we are today. We're here because word has gone around the community that he's a wizard. He must be burnt alive."

"Thank you for walking us along this difficult path," Ngaka said, "and taking us into the confidence of your blood. These are very difficult matters," he continued. "They can split this community apart, but we must try hard not to allow them to. We need each other."

I had mixed feelings now. Part of me wanted to get away from this, but another part wanted to stay. Was it a community matter, was it witchcraft or was it religion? Maybe it was just madness.

"What exactly is the problem?" Ngaka asked. "Why do nearly forty people sit here and go on and on about this? Who is this man's wife? Is there anyone from the community who wants to say something?"

"Yes, yes." A young man stood up to speak. "As the elders know, I come from the youth of this community; I'm the chairman of our movement. We heard that Ntate Thuso is a witch, and that witches kill and mutilate children and make *moriane* out of them. So we discussed this in the youth movement; it caused us great concern. We took the matter to the chair of the residents committee, Ntate Ngaka. Some among us wanted to necklace Ntate Thuso, but others wanted to ask him about what we'd heard, and about his rondavel that the community says is a witch house. Some suggested we get advice from the community elders before we call Ntate Thuso; others thought we should call the police. But we went to Ntate Ngaka. Ntate Ngaka has now called us all here to talk about this matter."

"The children in the community are terrified," the young man continued. "Mothers are angry. Fathers are talking about this. This has happened since the funeral; when Mme Masello was buried. Word came out that a bottle was supposedly put in the coffin, that people left the vigil that night feeling afraid. There is fear in our community; the children are afraid; the youth are angry; the mothers are angry; the men are pondering. All because of the bottle Ntate Thuso wanted to put in the coffin."

Ngaka spoke now. "I just want to ask Ntate Thuso one question. Do you really understand where we are?"

"Yes, I do," Thuso replied. "May I please say this: I intend no harm to anyone. I apologise for the terror and pain I've caused the community. I really have no evil intentions; I'm not a wizard. I'm concerned with the wellbeing of the human race. It is my calling."

"Your calling, your calling, what calling!" Mma Matshidiso burst out, fuming, shaking a finger at Thuso. "What human race? Who do you think you are? It won't work! A crippled man who can't do anything for himself, who depends on his wife for a living! Human race? What human race would come to you, for what?"

"Thuso," Ngaka asked, "what is in your rondavel?"

He was trembling, tears running down his cheeks "My ancestors are there."

Now a light, slender woman with longish hair spoke. "My name is Nomusa, as you know." She spoke Sesotho in an isiZulu accent. "I am Thuso's wife. A question was asked, and I haven't answered it," she said.

"You may speak," Ngaka said. "And then I hope Thuso will finish his say."

"We've been married twenty years," she said. "We have four children, a girl and three boys. They are here too..." She began to weep. "Ntate Ngaka, our life has been very, very difficult. My children have come home and asked about their father. Does he bewitch? Does he mutilate children? What's inside the rondavel? The youth movement has questioned them. They love their father, but now they are sad, confused and afraid."

"Have they asked him these questions?" Ngaka asked.

"Yes."

"And?"

"He's told them what he just told all of us."

"Do you think he's a wizard?"

"I'm confused," she said. "I've supported him, even when he lost his job and went to *thwasa*. I've stood by him when he was called a wizard; I've stood by the family when the children were traumatised and it seemed we were falling apart. Our only child at school now, our eldest, Nkele, she stands by her father. But the boys have become afraid. Ntate Ngaka, I'm happy this has come out into the open. I hope we'll find a way out."

"A way out of what?" Mma Matshidiso demanded. "You've said yourself you're a witch. Do you remember what Mother said before she died? Do you? I wouldn't be surprised if you killed her, if you thought you could slice her into biltong and do whatever with her!"

"This is a time for all of us to say what we want to say," Ngaka said. "We must open up our minds and our spirits.

We need to free ourselves from the evil among us; not allow it to settle in our lives and control us."

Thuso's wife began speaking again. "If anyone is guilty here, it is me and my daughter and my husband. My sons believe, as many do, that there is evil in our home. They're young, they're asking for peace at all costs. They've pleaded with their father to leave his ways. If we are not spared, they must be spared! But there is no shit in that rondavel; there's nothing in it that isn't in any *dingaka's* ancestral home. I ask that before you do anything to us, we go to the rondavel. You, Ngaka, as a *ngaka*, will recognise everything that's there. I've never ever thought my husband meant any evil. But if he has been evil, I say we deserve whatever punishment you give us. But I've seen no evil. I'm a Christian too, but I come from an Amazulu house, so I'm no stranger to what my husband has been doing," she said.

Silence.

"The matter before us is very difficult, very complex," Ngaka said gravely. "This is because it has produced anger and fear and strong emotions. I say this not to blame anyone, but so that we're aware of its impact. All of us must be aware of this impact. If we are, then we can do something about it. Already we've done something: we've come together to explore it, to find out what needs to be done. I'm humbled by the youth, because they felt, when they were confronted by these terrible feelings and emotions, that they should call the elders. As you know, elsewhere they don't do so; they take the law into their own hands. So we must be grateful to them." He paused. "Mma Lerato, I see that you wish to say something."

"Yes, yes. Thuso said something that I think we should follow up. He said his great grandfather was a *ngaka*. Is that true?"

"Yes," Thuso's uncle said, "that is so."

"That was your grandfather?"

"Yes," he said.
"Did you know him? Did he have an ancestral house?"
"He did."
"Did anyone enter that ancestral house?"
"Yes, but only with him."
"Was your grandfather a witch?"
Silence.

Dikeledi rose to speak. "While Thuso's uncle and every one of us is thinking about that question, I'd like to ask Thuso a question." She turned to him. "Why do you think the community is so suspicious of you, so afraid of you?"

"Because I am a cripple, I must look very strange to others. I am also a *ngaka*. In people's eyes I am surrounded by mystery. Perhaps some find me to be a social misfit. But I repeat to you all: I mean no evil. My ancestors wanted me to protect my mother, whom I loved dearly. By the time she died my mother was angry with me. She believed I was disgracing her. I ask forgiveness for causing you all so much pain. But I want to make one request to the community. I ask that you spare my wife and my daughter. They are innocent."

A loud cry of pain came from a young woman beside Nomusa. Nomusa held her daughter Nkele to her bosom. Silence, except for her weeping that now engulfed us all.

"Please," Nkele cried, "I plead with you, I beg all of you. Leave my father alone! If anything he needs your help, not your wrath. Why are you so afraid of a bottle that was going to be buried with a corpse? Why are you so afraid of sticks and skins? I say this with humility. I think it is enough now…" She went on sobbing.

Next to me, Thuso began whispering to himself, calling names as if in prayer. I thought of Nkosi.

Ngaka spoke. "There is too much pain in this community. We need strength, wisdom and counsel to deal with it. Let the Christians help us by praying for us. And let us sing…"

I want to work for you, oh Lord
While I am on this earth
It is filled with thorns, they pierce our bare feet
Even then, I say, I agree
I must work for you, oh Lord, on this earth
While I am alive.

Something heaved inside me. I began to sob. My weeping took me by surprise; it was uncontrollable. I wept and wept. I felt Thuso's hand on me, comforting me. What was the matter with me? I felt different hands hold me, embrace me. I felt hair touching me, and the voice leading the song was over me, hovering, strong and powerful, large as the sky; it held the roar of the ocean and the wind. It was Dikeledi; she gently rubbed my shoulder with her hand as she sang and sang and I wept and wept. What was going on? What was the matter? I struggled to stop, but I'd tapped into depths I'd never touched; gone down a slope where I'd never been; seen what I'd never seen before. Something had released. What was it about this song that touched me so deeply? Or was it the voice that carried the song? I had never wept, or rather, couldn't remember when last I'd wept.

These thoughts all flooded through me as I sat there with Seabe. He seemed glued to the TV screen, watching whatever was yapping in an American accent.

I was tempted to ask him to switch it off, but Teresa had taught me to be cautious when dealing with this young generation. Being cautious didn't mean not being firm, not questioning or not making certain things clear. Yet we had to be careful – careful not to lose these children of ours to drugs, to liquor, to the viciousness of the streets, to prisons; not to let them become corpses sprawled on the pavement with a bullet hole, or the gash of an axe or a knife. We had to take care. The American TV programmes, like the ships before them, were taking our children, snatching them by the scruff of the neck, leading them far from us into spaces and times not of our making, that we didn't know or understand.

At times it felt futile to keep talking to Seabe about my MK days. It seemed so long ago that I'd been a cadre. And the South African media – foreign to everything South African, southern African or even African – had buried everything to do with MK, the ANC and the struggle under heaps of words filled with innuendo, irony and hypocrisy. The media that had once called us terrorists and murderers later said that a miracle had happened in South Africa, that it had given birth to a lost generation of black children; and still later they accused those they'd once called terrorists – all of them black – of riding the gravy train as they took up responsibilities in government. Then they said they were running the country inefficiently and ineffectively, and that among them were many thieves, most of them black.

I didn't know why my talk with Seabe had brought this very private experience to the surface after such a long time. But now Dikeledi began to occupy my mind. She and I had a relationship that had begun in secret and it remained secretive still.

Back in those early days I'd trained Dikeledi in pistols, rifles, engineering and underground work. We'd established arsenals known as dead letter boxes in several areas. We would receive personnel from outside who then took over. Then one day the first operation was carried out: an attack on a military base, which was followed by an attack on a police station. Then Dikeledi began training young women, one of whom was Nkele.

Mma Lerato, I have to say, was the best commissar I ever had. She mediated between us and the community. When the operations began, I recommended that Dikeledi should leave.

"No," Mma Lerato had said, firmly but calmly. "She must not leave the country, nor the area. And you must report back to base."

I didn't agree with her. But I felt from her look that I had to comply.

Dikeledi and I continued to meet up on occasion. Whenever we parted we promised to meet again. We needed to. There was a lot going on in our lives that we couldn't share with anyone else at that time. We entered into a relationship that was very intimate and discreet, yet undemanding. It felt so mature because we had no obsession, no grand ideas about possessing the other, yet we derived considerable intellectual, spiritual and physical joy from being together. I still have no idea how we created that.

Dikeledi told me that after I'd left Villiers, Mma Lerato took her to Musina, a little town in the north before you enter Zimbabwe. In Musina she'd trained more young women. And there she discovered a person she'd always dreamed about but never met. She walked into a house and there she was. They were both shocked by this discovery, each wanting to tell the other their dreams about the other. I know this is a difficult thing to believe or understand. Dikeledi discovered that she was in the house of the best known *ngaka* in the area. And so she went to *thwasa* for six months, and became a *ngaka* herself.

I'd only once been back to Villiers. It was eight years after I'd first arrived there for a mission, and five years after I'd left. I was devastated by the disintegration of my marriage to Nomazwi, but I wasn't going back to my mother and father. I was too old for that. Even though I had a flat, it was empty, lonely: a single bed with some empty cooldrink cans, takeaway boxes and whisky bottles. I was drinking whisky with passion then. My whole being resisted returning, but at the time I had nowhere else to go.

My return to Villiers those eight years ago is a time that will stay with me until the day I die. Dikeledi and Mma Lerato gave me soft fermented porridge and we sat in the room of my past, eating in silence. Then Mma Lerato stood up, searched her dress pocket and pulled out three bangles: one silver, one gold, one brass, and gave them to me.

"If you find the time and courage to wear them, please do. I've had them since I was a little girl. I've enjoyed them tremendously. They came from my mother who was given them by her mother. Since I have no children, I give them to you as my son." She gave Dikeledi a golden necklace, and then kissed us both.

What was time, I wondered now, as I looked at Seabe in front of the TV set. No matter how I tried to answer that question, it was events, people, places, moments…

ଔ

These thoughts put me back on the highway the next day. I needed to go back to where too many unknowns were real, as real as the distance I was now covering.

The last time I'd seen Dikeledi, she told me that Mma Lerato had died. Now as I drove, the harsh landscape of the Free State running backwards past me, I recalled the soft porridge, the silence, the issuing of gifts, the embrace and the kiss. At the time I'd thought Mma Lerato was just being sentimental. Now, since time had decreed that I would never see her again, I realised that this had been her ritual farewell to two people with whom she'd put her neck on the block. It weighed heavily on my heart.

Villiers had changed. The shacks were gone and small houses had taken their place. There was electricity, water, proper sanitation. But something of the past still hovered there. Time is so strange, determined, unfriendly, so unflinching and cataclysmic. Time and change interact organically, leaving many things transformed and unrecognisable, yet bearing a semblance of what we have known.

Dikeledi was wearing high heels and a black skirt, with a white blouse and a wide belt around her waist. She still had her dreadlocks, and beads on her arms and ankles. She was as beautiful as ever.

"We've liberated our country physically," she told me. "Now we have to emancipate its spirit. Mark my words, more young people will be called to *thwasa*," she said. The things she was saying were beyond me. Then she asked suddenly, "Where are the bangles Mma Lerato gave you?"

I'd left the bangles and other small items at my parents' home when I returned to South Africa after Mandela suspended armed operations. I wasn't sure I could still find them.

"Why do you ask?"

"I dreamed you were looking for them," she said, "over and over! You must find them and wear them. They connect you to many past generations." Then she laughed. "Abuti Tshepo, why are you looking at me like that?"

I said nothing, wondering if she could read my mind.

Then she told me that she was married. She began to tell me about her husband and her child. It tore me apart. I thought then about Teresa. After some meandering small talk, I told Dikeledi I had to leave. I would come to see her again, I said, and when I did, I'd like to meet her family. She gazed at me with her large eyes. I told her then that I was her man forever, and she would be my woman forever. We said no more for a while.

"I hope by then I'll have finished my rondavel and set up my computer," she said. "Call me and I'll give you my e-mail address."

I kissed her and got into the car and onto the highway.

Chapter 8

BACK AT HOME, I found that Teresa had begun another dialogue with our children. We'd been leaving our children to the TV, the computer and the shopping malls, where pimps were waiting to turn them into prostitutes and drug addicts, Teresa told me in her calm and determined manner. We had to spend more time building our family. And we couldn't leave our relationship at risk, she said. It needed nurturing and cultivating. Only if we were prepared to do that would we be able to care properly for our children. It all depended on whether we were able to love and respect ourselves, she said, and keep on improving and developing as individuals.

Dikeledi came to mind as I listened to her. I had contemplated telling her about Dikeledi, but never had. As long as Dikeledi and I caused no harm to her, or now to Dikeledi's husband, I would keep it to myself. This decision had often troubled me, but I was sure that the worry was caused by my Christian background. So I'd decided to fight that background. As long as I had the capacity to relate to both of them with love, care and humanity, I was doing nothing wrong, I told myself. But I had to work hard at it, and remain conscious of this thought.

Teresa's lecture had sounded religious to me, and being averse to religion, I was careful to be noncommittal. Human beings have the ability, as they turn spirituality into religion, to become fundamentalist. To say that the Bible was written by God, was the word of God, was to insist that there be no discussion, no debate. But the Bible was written by human beings inspired by knowledge and wisdom. Its fame and popularity and the commitment of millions to its principles reflected that it had found men and women thirsty for an understanding of spiritual issues. It must have been inspired by spirituality.

But powerful men and women had tampered with the Bible and killed in its name. Despite its declaration of God as a friend of everyone, whatever their skin colour, it had created great insecurity and anxiety; it had been used as a symbol of commitment and belief, as a means to justify human action so as to render the cross innocent of bloodshed.

So I was always very careful. I didn't want to lose Teresa to an argument about religion. It had already been too costly for us as Africans. This young religion on the African continent, Christianity, had cost us dearly indeed, but we had made friends with Christ and asked him daily since then to liberate us from the West. I tried to find a way to tell Teresa that she had a right to think whatever she chose to, but that she should not bind us, commit us all to religion. I trod carefully, thoughtfully.

At times it troubled me, especially when I heard her pray. I hoped she wouldn't try to impose the idea on the children that the answer to all our challenges lay in religion. It was an honour that at one moment we had been children facing the inferno for our freedom, and now, in the next moment, we were the generation responsible for building our nation.

One day I felt it was time for me to have a talk with the children. Teresa and I took them to the Kwa Maritane Lodge in a game reserve in the North West, a peaceful place.

Teresa wanted me to talk to them alone; she told me. The topic was too close to her heart. She was afraid to talk to

Seabe and Mantwa about it, because if the discussion went wrong and they rejected what she said, she might not handle it, she might become hysterical, as she put it.

I tried to read Seabe and Mantwa's mood as we lay on the lawn. I was beside Mantwa, who was cutting her nails, and Seabe was next to her, doodling on a pad as I spoke.

I was uneasy too. What would I do if things turned negative? Our culture kept our children polite, something many had become sceptical, even angry about. I didn't know what it meant to be aggressive as a way of life. Should we be teaching our children to be aggressive, or perhaps proactive? Aggression and proaction seemed to me instincts that animals developed naturally in their environments. But what did I know of such matters?

"If you listen carefully to South African musicians," I began, "you'll find a tapestry of the traditions and customs of African people. We need to listen, and make up our minds about how relevant their words are to our lives."

Mantwa glanced up. "You mean musicians like Jonas Gwangwa, Miriam Makeba, Hugh Masekela and Caiphus Semenya?"

"Yes," I said, "and many others in the *mbaqanga* genre. But traditional songs and gospel music also reflect who we are."

"So music's not just entertainment?" Seabe asked.

"It's also for educating," I said.

"Why are you telling us this?"

"Because the world we're living in requires that we know who we are," I said. "It's not enough to say you're an African. You need to know what that means. I'm suggesting that part of the answer to that question lies in our music. Let me tell you some stories, and I hope that at the end you'll understand why I wanted to come here and talk. You also realise that I'm a bit uneasy as I talk to you, and so is Teresa, which is why she's asked us to excuse her. We love you very much, and we're trying to find a way to make you strong and prepare you for the times you live in."

I paused. "Has Seabe told you about his friend's father who was raped?" I asked Mantwa.

"Yes," she said. "And Teresa also told me."

"Let me tell you something else. You know, before Teresa and I came to stay together, I lived in a flat in Yeoville, in old Fortesque near Rockey Street. I was working in MK then, taking part in the negotiations. I used to drive to Pretoria every day. The flat is disintegrating now, but then it was my haven. The area was very quiet when I moved in, but gradually its face began to change. Drugs, robberies and many other things began to appear there, including prostitutes. For some reason this suburb became the bait point for these girls. The girls were black, but most of their customers were white men. One morning as I was leaving for work, I noticed this girl sitting on the pavement next to my gate. It was a wonderful morning; the jacarandas and other flowers were splashing their colours into the air, and the breeze was full of their perfume. People were getting on with their day, going to work and doing their errands. I wonder how many of them even noticed her, or that girls like her had come into this space where we lived."

Sometimes it's not easy to read the effect of what we say on others. I paused, wanting to see their faces, and to test if they were listening. They looked up, then cast their eyes down and continued with what they'd been doing.

"When I got back from work at the end of the day, the same girl was lying on the grass not far from where she'd sat when I left. As I got out of the car to open the gate, I heard her cough and cough and cough. When I got inside, Tshidi, who worked for me then, asked if I'd noticed the girl. She told me she'd been lying there the whole day, coughing and vomiting. 'Something's wrong, very wrong with her,' she said. I went outside to her, and she began to cough and cough again. 'Are you okay?' I asked her. 'Fine,' she told me. But she was so thin, her cheekbones, shoulders and arms were sticking out under her skin. She was struggling to stand up. I asked if I could help, and she said no. 'But you're ill,' I told her. 'Says who?' she asked. But I could see it. She fell back and lay there awhile. Then she tried to get up again, but she began such a bout of coughing that my own chest ached."

Mantwa was looking at me now.

"I phoned for an ambulance. It took half an hour to arrive, and I went to meet them and explain the situation. I made the mistake of pointing at her. She stood up then and forced herself to walk away. She's walking, the ambulance attendant said, so what was the problem? I told them how long she'd been lying there, about her cough, how skinny she was. Only then did he get out of the ambulance and go to her. They spoke awhile. Then he came back to say she was fine, and drove off. I watched her walk slowly to the pick-up point and stand there, waiting. A Mercedes Benz drove past very slowly. There was a white man driving. He looked at her, passed, came back and stopped. Then he picked her up and drove away. I just stood there, between the buzz of traffic and the silence of the trees. I was lost."

Neither of the children spoke, but I could see I still had their attention.

"This incident reminds me of another," I said. "It was far from here, in Alexandra where I grew up, in the early nineties, I think. The war in Alexandra had just ended, but the smoke, the rubble, the scars were all still visible. I was visiting some relatives when a cousin of mine told me they'd just buried Lucky that week. Lucky had come home late at night. Then the police arrived with a young man. He had blood around his mouth and eye, and his face was bashed and swollen. The young man pointed at Lucky, and the police grabbed Lucky and asked him where the gun was. Other policemen searched the house, the yard, the broken cars and the people in the house. Eventually they brought out an AK47 from one of the rooms. Lucky was bleeding now, and screaming that the police had planted the rifle. They dragged him into the Casspir, demanding he tell them where Joe was, and drove off with him. That was the last time Lucky's family saw him alive. The next day a young woman found Lucky lying dead in a donga, full of mud. His legs were broken and one eye was missing."

Seabe had stopped doodling.

"The girl with the cough and Lucky and his friend must have been nineteen at most at the time. They were maybe the fifth or sixth generation of Africans to live in urban areas. Lucky died around 1992; the girl with the cough was in 1999. Before then, we lost thousands of the 1976 generation during the protests. Later, the eighties generation were shot recklessly, while those before them were detained, exiled and killed. And since 2000, we've been burying the Aids youth. This hasn't just been happening in Jo'burg. It's been happening all across the length and breadth of our country, in rural and urban areas, but especially in the squatter areas that sprawl to the horizons like a spreading rash. The death of our youth in the squatter areas is a legacy of the apartheid system. When we fought for freedom I didn't know that when we finally defeated apartheid, we'd inherit all the devastation it caused.

"Not only have we inherited it, we've become responsible for undoing it, while those who created it try to hold the moral high ground and blame us for failing to heal it quickly enough. And they want to give us advice on how to shape the future from that past. In the meantime, we have to live with the mess and the dirt of the past system. The boys and girls I speak of are our own children or relatives. The blacks are in the pits while the whites live with the privileges of the past. As President Mbeki has said, we South Africans are two nations: one black, the other white. What then must we do to overcome this situation, which has the potential to become violent, to undermine the nonracial, nonsexist and democratic nature of our new South Africa? Black people in the new South Africa have political power, but the whites have the economic power. The political power of the blacks secures the economic power of the whites. How can we level the playing field?"

It seemed as if I'd taken a lifetime to make my point. A silence fell among us.

"Why are you telling us all these things?" Mantwa asked.

"Because we need to come to terms with the world we live in. Teresa and I would like to talk about these things with you sometimes."

I hoped that maybe, just maybe, something had been started today, something that could get us to communicate.

"I'm thirsty," Seabe said.

"Why don't we go find Teresa and get some lunch?" I suggested.

"Yes!" Mantwa said. "I really need something to eat."

As we sat there eating chicken, sweet potato, *ditloo, leraka* and fruit, I felt more convinced than ever that no one had the right to colonise or oppress anyone, and that none should allow themselves to be oppressed. Yet it had happened in so many variations throughout history, and was still happening, and others were still planning and plotting oppression. Well, let the wheel of time roll on, I thought. There was no one whose spirit didn't seek to take off and fly. Seabe and Mantwa, in their innocence, looked so vulnerable as they sat there eating thoughtfully after listening to my ramblings. But they were here with me, and as they sat, bewildered, pondering why we'd come here, why I was saying these things, I thought that this could be my last chance to spend time with them in this way. It might never again happen that we could sit like this, eat like this, talk like this away from home together. The chores of life might never allow such a time again.

I had to find a way to express who we were as South Africans. Our destiny was trapped within the depths of our identity. We were the meandering and shimmering shades all around us, the dappled light beneath the swaying leaves and branches, the splashes and shafts of light and shadow, weaving endless tapestries, as our many tongues sought the wisdom to express all the manifestations of life. Yet we were blind to the truth of who we were. Warmed by the heat from above, we were one with the breeze that swept over the valleys and mountains, over the rivers and lakes that sprawled across the land. Our character was woven into the ever-changing weather patterns emanating from the spinning of the earth. As the earth yielded its own motion, it fashioned the stillness that set us apart as humanity and bound us to everyone else. There was nothing we had not done. The elusiveness of who we were was engraved in all we did as human beings. The colours of our flesh were blended into the glittering mural issuing from the streams, the light and shadows and dancing sun rays that made day and night, and the heat that created the very essence of the plants, reptiles, ants, and all life that breathed beneath the blue skies...

We were so simple. We were so complex. We were like everybody else, held between life and death, constrained by the cruel brevity of life, the smallness of space and place. We knew the threat of being plucked out by the root like a weed. It was this that had taught us to meander into unreachable depths until we were woven into the fabric of time past, time present and time to come, to the point of stillness, the reality where we had said no and meant it, when fate pondered what should happen with us. Like all peoples, we had fought battles, we had built, we had gathered knowledge in its complexity. We had made choices, we had learned from our mistakes and from others, we were revisiting our destiny like everyone else. We had engraved ourselves into the winds of the land.

While we now determined our own direction, we'd been fearless in taking the directions fate had decided for us. This was evident in the visible milestones of our life. We'd been slaves, we'd been doormats for other people, and we prided ourselves on having survived. Who then were we that we were not yet a nation? The virgin eyes that now searched the space above my forehead, avoiding my eyes, absorbing what I'd just said, inflamed me with anger. I didn't want them to walk the paths I had traversed. I hoped they would have their own destiny, this young woman and this young man. I hoped that like me they would be able to say, we fought when we had to and did our best when asked. I looked at them. We gazed at each other.

I thought about Thuso in Villiers. Among those valleys that harsh winter, he'd had to make a decision, and he had done so. On that day the people he lived and grew up with held him by the stalk and tugged, wanting to uproot him. On that day he was shaking. Can our people make decisions? Can this community work out its story when given a brutal chance? Or will it collapse under a tumour and disintegrate? What will those like Thuso do, what will this community do, after it's had the chance to examine its life? If they come to know who they are, they will know what decisions to make.

I didn't know whether Mantwa and Seabe would know how to protect their backs after this talk. But at least I knew that Teresa and I had raised them together and would not abandon them when they became adults.

That night in Villiers, at the end of the meeting, Thuso had apologised to us all for causing us pain. And he'd said: "I'm disabled, but please don't fear me. I've heard all you've said. You don't want me to put a bottle in any of your coffins, so I won't. I'm not a wizard, I wish no evil on anyone, and because I don't, I will continue with my rondavel. I'm in the process of becoming a *ngaka*. With or without your support, *bongaka* will be present in this community."

And he'd begun to shake uncomfortably, his deformed arms hanging like poles at his sides, his twisted legs and feet jumping up and down in their ugly twisted shoes.

"With great humility I ask you to let me go now," he said. "I will go to my house, and take my family with me. If I'm evil, or a wizard, set us alight." And he struggled to his feet.

There was the silence of ages among us, the silence of judgment day, of life and death. It was like the silence just before the gunshots ring out; or the smouldering after the fire has gone out; after glass had shattered and the screams died down; after the tears have dried. It was a moment of thought and of choices, when anything could happen.

After his great struggle to stand and control his legs and shoulders, he turned and wobbled away. I stood and helped him along for a while. Then Nkele and Nomusa came to take his hand, and I turned back to see his other children following him. He had assumed the defiance of ages and generations. We remained in a kind of startled wonderment. He was gone.

"Thuso has made his decision," Ngaka said. "We have still to make up our own minds. Do we burn his house and his family? Do we ask him to leave our community? Or do we respect his calling, as he respects our own? We don't need to make the decision together now. Anyone can call on me, and I will convene a meeting. But only if there are corpses or evidence of evil Thuso has done," Ngaka concluded. "Bring this to me, and I will be obliged to take harsh steps against him."

When there was no response, he'd stood, taken me by the hand, and walked out of the meeting. Night had fallen, and as I lay on my bed in Villiers that night, I'd finally begun to think about the job I'd come there to do.

Chapter 9

WHEN TERESA, MANTWA, Seabe and I left Kwa Maritane, I was already preparing for a trip to Zimbabwe with Bra Shope. As we drove past Musina, I thought about Dikeledi. On the way to Beitbridge, Bra Shope became very talkative.

"History always repeats itself," he said, "with possibilities and chances for us humans to make a great leap forward."

"I don't see how that's a response to my question. I asked whether there's any room for what we call African institutions in the twenty-first century."

"That wasn't your original question, which arose from seeing the rock that reminded you of the Zimbabwe ruins, Mapungubwe and Thulamela, remember? Are you so absent-minded? You were saying that if these ruins signified civilisation, what happened? Why is Africa where it is now? Remember?"

"Okay," I said. "So, can we locate these institutions in the present so that they become catalysts not just resistance or protest structures? Can we recreate extended families, polygamy, *bongaka* and *magosi*, initiation and *lekgotla*? Do they have any relevance now?"

"My dear friend, Africa is practising all that now, right now in the twenty-first century. But is it working? Why were these institutions created? Are the reasons still relevant now?" Bra Shope asked. He was irritable.

"Well…"

"Don't say 'well'! You know what all this is saying to us?

It's asking us as African intellectuals whether we're relevant to our own lives. If we are, the questions we're asking would be asked, and the answers to the questions would come from us. These questions and answers would be our response to our objective reality."

"So are we relevant? There's too much TV, Harvard and Oxford in our spirit, we hallucinate about our lives…"

He looked at me, "I'm making a very serious indictment," he said.

"I know…"

"You know?"

"Yes I do," I said.

"There, then…" he said.

Bra Shope had insisted on holding his exhibition at the Catholic community hall in Gweru. We stayed at the Fairmile Hotel, again at his insistence, although it was ten kilometres from the Guinea Fowl air-force base and the Hwahwa maximum security prison, institutions where the issues of the past were alive in the warm sunshine of that beautiful country. There was something inexplicable in their stillness and quiet as they stood firm in time, and the presence of these walls and gates made Bra Shope and I talk about them. We also debated the future of this land, Zimbabwe, influenced by these silent, dormant symbols of its past, contemplating how life would be lived in the nurturing sunshine of this clear blue sky, among these vast, lush, undulating plains and veld that defied one's eyes to find the horizon. The land question that loomed large was to remain an issue in the region for a long time.

There was also something cruel in the air, in this land so many had died to liberate. Whatever that something was, an innocence seemed to cloak Guinea Fowl and Hwahwa prison. But if the walls could only have spoken, they would surely tell of the bloody price of that freedom and of the scars that still rippled through the beauty of southern Africa.

Bra Shope called his exhibition "The Truth about Truth and Reconciliation", and said that in the end he hoped the exhibition asked all us Africans "Who are you?" Bra Shope had appropriated the so-called arts and crafts into montages that combined drawing, wood carving, grass weaving, stone, beads, fabric, utensils, stools and papier mâché. He'd also used some of my photographs, especially of women. He spent most of his time at the hotel, reading, walking, asking the workers to teach him Shona, and flirting with women.

At the cocktail party to open the exhibition, Bra Shope got drunk and told some very off-colour jokes. Most people, however, were polite to him.

"Who do you prefer, Pinochet or Mugabe?" he asked a tall white Englishman, who held his glass as if he might drop it.

"The line between them is growing thin," the Englishman said.

"But why is England saving Pinochet and crucifying Mugabe?" I wondered then where Sarah was, where Dimakatso and Musa were. "England didn't crucify Pinochet," Bra Shope said.

"But Chile is, and Zimbabwe is crucifying Mugabe," the man said.

"If you're talking to me, please think, don't fart. I'm asking you a simple question. It's not even a political question, it's a common sense question. The breaking of law and order, as the Queen's people call it, arises over the question of land. Now, I don't condone the breaking of law and order, and I can tell you why, but for now it's safe to say I don't condone it. Nevertheless, if we don't address the land question in Zimbabwe, there'll be no law to break – the country will collapse into chaos! Is that not common sense?"

"I take your point, but when a government depends on breaking the law to reach its goal, who then will maintain the law?"

'I hear you, and that's why I say I don't condone it, but if those who know so much about law and order to the extent that they're its keepers in the world, why can they not see that Zimbabwe inherited the breaking of law and order when the land question wasn't solved?"

"Mugabe had twenty years to solve the problem," the Englishman said.

"I beg your pardon, what did you say your name was again?"

"Peter."

"Peter, please let's look at the facts, let's not be prejudiced."

"I'm not prejudiced at all. It's a fact that Mugabe had twenty years to resolve this issue, but didn't," he said.

"My question is, Peter, wasn't there already a breaking of law and order when Zimbabwe was liberated and the land question wasn't resolved?"

"Let's say that…"

"So at some point or the other during those twenty years this matter was going to arise. And even if Mugabe goes, it will still arise, do you agree? My question then is, what must be done? Fight Mugabe, or insist on solving this problem?"

"How do you insist on solving it?"

"The UK and the US must give the money they promised in Lancaster to compensate the farmers whose English ancestors stole the land from the Zimbabweans. How's that?" Bra Shope said.

"And pay the money to whom? To a corrupt government?"

"I'm glad you recognise that Mugabe is in government. If he is, why do the English think they must tell him what to do? Why don't they leave the matter to the Zimbabweans to sort out? If he's corrupt, put a system in place to ensure that he's accountable. Force Mugabe into a corner and mediate the process of proper land redistribution. Is this not the issue?"

"It may be, it may be, but at present we're dealing with rogues and lawlessness."

"Are we going to find a common point of reference, or are you going to maintain a position of presiding?" Bra Shope asked.

"I'm not presiding, I'm making an observation that there's lawlessness; there's corruption in government. Rogues are roaming the land, killing and destroying property, that's what."

"I hoped you'd see things differently from your ancestors, who not only thought Africans were rogues, but also believed we were primitive, pagan and uncivilised, and therefore behaved like rogues towards us. They pillaged, they appropriated land; they dehumanised, enslaved and subjugated us."

"It doesn't help to pay lip service to not condoning lawlessness. There must be action to prove it," Peter said.

I walked away then to survey the exhibition. It was Bra Shope at his most meticulous, but still it was an experiment. It had possibilities, but except for a few pieces, only possibilities. I thought about the title, and wondered whether I needed an education to appreciate the exhibition. What was I comparing it with? What was my point of reference? Could it have its own logic, its own aesthetics, patterns and forms that couldn't compete or be compared with anything else?

There was a large framed piece of a traditional dancer called *Ritual Dancer*. It was a colourful portrayal of a dancer moving at high speed, and included grass stalks, wood and fabric. Movement flowed from it; bright colours blurring in motion into a thunderous tapestry. Multiple images of the dancer's hands were superimposed to reflect speed as the dancer played the drum; the same was done with the legs, and the fabric seemed to fly like flames in the breeze.

Collectively, the exhibition attempted to shift swiftly to the past, harness and enhance it, and produce contemporary pieces that were elegant and dignified. But I wasn't at all sure if it worked. Music played: there were musicians from Zimbabwe, Angola and the DRC, and Miriam Makeba dominated. The event had a fashion show feel about it. Bra Shope had wanted Dimakatso to come and dance, but hadn't managed to persuade the organisers.

One of the themes of the exhibition was poverty: the cruelty of poverty as it wears everything down: clothes, fingers, hands, arms, faces, eyes; as it dulls the mind, blunts the spirit, breaks the body. Many people found this riveting. There was a large portrait of a barefoot woman in a vivid dress with ruffled hair and a ravaged face that seemed to ring out from its space. Her facial features were twisted and distorted, all portrayed in the finest detail. She had a wide toothless smile with one staring eye, the other having been gouged out. There was also a representation of a family: a husband in ragged trousers with neat creases; the boy in a shirt mended many times, and a girl in a boy's shirt whose shoe had no sole. The meticulous detail with which each item had been created evoked silence, emotion and wonder.

◌

When we got back to South Africa, Bra Shope began questioning me a lot about e-mail. He wanted to e-mail his friends, and I promised to find out how to do it. He asked me to go to Cape Town to request the gallery where he'd previously exhibited to buy him a PC with the money it owed him. He was adamant. His friend Jean was a computer expert in Cape Town, and I was to take lessons from her. I recalled how he'd been the one who taught me to use a camera – to replace my AK47, as he'd said then. I'd started by taking slides of his work. Then he'd sent me for a course on archiving. Later he asked me to photograph buildings, people and all kinds of things.

Jean and I met in the so-called Mother City. Nature in this city is luring, provocative, dappling things, promising tranquillity. The sky, vast and aloof, reflects the sea; the mountains ignore the sky but acknowledge the sea; the gloomy grey-blue sea reflects back the sky. Cape Town has a harsh, sandy landscape; it can be hot, it can be wet, and it can be hellishly windy. You sense the fish on the breeze, you hear the white birds, sometimes the black ones that croak, and now and then, the hoot of a ship. Cape Town can give you the sense of the end of the world.

During my three days in Cape Town, I was able to get the money from the gallery, and Jean advised me, in her husky, guttural voice, what type of computer to buy, and taught me a bit about computers. Jean and I worked well together. She was the colour of ginger cake, and her hazel eyes seemed to stare into me from her beautiful stern face, framed by straight black hair that shone like a mirror, cropped short beneath her ears. She dressed in miniskirts that revealed muscular legs.

When it was time to go, I walked through the city streets to get a taxi to the airport.

As I turned a corner I glimpsed Table Mountain looming in the distance above the skyscrapers. Then I stopped in my tracks. A ragged man had blocked my way. "I'm not begging," he said, tipping his hat, "but I can make you smile. Promise you'll give me five rand, and maybe some leftovers, something I can use. So I can eat." Then he turned slightly and gestured toward a passageway with a closed shop doorway and grill in front of it. There I could see a woman on her back and a man on top of her, naked and oblivious, groaning as they made love.

"You smiled! Now give me my five rand." He pointed at my camera. "I promise you," he laughed, "a picture of me is like a postcard!"

He posed with a toothless grin, and I took the picture. There were more groans from the passageway. To get away, I pressed a ten rand note into his rough, dirty hand and left. Before I turned the next corner I looked back. He had stopped a white couple and was pointing toward the doorway.

What was that about, I thought. How do people do that? And what would I do with the photograph, I wondered. I'd give it to Bra Shope, I decided immediately.

ଓ

I spent the two hours on the plane trying to make sense of what I'd experienced. It stayed in my mind, bothering me. As the plane landed I found myself rehearsing how I'd relate the story to Teresa and Bra Shope, determined to print the photograph that evening.

The weather was as bright as it had been in Cape Town. Teresa walked slowly up to me and held my hand tightly. "How was your flight?" she asked without meeting my eye.

"What's the matter?" I asked.

"I've just been to visit Bra Shope," she said. "Something's wrong."

"What! Should we go and see him?"

"We must go right now," she said.

The drive from the airport to Morningside took forever. We emerged from the airport, went under the bridge and back onto the highway. Signpost after signpost directed us with its words and arrows. The tyres were pounding like raindrops on the tarmac. The tension between Teresa and me felt familiar, evoking a mix of suspense, fear and anxiety. I wondered what lay ahead to be faced. I tried to pray, but before I could finish the prayer my mind drifted away, lost.

"I stopped by Bra Shope on my way back from swimming," Teresa said. She went quiet. She was concentrating on the road now, taking the off-ramp and negotiating an intersection, her attention on the traffic. "I don't want to be alarmist, but I want to know what you think…" She took a turn.

"What do you mean?"

Teresa was preoccupied. I knew her. I had to leave her alone, though I knew that she wouldn't leave me alone about whatever this was about. I knew I had to wait till we got there.

"How are the children?" I asked, trying to change the subject.

"They were fine when I left for swimming."

As we turned towards Morningside she said, "Let's buy some fruit or something for Bra Shope at the bridge."

"No. Take me there first, then go buy fruit…"

"But why? It's on our way."

"I know, but I'm in suspense…"

"About what?"

"Teresa!" I said. "You haven't said why we need to see Bra Shope before I even get home. I've been away four days, and the children are about to leave."

"I know, I know. But we have to see him first," she said. She passed the shop, then turned and stopped in a driveway. The automatic gate began to slide open.

"You've got Bra Shope's remote?"

"He gave it to me long ago," she said as we entered the yard and parked. We entered the house, Teresa almost running in front of me, calling.

"Bra Shope!" No answer. "Bra Shope…" She hurried along the passageway to the lounge.

There was Bra Shope in his gown and slippers, smiling. He looked at her and then me.

"You're my family, aren't you?" he said. His voice was odd, his face strange, his eyes not his own.

"What's the matter?" I asked.

He looked at me, then at Teresa. "Well, I'm an old man, you know," he said. "I'm not your age. Time moves on, and drags me along..."

His eyes were searching ours for clues. I realised somehow that Bra Shope had given in to something; something that, although it frightened him, he'd decided wasn't worth fighting. I knew then that this was what Teresa had wanted me to know.

Bra Shope sat there on his favourite sofa in his pyjamas and gown, smiling a kind of mock smile – a frightened smile, a hopeless smile. I wanted to take a picture, but I knew I should seek his permission. What if he said no? I unslung my camera from my shoulder. He stopped smiling and looked puzzled. I nearly didn't take the picture, but I clicked.

"You're committed to your photography." He smiled again. "You've swapped it for the AK, heh?"

What could I say?

"How was Cape Town?"

"Fine." I hesitated. "What's wrong, Bra Shope?"

"Nothing. What does it matter? I'm just fine. Bloody problem is when I ask my limbs to do something and they don't," he said.

I became aware then of a pool of water at his feet. Our eyes met.

"What can a man say?"

"Can I help you to the toilet?"

"It's too late," he said, and looked down at himself for a long time. Then he looked up at me, shook his head, looked away towards the window. I felt a great sadness rising like a sob in the throat.

"You must look after Teresa," he said. "Don't be like me, alone in this state. I've burnt many, many bridges, I know. I'm like that."

"What are you talking about?" I asked.

He looked away as if into the distance. Then he looked down at the pool of urine at his feet. I took his hand; it was cold. I pulled slightly, waiting for him to respond, to stand up, to come with me. He stared at me, not moving an inch.

"I'll pull his hands," Teresa said. "You try to lift him."

I went behind the chair. I slipped my hands under his armpits and tried to hoist him, while Teresa pulled. A stench engulfed us. Bra Shope had been trapped here, alone, the whole day...

BOOK TWO

BOOK TWO

The voices sing and sing,
and the dance, a tapestry of song,
goes on and on…

Chapter 10

BRA SHOPE IS GONE. He almost died in our arms. When he eventually passed, it was as if the whole world sighed in relief. He suffered before he passed on. Initially, he refused to go to hospital. He said he wanted to die at home. In the first week, Teresa and I took shifts to mind him. We made sure he took his tablets and ate the right food, and usually he just lay there or slept. It became difficult and frightening when he had to use nappies, because Bra Shope was such an independent person, such a proud man. I felt his humiliation whenever we changed the napkin. He never shed a tear, but I knew he was crying inside.

Surely, I thought, it wasn't just coincidence that Teresa and I were witness to this. His need for napkins humiliated him so much that he would try to refuse us entry to his bedroom when it was time for him to take tablets. There's a song of deep hurt and compassion that goes *uzangikhumbula mhla ungen'a mandla*. I would insist on coming in, although Teresa, being a woman, could not. There I'd be greeted by the fresh stench. When I made it clear that I was aware of what had happened, he would sulk. I insisted we discuss the situation.

"What do you want to discuss?" he'd ask.

"Bra Shope," I would say, "you're very ill. Let's try to join hands and co-operate, so we can get on top of the situation."

"What situation? There's no situation!"

"There's no point in denial, and I'm already getting help. The doctor's coming tomorrow…"

I discovered what large eyes Bra Shope had, as they bulged in anger and disbelief that I could call a doctor without his knowledge.

The doctor came in his white coat, carrying a briefcase and walking softly, the stethoscope around his neck. I wondered whether he'd be able to examine his patient. Bra Shope refused to see him at first, and then relented. But he complained endlessly that there must surely be another way, some alternative to napkins. We promised to find out, but in the meantime we had to use them.

Then one day he was swollen from head to foot. He was almost unrecognisable. We had to rush him without his consent to hospital. I sat with him in the ambulance. He asked for a pen and paper, and wrote down the phone number and address of his wife, Tembile. I was shocked: I'd never known that he knew where she was. Then he closed his eyes.

He was put on a stretcher.

"Does Sis Tembile know you're ill?" I asked him. He looked at me and then shook his head.

"How are you feeling?" I asked him. He shrugged. "Is there anything you need?" He shook his head. We held hands. I was very afraid. What would the world be like without Bra Shope? But something about him kept me hopeful. Once or twice as I asked him a question, I saw that familiar mocking smile of his. I imagined him one day saying, "When I was ill you were very afraid, right?" I didn't know that I would never again see Bra Shope walk, nor hear his voice again.

Early one evening, Teresa came back from the hospital looking very grey. She seemed unable to answer any question. I held her, and she let out a deep howl. I'd seen Teresa cry before, but not as she wept that day.

"Sis Tembile arrived at the hospital while I was there," she said. "When she held Bra Shope's hand, he wept..."

she said. She wiped her face; her eyes were red. I waited for her to finish, but she left me standing at the front door and went to the bedroom. When I went to check on her, she was under the blankets. She wouldn't talk.

I got into the car and drove to the hospital, expecting the worst. There was Bra Shope, lying on his back, with Sis Tembile in a chair, still holding his hand. There was something youthful about her. She gave me her beautiful smile and a firm handshake. I searched her face for a clue about Bra Shope's condition, and felt Bra Shope's glare. His eyes were large as the moon. What might it have been like if I'd known them together, I wondered. I gravely regretted that this thought should have arisen so late. Bra Shope's eyes were large, almost winking at me, but also very distant. I saw that Sis Tembile was not just holding his hand now, but clutching it. Here the three of us were then, she and I terrified, but he, with hindsight, was distant, no longer concerned with the flesh. He had already taken his decision to go. And soon he did: just like that, he was gone.

ଓଃ

Bra Shope's voice echoed still in many cities around the world. I no longer knew whether I'd really known him. Voices popped up on the computer screen in a variety of English forums to mourn his passing.

I should never have photographed Bra Shope in his coffin. I spent so long printing this image, it felt like the only picture that now remained before my eyes. It couldn't be the image of my friend. His eyes were closed, his mouth like clay; his forehead had lost its wrinkles. His face was passive and expressionless, frozen as if something terrible was about to happen. It was the colour of calabash; round, quiet, neutral, without laughter, pain, without a smile. It was a dead face without spirit or soul, surrounded by a wooden coffin with silver handles, on its stand in the middle of the green carpet.

I watched as people filed past, peeped and looked away. Some of them appeared in the photographs. Some showed surprise; some shock; others bewilderment; some gasped and others, even as they peeped, were already looking away.

The person who'd called all these people to file past and peep at my friend's corpse said, "*Bagaetsho tlang le tlhobogeng ngwan' abolona.*"

"My people come and forget your brother," an interpreter said for the many white people, and perhaps for the black people who didn't speak seTswana. I had to fight myself not to go up to the interpreter and call him a liar. That's what Bra Shope would have done. I was also tempted to ask those standing in line for peep what the hell they thought they were doing. I began to shake in my anger, and had to leave the room, struggling to stop the flood of tears.

When I came back, I had my camera, and began to take pictures. The filing and peeping seemed to go on forever. It was a relief when we finally put the coffin in the hearse and eventually into the ground, piled soil on top of it and began to walk back to our cars and drive away.

ᘔ

I got the idea, after the funeral, to look up the business cards I'd collected on my many journeys with Bra Shope. I realised then that his life and mine had become so intertwined that I didn't even know how some of these business cards had come into my possession. Using them, I began to send e-mails to inform people who had known Bra Shope that he was no more. I became so busy with this that I forgot all about my camera, and hardly left the room where Teresa had set up the computer. I'm not sure how long it took me to send out all these e-mails, but it felt like years.

The purring blue-and-white screen brought back replies from all over the world. Some asked who I was. Others asked when Bra Shope had passed, or said management had changed and they didn't know who he was, but regretted his passing. But some expressed deep pain at the passing of Bra Shope. Some even asked whether he had a will, while others asked about the whereabouts of his work. Some even offered pieces of his work that were in their possession. There were responses from places I didn't even know Bra Shope had visited.

Death is a part of us. It's as close to us as skin to bone; we're as close to it as to our own shadows; it's as familiar as the blood running through our veins. Yet when it presents itself, as it did to my friend, it's startling.

One day I began to cry. I cried alone, deep into the night as I sat in front of the purring illuminated screen, connecting with the different time zones of the world's cities. It suddenly struck me that all these e-mails were saying something or other about a friend of mine, whose friendship I couldn't measure in any time frame. I didn't remember and didn't care how long Bra Shope and I had been friends; it felt as if we'd known each other for centuries. And I would never see him again.

I didn't want Teresa to know I was crying. Bra Shope's death had left her devastated. She hardly spoke of him. There was something I couldn't reach in her. At times when I came into the bedroom, I'd find her staring into space. Many times I lay next to her in silence, incapable of helping her in her sorrow. At times she was irritable. Something told me to wait. And when I now began to cry, I became afraid. Afraid perhaps of the future that looked so blank, echoed with such emptiness.

What did it mean that I couldn't bear the sorrow and pain of another, someone I loved? We were examining something inside ourselves, something that yielded a blank, that had no answers to our questions. Bra Shope was part and parcel of our love. He was part of our lives and our being. Bra Shope had petered out. Period. Everything felt so empty, so surreal. Why was this man's passing so catastrophic?

But the vacuum also promised that it didn't matter, that soon it would no longer be there. Vacuums don't exist in nature. One day we would awake and there would be Mantwa and Seabe, on their own, drifting and clutching each other.

∞

Mantwa had become a very beautiful, tall woman. She was fully conscious of her womanhood. She carried herself with a feminine gait; she swung her body with ease, and gently. She watched without watching, and had become careful with words. Something told you, when she was with Seabe and myself, that she wanted us to know and recognise that a woman was present. I could feel that her education and her peers were influencing her. I challenged her a lot, and she took me on.

Seabe was more on the quiet side, but very considerate and friendly. He and Mantwa were engaged in a silent tug of war over space, roles, knowledge and their relationship with each other. They were each in their own way now entering the world.

Mantwa was a very neat, organised, and systematic person; Seabe seemed to be more searching. He was looking for something. He was uncertain, rather untidy, and often preferred to sleep longer and watch TV more than the rest of us in the house. He took longer to engage with issues and seemed to feel a little inferior. But his big sister seemed aware of this. She took great care of Seabe, chaperoning him and navigating around him in a way that avoided making him resentful.

Revelations

One day Teresa told me she'd been going for counselling. She'd been doing it quietly. I was startled. What did it mean, I demanded. What would counselling do for her? Who was counselling her? Counselling her to do what?

She shut the door in my face then. Anger is not only a reflection of helplessness, it is also reckless, and therefore dangerous. But the more I heard about what counselling meant, the angrier I became. And worse still, she dared one day to ask me to come with her. When I asked her what the counselling would do for me, she said it might help me with my anger.

That finished me. What should I be thinking about, I asked her, the anger or what caused the anger? Help me? Help me with what? To do what? What did these people know about Bra Shope? And when she told me that whoever was counselling her was white, I decided that my lady had gone absolutely mad. She was insane, she was out of her mind.

At times during the sessions they played classical music, she told me. It soothed her. I had to force myself to keep quiet, and hope that she never raised the subject with me again. At times of distress like this, the human mind can degenerate. It needs strength, it needs to know that we can still control it, without letting it become base.

Now I was the one who refused to talk about Bra Shope with Teresa. I confided to both Nkgono and Nkoko about this dilemma. One said I must pray, the other that I must see a *ngaka*. Nkoko kept telling me, in her eternal calmness, that an elephant never complains its trunk is too heavy; it carries it and uses it, at times even to amuse itself.

I heard them. And their advice occupied my mind. Somehow the resilience I'd learned during my initiation, and in MK while it existed, gave me great sense of responsibility. But I also needed something to hold onto, something to direct my mind in a more positive manner. I began to search.

Teresa and I spent time separately with Sis Tembile, in that now terrible house in which Bra Shope had lived. In so many ways the house spoke to us of his absence. Tembile was very deliberate in telling us that although we'd accepted that Bra Shope was no more, we were now responsible for creating a safe passage for his spirit. Teresa listened carefully to Tembile, who performed all kinds of rituals with the help of an old lady who guided them. I had to follow them. These two ladies who had been in Bra Shope's life were a great challenge to me. At times I paricipated, at others I didn't. I wondered whether they understood that Bra Shope was my friend, my comrade, my mentor, and would always be, forever. We were cleansed. We spoke to him together. We disposed of his clothes. We packed up his belongings, including his paintings.

Teresa was distant, probably because I too was distant. I abandoned the mad world and sat at the computer. I was now surfing the Net, scrolling through piles of information day after day. Whatever the information was, it nurtured voices in my head. Many times I felt as if I was watching ripple after ripple form and break, form and break, as if watching a boiling lake.

But useful and educational as it was, the computer couldn't save me.

Chapter 11

I HIT THE STREETS and the bottle then. In a drunken stupor early one evening, I got into the car and drove to Villiers. I had to see Ngaka. I had to find him, his quiet wisdom, that calm he had revealed to me. Perhaps it was also an excuse to see Dikeledi.

I don't know how I got to Villiers. Dikeledi opened the door. Face to face with me she stared, smiling softly, searching me with her eyes.

I sat down on her sofa, aware of the images on the TV screen, conscious of her husband sitting in the corner watching it, and the snoring of her son from another room.

"Who must I see," I asked her, "you or Ngaka?"

She was silent for a while, then, ignoring my question, tried to make her husband aware of me.

"I know him," he said. "He lived here for some time during the struggle. He's a comrade."

"Oh yes!" Dikeledi said. "Of course you know him. This is my husband," she said. I staggered over, nearly tripped, but managed to shake the man's hand. He introduced himself as Jomo. I felt very drunk, and very hungry. I wanted to leave and go back to Teresa. But I only managed to sit down.

"Where have you come from?" Dikeledi asked me.

"Jo'burg," I said.

"And where are you going?"

I was tempted to feel insulted by this question. But I answered.

"I need to talk to someone," I said. With a polite smile, Jomo stood up, excused himself and vanished into the semi-lit passage. Dikeledi followed him. She was away a while. Why had I come to Villiers, I mumbled to myself. Dikeledi came back, excused herself and went out. She was gone a while, years maybe. Then I felt someone shaking me gently and calling my name.

"What?" I asked.

Dikeledi was standing over me. "Come with me, I've arranged a place for you to sleep."

"Why?"

"You're tired. I won't let you drive in that state."

"Won't allow me? What do you mean you won't allow me!"

"Have you eaten?"

"I must go," I insisted.

"Have you eaten?"

"No, but, I must go." She went to the stove…

When I next saw her, she was shaking me again. "Here's some food." She looked me in the eye, and her face looked very sad.

"I'm sorry," I said. "I must apologise for troubling you like this."

"No. I'm glad you came," she said. "But now you must eat and then go to bed."

We sat opposite each other at the small table, the plate of food between us like a game we were about to play. The plate irritated me. I grabbed it and began to eat. The food was delicious, perhaps because I was hungry, and I demolished it shamelessly. She gave me a damp cloth to wipe my hands and stood over me, waiting. As I gave her back the cloth, I felt very drowsy.

In the morning, the old lady in whose house I had slept smiled. "You must have been very tired. You snored like a roaring lion!"

Her face was familiar. I tried to remember how I knew her. Something in the way she spoke struck a note. But what could I say? She gave me coffee and prepared water for me to wash, saying that Dikeledi would fetch me at eight. Suddenly I realised who she was. Nomusa! I knew then where I must be. I hoped to God that a volcano would swallow me up. I washed and dressed, feeling trashed. My body ached and I was light-headed, disoriented and bilious.

Dikeledi arrived. Something about her was still so attractive. We were both quiet. Our eyes locked briefly and the moment spoke volumes between us.

As we drove to see Ngaka, I told her I would always love her. She told me she would always love me too. I thought, then, that for what we'd just said to each other, the community could pile up wood, stack it neatly and deliberately so that the strike of a single matchstick would ignite the lot, and then throw us, bound and gagged lest we scream too much and too loud, onto the flames of the inferno. They could watch us burn until we were nothing but ash, all because we had declared our love to each other.

I said nothing more to Dikeledi, and we drove in silence until we reached Ngaka's homestead. I had found peace here on many occasions when I'd come to plan and prepare for missions. There was something about the homestead, its trees, plants, boulders, little stream, the smell of the incense, the orchestra of birdsong... At times when I'd come here, the healing songs sung and danced by the *dingaka* and others, evocative and insistent as they communed with the spirits, used to put me in dialogue with myself and my deepest conflicts.

Now Ngaka came out to meet us, and led us into one of the *ndumba*. Ngaka and Dikeledi sat on one side and I sat opposite them, with the grass mats and *ditaola*, or divination bones, between us. They began to divine, calling up the ancestors to preside.

I come from the Bakgatla, Ngaka told me. Otsile was my great grandfather's name. His father was Bareng, whose grandfather was Lepane, who was a general in Sekhukhune's army. Lepane had become a herb collector for a *ngaka* when he was young. He came to know the terrain where he lived and also further afield as he went in search of herbs. The *ngaka* he was working with was the *ngaka* for the royal kraal. He and *ngaka* Phasha looked after the soldiers when they were ill, so Lepane became familiar with the ventures of *mephato ya* Sikhukhune as the soldiers related their escapades while they were being tended. Lepane had risen in the ranks of *mephato*, and was then sent to meet other generals among the Barolong who were fighting the British, the Boers, the Matabele and even the Griqua. He had fifteen wives.

I was a tributary of that past. As I sat face to face with Ngaka and Dikeledi, it was like a film rolling before me as they related my past and linked me to my ancestors. Some of the issues they raised were familiar, for I had been told them during my initiation. As I sat there in the *ndumba*, I was shown the link between *koma*, *lekgotla* and *bongaka*. These were the institutions my people had founded to run the estates they had created. There was also a link among *koma*, *lekgotla*, *bongaka* and *mephato*: they were all linked to cattle, land and communal family on which communities were built. And all of these were threaded together by polygamy and by various institutions – *bogosi*, *bongaka* and *koma* for young men and women. The roles of men and women were institutions in themselves, such as boRakgadi, boMalome, boNtate, boMme, boNkgono, boNtatemogolo, boRaqngwane, boMmangwane, and so on. They were institutions with responsibilities to the family and the community. It was through this, and through their standing in the community, that they become *bagolo*, or elders, and were therefore always in council. These were the institutions that Western civilisations had destroyed with their colonial offensive of pillage and destruction, and their numbing religion preached as if they were the Almighty himself. But worst of all was that we had believed them, and come to despise all our own spirituality.

These institutions, Ngaka revealed, were harnessed and interlinked by a philosophy that could be paraphrased as *motho ke motho ka batho, kgosi ke kgosi ka batho*, a person is only a person because of other people. Myriad idioms and proverbs formed a tapestry entrenching the wisdom and observations of these so-called illiterate people, my people, and their understanding of intellect, spirituality, the universe, life and the way these all interrelated. Myriad structures were established to create harmony in life through ideology and philosophy.

The discussion and debate among the three of us became more intense as we progressed. Ngaka was a highly skilled facilitator. As I asked questions and as he threw the *ditaola*, he would pose a question, then probe, then seek a conclusion from Dikeledi. Finally he would comment, giving his view of the issues. The session was exhausting, and we occasionally took a break. Just before one such break, Ngaka spoke about spirituality, and plunged me into the dark sea.

The human spirit, wherever it was, was the basis of our humanity. The human mind was located in the head, it was said, and this was what made us human, different from any other living thing. Though we knew our physicality, we were hardly aware of it, nor in touch with it often enough to understand it, until eventually we discovered how fragile it was.

We walked into others' lives with a mixture of knowledge and ignorance. We wouldn't hear a loud bang, although we might perhaps feel it if we were receptive. Mostly we never heard it. A journey began. We adjusted. Two people, three people or more made contact, bringing to each other our knowledge and our ignorance. We entered into each other's lives. We saw and heard each other; we would speak, respond and interact; do things together and also apart.

Our interactions created a spirit among us. As our senses activated our minds, we began to know. For knowledge comes from the spirit of things, from the minds and physical interactions of people. But knowledge is only knowledge when it is dynamic; it is always relative. In its dynamism and relativity it accumulates not as knowledge but as the rules of what is known and understood, and what is unknown or not understood. And knowledge is only knowledge if we use it. Unused it is useless, unknown. When we use it, we create tapestries, accumulate what is known and unknown and structure this, and this knowledge forever replicates itself in the form of problems and solutions. It develops a history. Its present, past and future combine to create a culture; and as a current this knowledge creates the politics of the present. As Ngaka used the word politics, he was quick to add that he did not use it to mean conflict and strife, but the judgement of who we were and what we would be.

This collective of humans with their knowledge and ignorance, he went on, creates reflections out of the content of its knowledge. From that content its bearers emerge. Even its bearers, like the content, reflect knowledge and ignorance, for ignorance is stagnant knowledge. And the interaction between knowledge and ignorance, through action, create consequences.

From time immemorial, the people of this country had gone through these motions, moving backwards and forwards, stumbling and overcoming. And now we were here we had to ask, what is change? For this change had been very costly to some. For others, it posed a threat, a danger, something unacceptable that had to be stopped. Yet it had happened. But something was not yet right. It was as if we were standing on an unsteady platform that shook and shifted beneath our feet. Something was strange also, as if night had suddenly changed and become day. It was that drastic.

Change had taken place. Everyone was affected, even thieves, killers, hobos, the homeless, the poor. Everyone, black or white, knew something had happened. They too attempted to be multiracial, multilingual and multicultural. But what is change? Change means a break in what is known, and a shift to the new, the unknown. This is a way of sifting and seeking what must make up the future. The future is a new crop full of new leaves.

Ngaka's words no longer came from thoughts, but formed a stream to be examined and pondered as it flowed, to extract the meaning.

"How is Teresa?" Dikeledi asked as we sat outside during the break.

"She's fine. But Bra Shope's death has devastated us. We're traumatised. I don't know why his passing has been so overwhelming, so painful, so difficult to accept." For me, a master had passed; for Teresa a bosom friend. He had left behind a vast space. "She's taken Bra Shope's passing terribly."

"So why did you not come with her to consult?"

"She's gone to spend time with Nkoko to help her recover."

"Does she know you're here?"

"No."

"Come back with her soon if you can," Dikeledi said. "It would have been good for you both to hear what's been said here. Do you understand?" She looked me in the eye.

"I do," I said.

The relationship between Dikeledi and me had taught us things. She'd been young when we met, twenty four when I was thirty eight. She said I'd taught her how to be a woman; in turn, she'd taught me how to love, how to care. That was because she was such an African woman, so solid. One day I'd have to work out what I meant by that. Between us the bond was a very deep. Here she was now, my *ngaka*.

Ngaka called us back into the session. I sat there at the feet of these two people, my one-time fighting partners, while the whole of my past was being unfurled before me. A throw of the bones, then a question, a statement, silence, a discussion between them. Then a question to me. "Whose law was it that told me that married people, while not keeping secrets from each other, must not still have privacy between them?" Ngaka asked. "Each has the need for privacy."

My mind rolled back. Had Nomazwi not impressed this upon me? Even when she was a guerilla, whenever her monthly period came, she insisted on being alone. She would tell me a day or two before and then prepare for her exodus to another room, where she remained for four or five days. She would sleep there, and if it were a weekend I'd hardly see her. I adjusted easily, because my own initiation had trained me to understand that this happened to women, that they were "dirty" at this moment. Yet I didn't actually think they were dirty, nor believe that was what was meant at initiation. We were being told to keep away, to allow women time to go through their cycle in peace, without interference. When we asked about women and their periods, as it was explained to us, we understood what those old men were saying.

There were so many matters like this in African culture. Issues had been carefully thought out; traditional experiments had led to many truths. But once told, not the whole story was told, and because we were an oral people, when memory failed among some of the elders, they would say, "Do as I say and stop asking questions," or "That's how it is, don't question it."

Who was I? Had I really been in MK? And what had we fought for? I remembered when we came back from initiation how the *kgosi* had stood there in the ice-cold wind. He seemed unable to stop talking. There were close to two hundred of us. We'd been on the "mountain" for three cold months; we could still feel the ache in our bodies. We sang and sang and danced and chanted before the *kgosi* came. We were scantily dressed, out in the open in the middle of winter. The icy breeze snapped at our ears, but we endured all this because it was engraved on our minds that we were men now, no longer boys. The steps towards manhood had been painful. The bitter winds that whipped around our almost naked bodies caused none, not one of us, to utter a word of complaint. As a peer group we pushed ourselves to remain in rank; any sign of weakness made us rally around the weakening one, to encourage, to console, to urge, so that we might join the generations of proud fighters and warriors, the wise ones who had gone before us. We had come to the mountain to join their ranks. We were one with them now, at the end of initiation. We felt courage, pride and boldness course through our veins and our marrow.

And then the moment came for sitting down, legs apart, the spear in one's flesh, leaving a ring of red around our manhood, an excruciating pain and a shout of *ke monna* from us! Soon there were feasts and celebrations and pride in our community when we re-entered it.

And the old men, the wise old men who had accompanied us, told us that now we'd been initiated, we would sit with them at the *kgotla*; now we were men and must discuss the issues and matters of men in the village. We were ready to discuss anything and everything about life with them now. We should join them as they deliberated the issues of the nation.

Besides teaching us the secrets of our community, our society and our nation, we knew that in our very being we had become instruments of our nation. The elders had taken control of our very being.

Without my MK experience and the fight for our country, it would have been very difficult to know, as I sat there in that *ndumba*, the value of that initiation experience. But initiation had not only prepared me for the tough journey of MK by accepting that life was hard, that matters were always difficult and that patience was a treasure. It had also located me among my people, within my community, my society and my nation. I knew that I was of the people, but also that I was an individual. Many of my initiation peers later told me how, during severe interrogation, their initiation perseverance had embraced them and seen them through their pain and humiliation at the hands of the secret police. And during prolonged periods of detention without trial, they found they had an in-built strength. Engraved as if by fire into the hearts of initiates was the knowledge of how to survive, yet to succumb to discipline and control when necessary. And this had also played a role during the cruelly oppressive apartheid system. When I watched African men undergo severe whipping and humiliation, sometimes looking so broken, I knew that, even as they seemed so servile, those from initiation harboured a hidden and untouchable resistance, silent and waiting. I knew it.

In the distance I heard Ngaka and Dikeledi talking, discussing, asking me questions. What they didn't know was that they'd unleashed a trail of thought inside me. It was as if I was standing before an X-ray that reflected my very insides to my inner eyes. I was examining everything; interpreting all I'd experienced.

If you don't know humiliation, if it hasn't stripped you naked and exposed you, you cannot know integrity, you cannot know dignity. And I came to learn, as I sat there now, that the sense of belonging we always seek is really the seeking of our own essence. It is a pity indeed that adverts have transformed the world into a set of commodities we can buy, for love cannot be bought. Being socialised is receiving love. Believing is seeking love. This love resides in the spirit, which can drive us to killing, sacrifice, passion and compassion. As the African story of creation tells, after our creation we were given the power of creativity that belonged to the creator and the diviner, and the power to be merciful to all living things.

Now and then I entered into dialogue with Ngaka or Dikeledi or both. But I was also in dialogue with myself. I heard all my voices; I recognised them. Some were frightening. At times when I encountered them and almost wished they would pass and leave me alone, Ngaka would intervene.

"Speak to us, don't keep things to yourself. Remember what I've said. There's no such thing as coincidence; everything serves to nurture the fullness, depth and quality of our spirit."

He was saying this to an MK cadre, an underground communist cadre, an ANC cadre. He too was these, though perhaps not a communist. And I had recruited Dikeledi into a communist unit in my days in Villiers. At that time there'd been no space for anything spiritual among us. As I sat here with my comrades-in-arms, I was in constant transition from moment to moment. One moment things were lucid; the next they were obscure, shifting between light and shadow so rapidly that I almost despaired.

Then Ngaka asked me about Ntate Makgothi...

We were in the *lekgotla* right after my initiation. It was my last day of joining the elders before returning to Alexandra where my parents were. Ntate Makgothi, a thoughtful, reserved man, was asked a question about land that Saturday afternoon.

"*Ba go gana go buswa, re ba kgalema ka morwetla, ga ba pala, re ba kgalema ka lerumo,*" he said: there is no land to talk about; we are living in the wilderness; the best of our land is in the hands of white people. Our *kgosis* are just like trumpets," he went on. "They make the sound of the one blowing them. The white people call the tune. We must decide if we are men. If so, we must tear our trumpets from the blowers, and blow them ourselves; or smell the saliva of the blowers. We must not just sit here, we must replan the institution of initiation to supply fighters to the fight. We must tell the initiates that we are making them men for the life-and-death battle of this land."

There was a moment of great silence.

Then the *kgosi* spoke. "These matters must not be spoken in anger or with such ease. For they will stir dust into the sky and draw attention. But we hear what you are saying. And those who have heard you, I hope they have understood you." He then moved on to speak of other matters.

I remembered this as I sat there in the *ndumba*. Ntate Makgothi's words had remained with me for a long time. They came back to me the day Mafuma told me he wanted to leave the country to join MK. Together we went to look for Ntate Makgothi. We found him still in that harsh, arid landscape of the rural area, and told him what we wanted to do. That same night, we got onto a truck from Dinokana and crossed into Lobatse in Botswana.

In Botswana we made contact with MK. We received three weeks' training in the use of grenades and AKs, and were then sent back to South Africa. There we attacked the house of an informer, along with Jolobe who'd come with Mafuma. We returned to Botswana, and were sent on to Angola. So began our lives as MK cadres. Mafuma was later captured during a mission in Swaziland. I heard later that he died, and was tied to a helicopter by his captors and flown over a village to show the villagers who'd been assisting him what would happen when they were captured. Jolobe died with many of our comrades in Lesotho when the SADF attacked. I was the only one remaining from my original team and unit.

The *ditaola* had made me traverse my life as if it were a landscape.

"Did this man not change your life forever?" Ngaka asked. "The *ditaola* are requesting me to ask you that question."

Chapter 12

On the road back from Villiers, thoughts reeling in my head, I realised that I hadn't communicated with Teresa in three days.

I called her. She told me that she and Nkoko had gone off to some place in the rural areas.

Our home was deserted. Mantwa and Seabe had been deserted; Teresa and I had deserted each other. It felt almost as if our lives had ground to a halt since Bra Shope's death. The cobwebs dangling in all corners of the house said so. The food in the fridge had grown mouldy.

I called Ngaka and told him about the state of the house. He laughed. I didn't see anything funny in what I was seeing, but he did. I began then, as the saying goes, to clean out my house.

Nkoko had taken Teresa to another *ngaka*. She stayed away for six months. Seabe, Mantwa and I missed her a lot, but we did all we could to cope. In her absence, we created a little nest for ourselves.

Teresa came back home after her *thwasa*, and completely turned our lives upside down again. I'd never seen so much blood spilled: the blood of chickens, goats, sheep and cows for rituals and ceremonies to reintegrate her into our home. Now there were all these strangers in our lives: many *dingaka* came to our house wearing their different regalia. There was ceremony after ceremony. I had never in all my life witnessed so much drumming and chanting, dancing and singing. We had no choice, Mantwa, Seabe and I. We had to follow Teresa day and night around the house and the yard as the ceremonies unfolded.

I saw Teresa dance once. She seemed in a trance; she was speaking in tongues. During those three days after her return, accompanied by what seemed to be thousands of healers, some of whom were extraordinary singers, dancers, percussionists or diviners, Mantwa clung to me. Seabe, however, disappeared right into the crowd, staying up late and refusing to go back to his other home. He seemed at home with all the happenings. He spoke to the different healers, and at night when we were together he'd share these discussions with us. Mantwa became most reserved; she even began to suck her thumb. Mostly she sought me out and held my hand. I tried to encourage her to speak to Teresa, but she refused.

Although Teresa had come home, she stayed out of our bedroom, away from our bed. She spent a lot of time in a room she'd chosen, and had possibly prepared before she left for *thwasa*. She mentioned, during a break from the rituals and ceremonies, that she wanted to discuss building a rondavel, a *ndumba*. I wondered at times whether I wanted a *ngaka* for a female partner, and whether she'd forgotten she was a lawyer.

I also wondered if she'd forgotten me, and forgotten that I was a man. I waited, watched, listened, and made Seabe and Mantwa my bosom friends. I also picked up the camera again. And now I began to study new topics on my computer, like biodiversity and intellectual property protection. And I shuttled between home, MHQ and the government offices.

From the look of things, we were going to have to put our lives together from scratch. There was a silence in the house once all the others had left, especially when Mantwa and Seabe weren't there. Teresa never invited me into the room she'd chosen for her work, but I went in sometimes.

Teresa was very welcoming. She would explain things to me, and ask me to join her in her rituals.

Not long after Teresa had settled back in, she told me that the *dingaka* had been invited to the institution. She was going there as a *ngaka* and also as a lawyer. She wanted me to accompany her. I wasn't at all sure about this, but eventually I went.

༺

"Doesn't this bell remind you of the combat bell in the camps?" I asked Phumzile, as she met me at the entrance to Parliament.

"Strange you should ask me that. I was just this minute thinking that the last time I saw you was in Angola," Phumzile said. "You'd just come from Kakulama, isn't that right?" I nodded. "When I came here in '94 as an MP, it took me back to Angola whenever it rang. We're still in combat here," she added.

"What are the flickering lights for?" I asked.

"The red is for the National Council of Provinces; the green is for the National Assembly. Do you have your gallery ticket?"

I showed it to her. We were walking along a maze of corridors. MPs were walking along hurriedly to take their seats in the National Assembly, black and white, men and women, murmuring. Oddly, the atmosphere reminded me of my university days.

"I hear you've been jet-setting round the world?" she asked.

"I don't know how it came about, but I've been going all over with the artist, Bra Shope. And you've also been travelling a lot."

"I have," she said. "I met Nomazwi the other day. She told me she'd remarried."

"Uh, yes, she has."

"You say it in such an uncertain manner," she said.
"Do I?"
"Yes. And she seemed rather sad about it."
"I am too."
"Was there nothing you could have done to save your marriage then?"
"Does anyone know how to? Divorce seems to be fashionable."
"Well, I approach marriage as a management contract," she said.
"How's Sello?" I asked.
"Fine, he's a general in Pretoria now." With that she had to rush in into the House.

The gallery was packed. I barely got the last seat, next to two old black ladies. Down below, there seemed to be hundreds of MPs. It was as noisy as a lecture room before the lecturer arrives.

Suddenly there was silence.

"There will be a moment of prayer or meditation," said the Speaker.

I could see Teresa on the other side of the gallery, sitting beside a group of men and women in all their regalia. When President Mbeki took the podium, the ANC members clapped. Then there was silence, except for the president's voice filling the packed concave oval of the house. I was facing the opposition parties. Except for a cough or sneeze and the occasional bellow from an MP, the silence was stunning in this vast house filled with over four hundred people. For some odd reason, my mind conjured up the Berlin Conference of 1884, where the Europeans had sliced Africa up among themselves.

I watched the leader of the opposition, a white man, wag his finger arrogantly at the president. At MHQ an MP had told me that this gentleman had served as a sergeant in the apartheid army. In his dark suit and spectacles he looked like a university student, though he behaved like an angry lecturer. His right hand remained in his pocket, but never still, so that I began to wonder if he was playing with his dick. His party cheered while the ANC members howled and heckled. He was beginning to appear like a movie star taking the role of a lawyer in court, making measured gestures, wagging his finger or touching his spectacles as if they were foreign to his face.

The National Assembly grew very rowdy. Now and then, opposition or majority party members interrupted to ask if it was parliamentary for so or so to say such and such. Many spoke in angry tones, shouting and gesturing widely.

Here I was now in Parliament, I thought, sitting in the gallery: Teresa's career as a *ngaka* had helped me to retrace my life. I had imagined that my first visit to the first democratic Parliament in my country would be a celebration of victory over evil. Instead I was listening to all these shouting voices. I didn't follow what was being said, but I sensed the racial undertones. We, the black people, had brought the apartheid system to its knees, and scattered its proponents helter skelter. We'd created a home for all, black and white. Yet the white opposition members were aggressive and arrogant, and seemed not to hear the heavy vocabulary of racism in their own words. As Phumzile had said as we walked the maze of corridors, the struggle continued. And I recalled Nkgono's words: there was a war that still had to be fought.

Why had black people, Africans, allowed the Europeans to carve up Africa? Why were they so trusting, so foolish, to exchange land and gold and diamonds for cloth, beads, spoons and other trash? Eventually we'd given up everything, even our minds. Looking back, it was as if the African continent had been through a nuclear war. We were not only slaves but professional students. Everyone who was not

African believed we should listen to them, learn from them, take their faith. They found ways to take still more from us, to tell us what the twenty-first century was and where we fitted into it. We'd been left poor and vulnerable to disease; our children thought they should become prostitutes rather than die, or be the garbage collectors of others. Some had left the continent to do this work in distant countries and cities we could otherwise not name, and hardly thought of coming back. If they did, they came back like the gold that was taken from our soil: changed, expensive, no longer our own, like those who used our gold to give themselves status to lord over us.

The lawyer mindset Teresa used in *bongaka* to listen to those who consulted her must, I thought, be a great innovation. I searched for her in the opposite gallery. She was smiling, talking to her *ngaka* colleagues. Did she know what I'd just realised? I waved and waved to try to catch her attention. She didn't notice me. She was engrossed in whatever they were whispering about. I became very animated. Even this struggle now unfolding before my eyes was worth engaging in. What we needed now was to shape new weapons. The old women beside me looked at me as if I'd gone mad.

"That concludes the deliberations," the Speaker said. "The session is over for today."

I'd heard the questions posed by the opposition; I'd also heard the president's answers. Now the MPs rose, and there was noise as they shut the lids of their desks and filed out into the foyer.

"Sorry I missed you," Teresa said. "I was late because of a meeting with the Minister of Health…"

At that moment Phumzile joined us, and I introduced them. Teresa introduced us to some of the *dingaka*, and then Phumzile invited us to join her for tea in the restaurant.

Never had I embraced so many bodies all at once as I did now, meeting comrades I hadn't seen for a long, long time. The foyer was a flurry of noise and embraces as we rushed through time, asking after others we hadn't seen. My comrades were shocked to hear that I'd been to Cape Town on numerous occasions without contacting them.

Then we were packed into the lift in silence, watching the numbers flash above our heads. In the restaurant, we sat at a long table reserved by Phumzile.

We were about fifteen at the table, drinking tea, coffee and juices and eating cake. In the restaurant were many white, coloured, Indian and black people, and many languages were being spoken: Afrikaans, Sesotho, isiNdebele, isiZulu, tshiVenda... All of South Africa was here.

When I asked Phumzile what her work entailed, she said they made the laws of the nation with the nation. So here were the law makers, I thought. If one tracked their histories they would lead back to slaves, kaffirs, Boers, British, Griquas, Khoisan... a bloody, embattled trail, linking the comings and goings to and from Africa, and the treks, terrifying and bloody, across the plains, the veld, the hills and the mountains, under the blue, blue sky.

"Tsile, where are you?" Teresa asked. She was sitting diagonally across from me, next to an old *ngaka* who spoke only isiXhosa.

"I'm here," I said.

"I know. I knew you'd come back to us," she said.

Phumzile looked at Teresa, then at me. "I'm happy to have met you," she said to Teresa, "I've known this man a long, long time."

"I'm glad to meet you too. He keeps his old friends away from me. I must take your number," Teresa said.

As they were exchanging numbers, my comrade Molefe asked with a hint of raw humour if I'd split with Nomazwi.

All I could do was nod. "Is this your new wife?" he asked. I nodded again. "What's her name?"

"Teresa," I said.

He stood up, shook her hand and walked around the table to embrace her.

"We lived a fine long time with your husband," he told her, "a time I'd gladly relive if I were asked to."

He came back round the table to squeeze in beside me.

"Tsitsi," he whispered to me. He was the only person who for some unknown reason called me this, and he could make it sound vulgar or joyous or angry, according to his mood and intent. Now it was secretive. "Where did you meet such a beautiful woman? A tall, dark beauty with a smile that melts my heart?"

Only Molefe could say such things. It was an absolute joy to meet up with him again. In a sense, we were the only survivors from our unit of comrades who'd arrived in Botswana just before June 16th, 1976. The comradeship between Molefe and I ran very deep. We'd been on the front together.

As I talked with him, I thought of my difficult discussion with Bra Shope – that time that felt long ago yet had never faded – when he took me to task about Nel and about being a soldier. I also recalled his discussion with Peter, the Englishman in Zimbabwe, and pictured Bra Shope then, obnoxious and arrogant. I told Molefe about him, and about Sarah, Dimakatso and Musa.

Now the experiences I'd shared with Molefe came flying back to me. Driving on those perilous missions, in Gaborone, in Francistown five hundred kilometres later, then the Chobe Game Reserve, and then the veld: quiet, with its distinct sounds, the wildlife and the moonlit sky with its millions of stars. And then the contact: men, the weapons, the message from HQ in Lusaka.

Those were days when we lived a harsh reality, for the ideals we shared then, while greatly inspiring, were hidden in the future, and in our ability to push through to that future and shape them into reality. It was also a time when to wake up alive for one more day was a beautiful experience. They were days when no challenge was insurmountable. Our determination to fight and be victorious was the rock on which our lives were anchored. We could be many in the kombi or we could be two. There came a time when you grew quiet, embroiled in thought. And as you glanced at the relaxed faces of your silent comrades, even as they slept, you sensed you were among human beings who could make tough decisions in a split second, who could be leopards if provoked. They could sit for hours, waiting. They could walk the longest distances with their cargo, if necessary, determined to reach their destination. Their eyes, ears, their very fibre was listening, seeing, feeling...

Seeing Molefe again had shifted me back into the feelings and thoughts of those days. He was a naughty man with mischievous darting eyes. As I put my hand on Teresa's lap, Teresa noticed his eyes dart towards her lap, gave me nervous glance, and then sighed.

Why had I been unable to explain the camaraderie among soldiers to Bra Shope? Perhaps because Bra Shope was trying to express his immense dislike for Nel. But Nel had tried, and in a sense, this is also what being human means: Nel had tried hard to be courteous, friendly, to serve us efficiently, and as far as possible, to be honest. Yet he hadn't succeeded with one of the kindest and most sensitive men I'd ever known. Nel was white, and from some of the things he'd said, he could easily have been a soldier in the apartheid army. According to Bra Shope, then, they should not dare talk as friends unless they had experienced the same clearly defined rite of passage.

It was through learning to watch by sniffing, feeling, sensing and touching that Molefe had become my comrade. Time had placed us in that reality between heaven and hell. There were no frills, although we were preparing for a joy that would make us answer, if asked, who our brothers were. Molefe and I came from that time, those circumstances. I loved him; I respected him. But I didn't understand what it meant for him to be an MP. He told me he didn't think I'd be a good photographer, and I told him of my passion for the computer.

The conversation at the table was diverse. I kept catching snatches of it: old friends and new acquaintances all feeling each other out. I wanted to be with Teresa. I wanted to share with her my realisation, which felt so extraordinary to me. I wanted her reaction to it. For Teresa was so particular about detail and had this ability to probe things. Now, as a *ngaka*, she probed things to their very depths. But as she did so she would construct a picture. And I was always fascinated by how she would search and search and then take time to construct each thing, with all its reasons for being as it was.

When traditional healers are at work among people, their methods of probing can be disarming. Ngaka had not been surprised that day when Thuso stood up in anger, took his family, and left the meeting. Ngaka had long realised that the problem was not Thuso, nor what he did as a *ngaka*. The problem lay in the hearts of those who accused him. For if they were so committed to Christianity, why did they fear Thuso as a *ngaka*? Did they think Christianity would be overcome by wizardry?

As we left, Molefe and I promised each other to keep in contact through MHQ. Off he went, his suit and tie so neat, just as he'd kept his combat kit neat and his boots shiny, his face always sparkling, even after a long march. That was Molefe.

Teresa and I then left for our hotel, where Phumzile said she'd join us later. Our hotel was just around the corner from parliament, where Bra Shope and I had stayed several times.

That morning I'd got in touch with Jean, who'd taught me how to use the computer. She'd sent a long e-mail in reply to mine about Bra Shope's passing, and she told me now how sorry she was about the old man. I thought of the time we'd spent together when she was teaching me to use a computer. Something Bra Shope had said in Maputo came back to me now: that a golden chain binds people together, whether they know it or want it, until they've completed the chores fate has given them. The earth spins and carries us to destinations we cannot foresee.

Jean and I had arranged to meet for dinner that evening. But I hadn't yet told Teresa. I had a sense of the type of women Teresa didn't like, but I hoped she'd at least get along with Jean. Teresa told me that I should go down to meet Jean, and she'd follow.

Jean was seated in the foyer talking to a waiter when I arrived. We embraced, kissed and sat down.

"How've you been?" she asked.

"Well, very well," I said. "And you?"

"I'm good," she said, and there was a hot silence. She then looked away through the large hotel windows into the dark night outside.

"Do you live far from here?" I asked her.

"Not far," she said, not really looking at me.

"We haven't seen each other in a long time," I said.

"I didn't think I'd see you again after Bra Shope went," she said. "But I do understand. Cape Town's the end of the world."

"I'm with my wife. She'll join us shortly. She's in Cape Town for a consultation with the government, so she dragged me along because we've always wanted to visit parliament.

As it was the president's speech today, she thought it was a good idea for me to come," I said.

"She must be a smart woman to be able to drag you along."

"I'm not that bad," I said.

"Do you still take photographs? It's strange to see you without a camera."

Just then Phumzile walked into the foyer, and she and Jean leapt toward each other, laughing and hugging.

Phumzile turned to me. "Baby and I go back a long way, you know," she told me. "How do you know each other?"

"We were introduced by a mutual friend, the artist I told you about," I said.

"The artist? Don't be so impersonal! It was Bra Shope, not just some artist!" Jean insisted. "You make him sound like he belongs to the coffin," she said.

"Ah!" said Phumzile. "Was this the artist you used to tell me about?"

"Yes," Jean said, "that's him. Bra Shope."

"And you, Malome," Phumzile always used my combat name, "you know Baby through Bra Shope?" she asked.

"Yes, but why call me Malome, when I've told you my name's Otsile? And why call Jean Baby?"

"She has a hard head, this one," Jean said.

"It's not that. He doesn't look or feel like Otsile to me, nor do you look or feel like Jean."

"But I am," I insisted.

"Oh, Otsile, leave Phumzile alone, I gave up long ago…"

Just then Teresa arrived. She was out of her regalia except for the beads on her ankles, wrists and neck. She avoided shaking hands with Jean and Phumzile; instead she politely clapped her hands together. I suggested we go up for dinner.

Teresa glanced at both women. "I'm glad to meet you both," she said. "This man's been hiding you. What a day. I'm so glad I asked him along."

"According to him you didn't ask him, you dragged him," Jean said.

"He's such a performer, this one," Phumzile said.

"Well, I'm glad I dragged him then, because now I've met you," Teresa said.

There was a silence, that moment of sniffing, I thought, wishing I'd asked Molefe to come. But it wasn't too late; I remembered I'd taken his cell number. I excused myself and went up to the room. He promised to join us a little later, and I returned to the table.

"Why must a person first become ill before they become an *inyanga*?" Phumzile was saying.

"I don't know anyone who willingly becomes an *inyanga*," Teresa said. "We all feel it's backward," she said.

"So they drag you into it?"

"You could put it that way," Teresa said. "Perhaps it's also a rite of passage."

"Has it always been like that?"

"Yes and no," Teresa said. "You have to live it, you see, you live as a *ngaka*, it's a discipline. It requires sacrifice, great morality, commitment to service. Not many people want to take that on, to live a life that's almost like being a nun or a monk. The most difficult part is the link to the ancestors. Shoo, it's been a struggle."

She paused briefly. "A long time ago, an old lady who was visiting my great grandmother told me I'd become a *ngaka*. And my grandmother, Nkgono, has never failed to remind me. I also had many dreams about it. Tsile here thought I was going mad whenever I shared them with him. I read people; I carry their aches. Then when Bra Shope died, I got a strong feeling that now I had to do it. I discussed it with Tsile and I'm glad he was encouraging."

"This one encouraged you?" Phumzile asked in surprise.

"You said you're also a lawyer?" Jean asked.

"Yes, I still practise as a lawyer. You know, when I came back from *thwasa* I had to go to court, and on that day I wore full regalia. I put the gown over my *ngaka* clothes and defended. There were shock waves in the courtroom. The magistrate interrupted the proceedings to talk to me. When he asked I said he should regard it like a doctor's white coat; that my clothes wouldn't bite anyone," Teresa said.

"That must have been a spectacle! *Iinyanga* are regarded as dirty, smelly barefoot people."

"Now I'm another barefoot, and I'm sure the herbs I use sometimes have a strange aroma, but that's it. I do wash, although at times I'm not supposed to," Teresa said.

There was silence. The two women contemplated what Teresa had just said.

"Even among us coloureds there's traditional healing," Jean said. The old people still practise it. And if you look at the Muslims – their symbolism, their rituals, their dress, their manner of prayer – they also have influences from traditional healing."

"There's a need for spirituality," Teresa said. "The twenty-first century is a century where we as humans will have to come to terms with our spirituality. The sciences have challenged our intellect almost to the limit. And our bodies, what haven't we done with them? But how often do we engage our spirituality? There is knowledge, there are phenomena that are part of our knowledge that reside in spirituality but remain unexplored, feared, denigrated and despised. But at times it demands that we engage it."

"And why should a spiritual commitment be seen as a threat?" Phumzile asked. "Why shouldn't we be able to just engage with this need without fearing repercussions?"

The waiter serving us never took his eyes off Teresa. He was listening to her.

"Sir," I teased him, "do you have enough *lobola* for her? I'm her uncle. Propose, and I'll oblige." He laughed slightly and then said politely: "I've never seen an educated *inyanga*."

"You have," Teresa said. "But you didn't realise they were educated. You can't be an *inyanga* and not be educated."

"Not like you," the waiter said.

"What's your name?" Teresa asked him.

"Solomon," he said.

"What do you really mean, Solomon? Are you saying you've never come across an *inyanga* who speaks English?"

"Yes," he admitted.

"I'm a lawyer as well as an *inyanga*," Teresa said.

"This *inyanga* issue dominates everything lately," I said, meaning to provoke Teresa. "At home, at work, with friends, we seem to discuss nothing else..."

Just then Molefe walked in, apologising for being late.

"Solomon, could you prepare a corner of the table for Molefe and bring him a chair...?" I said.

"Well, today's my day!" Molefe said as he sat down.

"Meet Jean," I said.

"I know Jean," he said. "That's why I said that. We know each other, but she avoids me."

"This one just wants to take me to bed," Jean said.

"At least it's not to the slaughterhouse, wouldn't you say, Tsitsi?"

"I agree," I said.

"It *is* a slaughterhouse if she's not willing," Phumzile said.

We were all laughing, and Molefe was rubbing his hands together, half to warm himself, and half implying that he had a great appetite for what was before him.

"Jean, if you agree, I'll marry you. If you want me to bring *lobola*, I will..."

"I'm amazed by your politeness today." Phumzile turned to us. "He's always so crude when he talks to me, since way back."

"You know each other from long ago then?" I asked.

"Oh yes," Phumzile assured me. "When Mampuru – that was his underground name – couldn't survive in Mthatha, he came to Cape Town. Baby networked for him and me, and we were given permission to link up to work. Baby and I were eventually arrested. You remember the Trial of Six?"

"So Jean was one of you? And Molefe?" I asked.

Phumzile nodded.

Solomon brought Molefe's plate and he immediately pounced on it, between sips of whisky.

"I trained in Zimbabwe and then went on to the Soviet Union," Jean said looking at me. "You don't know me like that."

"So I'm here among soldiers?" Teresa asked.

"Yes ma'am," Molefe said. "And I'm so curious to know how you and Tsitsi met." He laughed loudly and nearly fell off his chair.

"Why do you want to know?"

"A beautiful woman, a lawyer, a *ngaka*! That doesn't happen every day. And on top of that, to my *phekula* brother! How did all this come together? I've never heard of such a thing!"

"He overpowered me, this one," Teresa said. "I don't even remember him proposing. He posed as a friend and the next thing he was in my bed," Teresa said. "He tricked me."

"How can he trick a *ngaka*?"

"I wasn't a *ngaka* then. I was doing my finals. I'd just got divorced, and he appeared and took me to dinner. First he hid the fact that he'd been a guerilla. He never said a word about it. He was prone to discussing politics, though, and he seemed to know a lot about the world. But there was also something thuggish about him, crude; I was enchanted. He asked me to his flat once. I didn't trust him. He said nothing would happen against my will, he was man of his word, an ANC man. I got curious then, though I still didn't trust him. I called loudly to my daughter that I was with uncle Otsile, whom she knew by then, and would be a bit late. We got there and he started drinking whisky and telling me all sorts of things, not what I thought he'd say. I expected him to propose. Instead he showed me all his photographs of paintings and the places he'd been. He found me lacking when it came to the world of art and creativity. I was curious and wanted to meet Bra Shope. And he was such a darling when we eventually met. That night Otsile played the gentleman: he took me to my car; followed me home and opened the gate, kissed me on the cheek and then left."

Phumzile was laughing herself to death.

"Tsitsi!" Molefe said. "The boy from the dark city in action. Man of honour? This is a killer man, what honour?"

"Otsile's a perfect gentleman," Jean said.

"I won't say a word about how he behaved in camp," Phumzile said.

"He was feared like hell!" Molefe said.

"I know something about that," Teresa said, "but it doesn't bother me."

"Jean, why haven't you answered my question?" Molefe said. "You can't say I've never proposed to you!"

Jean blushed, her eyes dancing. "Why would I think you were serious?"

"Okay, okay, let's leave it at that," Molefe said in earnest.

"Oh gosh, I didn't mean it like that," Jean said, blushing again. "I meant to say please leave me alone."

Phumzile began to laugh.

"Baby, you look like a schoolgirl," Phumzile said, "all red in the face!"

"I wish I wasn't coloured," Jean said.

"Well you are and it shows," Phumzile chuckled.

"Hey, hey. Please leave Jean alone, and let the subject go," Molefe said.

"What do you mean?" Jean asked again. We all laughed.

"Just that. Subject closed," Molefe said. "I'm happy to meet you Teresa. I hope my rogue brother will look after you. I have no doubt he will."

The conversation turned to politics, and Teresa and Molefe soon became embroiled in an intense discussion.

"But then they're misleading the masses," Teresa said. "The liberals and media are using the plight of the masses opportunistically; they're not interested in addressing their plight."

"Well it's our democratic right to enter that battle," Molefe replied. "We can't control what they say, but we must come up with better strategies to talk to the masses, to let them know what our problems are and what we're doing."

"They've used their opportunistic criticism to occupy centre stage," Teresa went on. "They've seized the agenda setting, the platform the liberation movement should be occupying. Every time we set the agenda, they seize the offensive and put us on the defensive."

"But it's what we do on the ground that speaks loudest, not what's said," Molefe countered. "The people aren't foolish. There's so much poverty; we must address that in a manner the masses can relate to."

"But, Molefe," Teresa insisted, "are you aware of the impatience, the expectations and the cynicism among the people?"

"I am not. I agree with you that people expect us to move with speed, and that at times they think we take too long," he said. "But we're still fresh in the minds of the masses. They know what we stand for; they see what we're trying to do."

"Really?"

"I admit that at times we lose them. We say we'll do this or that, and then it takes time, or gets scrapped because it's unrealistic, like the Reconstruction and Development Programme. We were moving full speed on it, then came to a halt. It got bogged down in bureaucracy."

"You're an optimist in this regard," Teresa said. "I'm not. I sense the vocabulary the liberals are using is permeating the masses. They're using it because it corresponds with their plight."

"But what can the liberals do to improve the plight of the masses? Do they have the political will? What of their fears and insecurities? Aren't they based on white domination?"

"They may be, but how would you know that if you had no house, no land, you were unemployed and lived in a shack?"

"We must act and we must explain," Molefe said.

"I must go now," Jean said. "I'm exhausted." I agreed.

"I agree with you, Teresa," Molefe continued. "Your basis is still revolutionary. You're talking to the plight of the masses. We should be talking more about how to alleviate poverty than what the liberals are up to."

"But we mustn't have our heads in the sand," Teresa said.

"People, I must go." Jean stood up.

Soon Teresa and I were on our own in the lift.

"You look tired," she said.

"I am. You look tired too. But you seemed to have the energy to go on and on," I said.

"Curiosity, not energy. Where does Molefe live?"

"Cape Town and Jo'burg," I said. "Like all members of Parliament."

"You know, Tsile, I don't think we're addressing the issue of the white tribe in South Africa properly. There needs to be a special section in the movement that addresses this issue. Yes, the white tribe is fearful, aloof, insecure, privileged, and seeks to preside and dominate. That's true, but it's not enough. The white tribe isn't homogenous. There are Jews, Afrikaners, English, Portuguese, Greeks and so on. Why aren't we focusing on each sub-tribe to mobilise them to at least support key national priorities?" Teresa asked.

She took off her shoes and stockings, undressed and put on her nightie. I sat on the bed, watching.

"No one can quarrel with what you're saying," I told her. "But I must add that when the movement was still outside, that *was* done. There were various white organisations and we also focused on the various sub-tribes, to use your term. And an initiative emerged at the recent racism conference to mobilise white people around issues and projects. So it's not as if nothing's been done. But you're right, the movement must engage this issue."

"But when, how?"

"I hear you," I said. "I must find a way to raise this with the Secretary General." Teresa switched off the lights and lit the candle. She put the snuff and *mpepo* on the plate and knelt.

"Are you going to join me?" she asked.

I knelt beside her, facing east. She began to call her ancestors. She called my ancestors. My mind was wandering, refusing to focus, to listen. It was such an effort to pray or to *phahala*.

"We're in Cape Town," Teresa intoned. "We have done the work we were supposed to do. We believe we did our best because we want to serve you. We ask that you protect our leaders, and give them wisdom to rule in these difficult times. We ask that you hold council, and represent our wishes and hopes to the God who created the heavens, the earth, the seas, human life, plant and animal life and the universe as a whole. God must hear us. Africa must not be the playground of rogues, whether African, European, American or others. We need to live. We need to do away with poverty and disease. We need to rally around the Renaissance of Africa. You are our ancestors. If you gave an account of your lives, it would be a tale of suffering, hunger, poverty, abuse and humiliation, of discrimination, exploitation, detention, prison, loss of land and loss of family. You know all this and more. But even then, you gave us customs, tradition, culture, resistance, revolution, liberation and wisdom, and above all, you ingrained in us that a human being is human because of others. You paid dearly for this belief, but you insisted, and even today you insist through us. We hear this challenge. We are conscious of the price we paid for it as a people. We must find a way to live the belief but also to protect who we are. Some have turned the world into a jungle.

"The whole of Africa is now free. We your children are still here. We are well. We are unchanged. We are working, planning and building, seeking knowledge. We seek to use this knowledge for the poor, the ill, the hungry, the suffering; we seek to re-establish and emancipate the African spirit.

"We submit ourselves before you to serve you. We ask that you hold council with our white ancestors. Through rape we are now related. Through marriage we are linked to the white tribe. We seek a solution to the racism that still exists in our country and in the world.

"I have made my requests. I have humbled myself before you. I beg that you hear me. You have asked me to be a *ngaka*. I have submitted. I thank you for allowing my partner, Otsile, to support me in this difficult calling. I will work for you."

She sighed heavily and was silent. Then she took out the snuff again and began to spread it. "We are going to bed now. Be with us in our sleep and show us what we need to do to serve. Give us a peaceful sleep and come with us tomorrow when we fly back to Jo'burg, as you came with us to Cape Town. Rest in peace."

She gave another deep sigh. Then she stood up and embraced me. She kissed me and then got under the blankets.

Chapter 13

I LAY AWAKE MANY nights, thinking. I wasn't complaining. My people had a saying that there was no way one could grow too old to learn. Maybe this was what kept me awake at night. Teresa seemed to have brought the ancestors into our house. At times I thought I saw them, heard them. She talked to them about current issues as if they were here with us, knew all we knew, and understood her causes just as we did. The other day she was talking to them about Mugabe and Joseph Kabila, whom she called a boy. She came up with terms I'd never heard before, like white tribes and sub-tribes.

She referred to Lepane as if she knew him. But it was I who had told her about him. And I'd been told about him by a councillor of the royal family in Sekhukhune. These councillors had the history of all their people in their heads. They recited it or said it in praise poetry. They went back in time in their minds. But at times as they said it, I thought about the fragility of memory, that sometimes it could fail. But they were very confident. The old councillor, Tolo, sat pointing earnestly at the veld, its boulders, bushes, ravines, rivers and mountains, where he said Lepane had climbed, walked, slept, dug roots and sought herbs; where Lepane learned to fight and to grind herbs, where he was initiated and circumcised. These were the footpaths he walked as he fought leopards, lions, elephants, where he hunted and worshipped the ancestors, where he attended *lekgotla*, commanded *mephato*, built huts for his wives, kraals for his cattle, sheep and goats, kept his chickens, harvested his fields. He fell far from his village, the old man told me, in a fierce battle against the British in Mafikeng. He'd fought in the leading groups of *mephato*. If I weren't a soldier myself, I wouldn't have believed he could have walked so long, so far. But I knew it was possible; I'd done it myself. On my many trips to meet Tolo, to whom my father had referred me, I had a sense of déjà vu as he spoke, leading me over mountains to the veld. He was vague about where Lepane was buried, but precise about where he fell. It was on the road from Mafikeng to Lobatse in Botswana, where many of my comrades had also fallen in battles against the security forces.

I thought about these things in the darkness of our bedroom instead of sleeping. I didn't know what I should do with this knowledge, but I knew that I needed it. I was startled at times that as a people, we'd been fighting for so long. Three hundred and fifty years was a long, long time. So much life wasted. More startling was that the issues that occupied Lepane and his *mephato* still occupied us now, still arose in Teresa's bedtime conversations with our ancestors.

Teresa began speaking to the ancestors about my having to pay *lobola*. Then one night she asked them if she should find me another young wife. This shocked and alarmed me. For a long time I didn't know how to raise it with her. Was she preparing to leave me? Was she going to replace herself with another young partner for me? Two words in particular stuck with me: "young" and "another".

Why did she say these words to the ancestors? For the first time, in secrecy, I even spoke to my ancestors myself, and to Bra Shope. Was this woman planning to leave? To go where? Yet she often spoke about the importance of *lobola* as the ritual joining of a couple's ancestors, for their own sake and for their offspring. Ngaka had said that once the ancestors were joined you could then know them. The family tree in the land of ancestors continued the living tree on earth, and generation upon generation was then joined and held council when you spoke to them. I'd never questioned this; I think I was afraid lest it turn out to be untrue.

But Teresa the lawyer believed it with all her heart. And she was actually contemplating another young wife for me. Yet it was hopeful that she also spoke of my paying *lobola* for her. I'd already paid *lobola* for Nomazwi when I came back from exile. These things got so complex! I was sure that was why Ngaka had said that trouble doesn't make sense. Seabe's ancestors were mine and Nomazwi's; Mantwa's ancestors were Teresa's and Joel's. Now, if I paid *lobola*, would I be joining mine with both Teresa's and Nomazwi's? I didn't know, but at times it seemed a good possibility, yet also somewhat unrealistic for people living on earth. If it worked, it would be good for us and for the children. But Teresa spoke also of white ancestors, some created by *rape*? At times I really didn't know what to say or think. What had we gotten into? What did it all mean? Yet Teresa was so serious about it all.

I'd never seen her speak to the ancestors in her office, and I didn't know that I wanted her to. What would people say? But I was sure there were moments when she performed rituals at the office, because when she started at home, she even mentioned some of her client cases to her ancestors.

I got so confused at times. Maybe confusion was preferable to fear or cynicism. I didn't want to become cynical. While I accepted that fear was human, I didn't want it to control me. Fear can make one very stupid, especially when it's born of ignorance. I needed to examine all these things. One couldn't examine one's life without examining all these things instead of just believing. But it kept me awake. I felt so tired, but my mind kept on and on.

Since we'd returned from Cape Town it was worse. I spent days drifting in and out of reality and the world of the ancestors, especially because this was all present in our home, our bedroom, our conversations, everywhere. What must it have been like when Teresa met her *ngaka* colleagues!

Well, if all this would emancipate the spirit of Africa, what more could one ask? Imagine, just imagine! I saw no conflict with what I'd learned in the liberation movement or in MK. And if the spirit of the continent was now liberated, it would be liberated both physically and spiritually. It was exciting, mind boggling, to contemplate. Cabral, Nkrumah, Lumumba, Mondlane, returning in another form, in a form superior to council, this time to liberate the spirituality of the continent where the human race began.

At times I felt I had no tools to grasp all this. But Teresa was there. I would talk to her. She always had an explanation, or she'd phone a colleague to raise an issue I'd raised with her, and then come with an explanation. Sometimes they made sense; at other times they made me feel I should keep quiet. When Teresa spoke to the ancestors, she really challenged me intellectually. She even spoke to them about intellectual property protection. And, she said, she wanted to specialise in that kind of law.

She spoke to the ancestors about social issues, biodiversity, technology and biotechnology, and about the institutions and experimental processes they'd left us as our heritage. I imagined universities, science councils and parliaments in Africa applying their minds to these things, considering how initiation informed education; how the wisdom of African languages informed knowledge and gave it richer meaning, understood its inherent logic.

I lay awake dreaming while Teresa slept. I looked at her, so innocent, and asked quietly if she realised what she was doing. Did she fully understand its meaning? I realised I was dreaming when I began to wonder how one would engage Africans with all this. But aren't our dreams related to our passions? Doesn't passion, like perception, drive humans to action? I felt so tired. I wished I could sleep. I would think about all this and discuss it with my sleeping beauty the next day.

☙

Seabe called me from outside the darkroom door. I was examining and archiving the photographs Bra Shope had made me take when he'd said that people who are too quiet die of heart attacks, diabetes and liver failure. I'd met all the people in the photographs as I took their pictures, but I'd never seen them again. From now on, I thought, when I took a person's picture, I'd try to get back to see them, and give them a copy of their photograph. It seemed only right, or else I shouldn't take their picture.

Seabe said that an uncle and aunt wanted to see me in the house.

It turned out to be Molefe and Jean. There they were beaming at me, searching my face, looking like they'd emerged from a nest they'd just built for themselves.

We hugged, we kissed. I held Jean by the hand and led her to the lounge. For the first time, Jean looked to me Chinese, or Malay, or white, or a combination of all these. She was neither white nor brown nor yellow. She called herself black, and sometimes coloured, but she was neither: she was honey.

"What's all this?" I asked.

"What do you mean?" Molefe asked.

"Where have you come from?"

"Cape Town," he said "And don't ask us where we're going. We're here!" he said.

"But…"

"Stop, you! Where's Teresa, Tsitsi?"

"At some *ngaka* do in Soweto."

"*Ngaka* do? You mean she's bewitching somewhere?"

"Molefe, don't say that!" Jean said.

"Come on," he teased. "You don't object when I call you a terrorist. And you *were* as far as the whites were concerned."

"Hey, hey, don't come and fight in my house! First tell me why you look like you're about to lay an egg in your nest."

"Tsitsi, let me tell you. This woman, I've been after her since I was underground, and now I'm an MP! It's a lifetime, man! So, don't spoil things for me. I think Teresa has some muti to help me. I love this woman, I want to marry her. We're here because I want you to go and pay *lobola* for me at her mother's."

"Jean! Are you marrying this rogue? You must be out of your mind."

"How does that song go?" Jean asked. "He makes my heart skip a beat, I'd rather marry him than die…" she grinned.

"You're becoming a poet and marrying a rogue?" I said. "What a combination!"

"No, seriously," Molefe implored, "I want you to help me speak to her mother, and handle the *lobola* thing, you and Teresa."

"These things are done by uncles. I'm hardly your uncle."

"But my uncle doesn't speak English. He asked me to find someone who does to accompany him. We've just come from him."

"Jesus!" I said. "You've barely settled down, and the first time you come here, you drop a bombshell on me. What do I know about asking for a wife for someone, let alone negotiating *lobola*?"

"Where's your whisky?"

"Molefe!"

"Or don't ancestors allow whisky?"

I pointed to the cupboard. Jean opted for a glass of red wine, and Molefe lit a cigarette as they settled down.

"We must talk," I said to him.

"You must do it for me. There's no one else who can, but you and Teresa."

"I must meet your uncle first."

"No problem. He said if you're a freedom fighter, you'd have no problem handling this. Oh, and do you know the movement's decided to hold its fifty-second national conference in Polokwane?"

"I sort of heard that. But why Polokwane?"

"Polokwane means a place where people bury each other."

"Is that so?"

"That's what's in the air," he said.

We looked at each other in silence. The air carried many tongues we'd never heard before in the alliance. For the first time as cadres, we were speechless.

"Polokwane came to mind because my uncle's there..." Molefe said.

I didn't have the heart to ask Molefe why he wasn't asking a relative to help him with the marriage procedure. These things have to be done properly, not hush-hush. But I dared not say so. I knew why he'd chosen me. I hoped I could do a good job. Teresa, if she agreed, would be very particular about how we did it. I knew she liked them both. She wouldn't allow any short cuts: she was a *ngaka*, and this was a *ngaka* matter.

Teresa still wasn't back by the time Molefe and Jean left, and I went back to the darkroom. There it suddenly dawned to me, looking at the pained faces of the old people in my portraits, that these were the lives on which so-called civilisation had been built. This civilisation, brutal and ruthless, had not only despised my people, but abused and humiliated them, excluded them from anything to do with development, taken from them all that mattered in life, and left them to merely exist. Their faces were living evidence of that bloody trail.

But when I looked at Tolo's face, I saw a face of steel. His expressive frown was engraved deep into the flesh, his piercing eyes showed pride, dignity and defiance. It was the face of one who bore knowledge and vision. This was why my generation had survived. We came from these loins, from this deep defiance in the face of abuse. But there was something else, I realised. I understood now what Ngaka had meant about the Bible being written by wise prophets of a written culture: he meant that ours was an oral culture. I saw now that Tolo, the councillor in the royal kraal, was a prophet too, a wise man, a custodian of the ages. These were the people, Tolo and his generation, who had eked out their lives from nothing, who through the rites of passage of initiation, *lekgotla*, extended family, and the social institutions Teresa spoke so much of – *bongaka*, philosophy, culture, the arts, customs and traditions – had withstood the harshest of odds. Even genocide.

Tolo had told me, as he unfolded my family tree in amazing detail, beginning with Lepane, that one of Lepane's wives, who left with him for the land of the Barolong, was his great grandfather's sister. Tolo was therefore my uncle. He told me that he went before my father to the *koma*; and the way he said it revealed pride and authority. I didn't know why he thought my father was educated. My father, who like Lepane had married a Motswana woman, seemed to have roamed South Africa. He spoke with great familiarity about what was now Mpumalanga, and occasionally still attended land restitution meetings there. He claimed to have owned land in a place called Mashishing. He wasn't educated in the conventional sense, but was taught by his people, his community, the institutions of his culture. I think he learned his English on the road as he worked from one place to the other. He also read newspapers regularly, and liked listening to the radio; even now when others watched TV, he would withdraw to his bed to listen to his radio. He'd wanted me to become a lawyer, because, as he said, if he'd had the chance he'd have done so. He fancied himself as a lawyer, and worked as a messenger for lawyers for a long time, sometimes stealing into the courtrooms to hear his employers defend cases.

Tolo, I think, felt my father was not his peer in terms of *koma*. Although just six years older than my father, he made it clear that if they were to see each other, my father would have to come to him. But my father had a car and loved driving. He drove slowly always, liked long distances and took ages to get wherever he was going. His car was almost fifty years old but he loved it, cared for it well and spoke of it as a second wife. Its purchase required great sacrifice from the family, and no doubt cost many battles with his wife. But once my father made up his mind, nothing would stop him. He would discuss the consequences of his action beforehand, but do it anyway.

From when I was little, I learned that it was in the bedroom where all things got sorted out between them, away from us children. When I'd told my parents, during my second year at university, that I was involved in the struggle, implying that I was about to leave, my mother was totally against it. I think my father was too, but understood why I had to leave. He was very quiet as my mother went on about it. She would demand to know what he thought. "When I know, I'll tell you," he'd say. I watched him keenly. Then one day when my mother wasn't there he called me. He said he was aware that they might never see me again: that the struggle might take me to faraway lands; that I might die.

"The road is long and rough," he warned. "Your ancestors walked it. We tried, and now Mandela, Mbeki and Sisulu rot in jail, Luthuli in Natal. We're just the debris of the white man's work." He sighed heavily. "But if you feel you must take part in the struggle, so be it. Never raise this with your mother, your brother or your sister. This is between us. My advice is that you go soon, rather than later, to see Makgothi. Remember Ntate Makgothi? Go to him about this matter."

He looked weary then, and sorrowful. I remember hugging him. Naming Ntate Makgothi was the revelation of a deep secret, which I held inside me. My father and I regarded each other differently from that day on. When he was home alone I would hover around him. He understood, but never said a word. We were becoming very close. There was sadness in it, but also something beautiful. I knew I had a friend. During my training at the various camps, these moments stayed with me. My father had trained me in military combat work without saying a word. By putting me in touch with Ntate Makgothi he had linked me to an ANC underground unit, and changed my life forever.

When I came back and was going through major troubles with Nomazwi, I reclaimed this space he and I had created between us those many years past. I kept returning to him, sharing in detail how Nomazwi and I were losing grip on our marriage. He took me to Tolo. But Nomazwi shocked us all by refusing to involve herself in traditional matters. The old people would be of no help, she felt; their wisdom held no relevance for us.

"She's very angry," my father said. "What have you done? Whatever have you done?"

He listened carefully to me, and one day he said, "You must look after Seabe. You know his name means treasure. Never lose sight of him, no matter how poor you become. Even as a hobo, you must look after him."

What did he mean about being a hobo? It was alarming; it seemed like a curse on me. Later, when I was on the streets, in hovels, and all was lost between Nomazwi and me, his words would come back to me when I was in a drunken stupor. And in that state I finally made a decision that the little money I had I would invest in a flat. It would encourage me to be responsible.

I knew my father was enchanted by Teresa, but my mother, who was very stubborn, preferred Nomazwi. So my father hid his regard for Teresa, for fear of offending his wife. I must go to my father, I decided, to discuss Teresa's *lobola* with him. I must involve him. I couldn't do it without telling him. But as soon as I thought this, I became afraid. I knew he'd refer me to Tolo, because something inside me was uncertain about taking this step. But what would I do, I wondered, if Tolo went the way of Bra Shope before I could resolve this matter? What was holding me back? Were matters unfinished with Nomazwi? Wasn't I sure where Seabe fitted in all this? What was the matter? Why couldn't I make a decision? Teresa was now contemplating another young woman for me: what would my father say about that? When I kept going to him during my troubles with Nomazwi, he'd said that in our tradition there was no divorce. I believed him. But love was two-sided; if the other insisted on divorce, what could one do? When I told Nomazwi what my father had said, she'd looked at me as if I was out of my mind. Not long afterwards the divorce papers had arrived. What could I have done?

"Say it and keep saying it," my father had told me. In private I called him by his name, Bra Kgathi, for he had become my friend. "You may not prevent her from divorcing you, but say it. Make it clear to her that you come from that tradition. We don't divorce. That's all you can do, but don't shirk that responsibility. There are things, if you believe in them," he'd say, "that you must die saying, even if it doesn't change anything."

With these words, he handed me the greatest responsibility of my life: to die telling the truth. This was surely the heaviest, bloodiest and most backbreaking responsibility of life on earth. I understood the consequences. It was like taking an oath of commitment, of loyalty a second time. It was then that I gained a deeper understanding of my father. I experienced the breadth of his emotional and intellectual capacity, his spirituality in moments of difficulty and pain. He knew what I was going through; that I was hurting. I knew that he knew.

He watched me, and before we parted he always said, "Come home and see me, come back to me." At first I kept my promise. But later, when the loss set in, the deep sense of failure, I couldn't face him. I went to dwell in hovels. I suspect that I replaced him with Bra Shope. Now I had to find my way back to him. I knew this deep inside. I'd kept my faith, so I could face him. It was my only salvation; I knew it in my gut.

The first time I'd tried to tell him about Teresa, he didn't look at me, didn't answer. "Go and tell your mother," was all he said.

And so I did, and she threw me into hell. I tried many times, until one day I asked her, "Don't you forgive in your Christianity?"

"There's nothing Christian about divorce!" she responded.

I wanted to remind her that I was her child. But what if she spat at me, as I feared she might. What would I have done? So I kept quiet, and kept away. I ached, but what could I do?

I would go back to my father. I'd tell him we could no longer discuss this with my mother, but that I needed his advice. Teresa had continued seeing them, but then she too had stopped. We'd never talked about my parents again, except occasionally when she'd say something about Bra Kgathi. I could only hope that one day something would happen. Although Seabe occasionally visited my parents' home, he was always brief about what happened when he was there. One day, when he was already at university, he asked why Bra Kgathi kept asking him if he would go to *koma*.

"Talk to your mother," I said.

He never spoke about it again.

Chapter 14

ALEXANDRA WAS BURSTING at the seams. There were new houses spreading across what used to be veld; there were golf courses, a cemetery, white, coloured, and Indian areas, industrial areas. It was like a wound in the flesh with the immune system under brutal attack. The wound was deep and septic; it was raw, painful, filled with pus. It had spread beyond all imagining, and its growth seemed unstoppable. There were the old, old houses, a signature of the spirit of the old people struggling to make sense out of senselessness, expressing something harder than diamond, more stubborn than steel, yet pliable as gold; rooted, engraved with the spirit of humanity, confirming that humans were the highest form of life on earth. Borne within all this were both salvation and conflict, the total experience of human emotion, belief and intellect – life residing in an endlessly unfolding story of human expression in all its variations, both outward and inward. There were the tenement houses: row upon row in single file like stationary trains whose windows, open or shut, expressed their inhabitants' moods and temperaments through reflections of light and shadow, the colours of curtains drawn or undrawn, voices, silences and weeping. There was such a multitude of windows and doors that they crowded even the movement of the breeze.

And there were the shacks occupying any and every little nook available, meandering along streets, pavements, the river, the cemetery, around trees, shops, churches, penetrating everything, shutting out the light. There were colours dull and bright, dappled with shadows, made of anything that could be put down, pasted, made to stand, held fast and stopped from flying away. All these shacks were claiming space; shoulder to shoulder; buttock to buttock; throat to throat, proclaiming the presence of human life, flesh and spirit. Spaza shops, shebeens – called taverns now – and various entrepreneurs all screamed relentlessly that there was life here. And not just human life: dogs also roamed the landscape like ants, and there were donkeys, cows, cats and horses. There were also Pajeros and Plymouths, Volkswagens and Valiants. And everywhere adverts, howling at some of the poorest people in the world, cajoling them to hand over every cent they earned for nonsense like cooldrinks, sweets and cosmetics; screaming with bright colours and words, or mixing their sounds with the drums, *mbaqanga*, *marimbas*, *kwaito*, jazz, gospel music, church songs or Afro-American lyrics. In among all this there were trees, grass and flowers, and tarred roads and pavements as narrow as ropes. And there were the taxis: kombis hooting, roaring, hurtling, loaded with people trapped without space to breathe, staring wordlessly through the windows as they moved. All this said there was human life here, very busy human life, moving at times like lightening, at other times as slowly as a painful death.

In the morning a torrent of human life – boys and girls, young men and women, adults and the elderly, all of them black – spilled out of their dwellings to find space and socialise on the paths and in the alleyways. There were all kinds of people about, on errands or just hanging out on the streets, at street corners, climbing in and out of kombis any- and everywhere. In these dwellings it was a chore just to make space, to give way for others to wake up, dress, wash, sleep.

Then the sun or the chill wind and the changing shadows would mark out time, and finally the sun would set, the dark come, and the dogs bark and bark in the echoing silence. The streets would empty and the street lights keep watch, to the lone sound of a speeding car, a siren, a gunshot, a howl. Somewhere in among all this my father and mother held the fort, kept a home for their children, who came and went and came and went. Many of us who came and went didn't really know what else to do.

Molefe and Phumzile were making laws. Many in this country were spending sleepless nights wondering what could be done to methodically eradicate the horrific, inhuman conditions of Alexandra, crammed with poor, landless, underdeveloped African people. Some of our leaders travelled the world, sure that an answer lay somewhere among humanity, sure that somewhere people with power would come to understand this common-sense issue: that a world in which the majority have lost everything could explode. Could people not grasp this? This was the question former freedom fighters were asking within the corridors of power.

Time was moving on; the world kept turning. I said as much to my father. I wasn't explicit, but I hoped he'd got the gist. He was ninety four, an old man. We were sitting on his stoep on a Sunday afternoon. The stoep faced the noisy corner of Vasco da Gama Road and 22nd Avenue, where people, cars, kombis, bicycles, motorcycles, donkeys, cows and dogs all mingled dangerously but mostly survived, except for the odd chicken or dog, or a sometimes a child still learning the rules of that corner. Opposite his house was a shebeen, a recent development, from which music blared. No one complained about it. People coped with the music, one way or another. My father had just come back from church, and was waiting for his wife to come home and dish up. She was in church too. They'd agreed, for some reason, to attend different churches. He never spoke about it, and I didn't ask.

"But this sickness, Aids, where does it come from?" he asked. Before I could answer he asked another question. "Why is it plaguing mostly black people?"

I shrugged. I didn't know.

"And when are you going to give us back our land and property and do away with this crowded hell called Alexandra? Why is our freedom like this?"

"It will happen," I said. "We'll get the land back."

"When?"

"It'll happen," I said again. He looked at me briefly, and looked away.

"Mandela's a good leader, a good leader. But what about Thabo?"

"He's a good leader too," I said.

Here came my mother wearing a hat, walking slowly, taking her time, clutching her Bible. She was in her church uniform: a white blouse and black skirt, stockings and shiny shoes. I always used to tell her that the white people who owned Christianity didn't require white women to wear uniforms to church. At first she used to swear at me, but eventually she'd just glare. She walked up the steps of the stoep, holding onto the pillar as if carrying a heavy load. In reality she carried her handbag, her Bible and her hymn book. My mother. And my father was watching, waiting for her.

"Shoo," she said, "I'm so tired!"

"Shall I get you a chair and some water?" I asked.

"No, I have to feed your father first. I'd better first go and change. If I sit down I won't be able to stand up," she said, breathing heavily. This scene would make the feminists scream, I thought.

"Your mother's very old," my father said. "By this age, in the old days, she'd have depended on her daughters-in-law. But there it is," he said.

I thought not to raise the matter: it would be bad timing. Where would those daughters-in-law stay? It was a pointless thought. It didn't address the question at hand. She passed us, sighing and dragging herself through the doorway. My father and I watched silently.

The extended family had broken down, I thought. It was a myth. Teresa was mad to think it could be brought back by looking at indigenous knowledge, or whatever she called it, that had now made her a *ngaka*. Old people lived alone. Their children were gone; they'd left. Seabe would go too, and Mantwa. Would we still be together then, Teresa and I? The answer to this question seemed out of reach.

The jingling of cutlery rang out, and my father went into the house. When I joined them at the table, he'd taken off his jacket and loosened his tie. He was sitting as his wife dished up for him. He no longer hunted, I thought, he no longer looked after cattle or sheep or goats: he looked after the car. And his wife looked after him as he looked after the car.

"Enough, Kgathi?" she asked, showing him the plate.

"Yes, Mma, it's enough," he said. "This young man is being elusive whenever I ask him about matters of the nation."

"The good thing about him is that he listens," my mother said.

"He does, but then he talks in circles instead of answering me directly," he said.

"Yes, but the nation is faced with different issues now," she said, still on her feet.

"That's true," I said.

"I was asking him when they're going to get our land and property back."

"But, Kgathi, the problem is so huge. We must pray for them, we must pray for Thabo."

"Our ancestors will stand by us," I said.

"Ancestors, ancestors… we never taught you that! Where do you get that from?" she asked.

"He's pondering, searching, that's what he's doing," my father said.

"There's a lot you didn't teach us that we're discovering as we go along," I said.

"Well if you discover wrong things, you're doomed," my mother said. She was dishing dessert for her husband.

"Pray that we not be doomed," I said.

"We could pray forever, but you won't be saved, not if sin is in your blood or in your habits. You have to believe, and to believe means you can't worship images of God, only God," she said.

"I have no quarrel with God," I said.

"Good. Good for you," she said. "You'll be saved."

"God will forgive us if we're wrong, we mean no evil," I said.

"A cow in the mud will die," she said, "if it just lies there saying 'I'm in the mud, help me'. Soon we get discouraged and leave it to die."

They hadn't asked me about Teresa or Seabe. I decided I should go. After we'd moved from the table and I'd given them tea on the sofa, they both began to snore. I sat there watching them. They had each other and nothing else, I thought. I wondered where my brother and my sister were – in a different world with different demands from my parents. And they, the elders, were holding on to what they knew and had lived for.

The old and the new life were both making their demands on us, the generation that had to take over from them. Would they listen, these two, when I spoke to them once they were ancestors, and asked them to look after Teresa and me, and Seabe and Mantwa? I must get to know my parents, I thought. I must know what they can't cope with while they're still living. I must know their strengths. I must use these and find a way to change their weaknesses. I will ask their help in changing their weaknesses, so I learn from them. As ancestors they'll listen to me. They'll know better what I'm talking about from a higher level. What was I really saying?

I needed to wake them up and tell them I was leaving. But they really were tired. Their tiredness was also the weight of their age. My father's snoring was backfiring, as if he were changing gear. My mother was snoring more peacefully...

It was my mother who woke me. I'd dozed off on the sofa, drifting in thought. She was walking like a duck, carrying her weight heavily, her aches making her sound like a choo-choo train. This also woke my father, who looked around, working out where he was. He looked at me as if he'd never seen me before. I saw myself in him then. It wasn't the similarity of features but something else, perhaps his body language: a gesture, a sigh or the way he carried himself.

"Still here?" he asked. "Miracles never cease. What do you want?"

"I need to speak to you," I said.

"Go on. I'm listening," he said.

"I need to speak to you about the *lobola* you need to pay for Teresa," I said. He looked around nervously.

"Where's your mother?"

"She went to the bedroom, I think."

He stood up and vanished into the passage. After a while he came back without his tie, and with his Sunday shirt unbuttoned.

"Let's sit on the stoep," he said, and went to the kitchen. I heard the fridge door open and shut. He returned carrying a litre of beer and a glass, and went straight to the stoep.

My father had done a lot of things on that stoep. He'd sulked, dealt with sadness, talked to his loneliness and tackled his demons and ghosts there. He'd sat on that same chair as long as I'd known him. It was as old as he was; it looked like him. Anyone who joined him had to find another chair. I was always the one he used to call to bring extra chairs if he wasn't going to be alone on the stoep.

After I'd settled opposite him, my back to Da Gama, and he'd poured his beer, he spoke.

"What are you talking about?" His voice was a little harsh, tinged with hostility and mockery.

"I need your advice. I humbly request that we discuss Teresa's *lobola*," I said.

"*Lobola?* You want to *lobola* twice in your young life?" he asked.

I thought about Teresa's "another young woman". How could I dare raise that if he put it this way?

"I'm asking you to advise me," I said.

"You're not answering my question. Do you want to *lobola* again?"

I felt he was putting a noose around my neck. Yes would send me dangling, but no would too.

"I request to discuss all this with you," I said.

"All what?"

"I find it difficult to raise it in any other manner than this," I said. He looked away, and sipped his beer thoughtfully. Then he looked at me.

"I'm happy that you know it's a difficult matter," he said. I looked back at him, stood my ground. He shook his head, shrugged slowly and frowned.

"Where is Teresa's daughter?"

"With her father" I said. "She comes to us on alternate weekends, like Seabe," I said.

"The Bible says future generations will suffer the sins of their forebears," he said. "I never thought I'd live to have to come to terms with this. You've always had a home and parents, without confusion. Your brother and your sister too have always had me and your mother. It helps children, that," he said. I kept my silence. "It must be different for them," he said.

"It is," I said.

"Now where does *lobola* come into all this?"

"I need to pay *lobola*, because then I believe Teresa and I will have tied a knot for our home. Then we can find a way to deal with the children."

"Children must never be a problem to their parents. Why should they?"

"I agree they mustn't be a problem."

"But Seabe and Mantwa are, aren't they? Or am lying?"

"*Lobola* is a step to solve these problems," I said.

"This is not the first time you've come to talk to me about this. I told you to talk to your mother and then to Tolo," he said, "didn't I?"

"You did," I said.

"Have you?"

"I have."

"So what should I do?"

"I had no success talking to my mother about this, so I didn't think I should go to Tolo."

"I see. So what are we going to do, if you haven't done the things I asked you to."

"I have."

"But you yourself said nothing came of it with your mother," he said. He looked around searchingly. He appeared to be listening, perhaps for my mother's footsteps. "I think you must talk to your mother. I will hear from her."

"I have."

"Go back."

"I know nothing will come from going to her; we will fight if I raise it with her again," I said.

"You must not start a battle between your mother and me." He was emphatic, final.

"I ask your help to find a way to handle this with my mother," I said.

"My advice is that you talk to her. Let me tell you something. If you go to your mother's wardrobe, you'll find a brown *muchikisa khiba*. It was given to her by Nomazwi. Are you asking her to remove it?"

"I can't do that."

"You want her to hang Nomazwi's *khiba* and this woman's in the same wardrobe? That is your mother's problem. She feels she will betray Nomazwi if she does that. What are you going to do?"

"I don't know what to do," I said.

"So talk to her."

We were back where we'd started. Because of this discussion with my father I was even more afraid to raise it with my mother. It would be like sealing a coffin. My father sipped his beer and seemed resigned. His role in the matter seemed to be over.

"Maybe I must call mother to talk this over," I tried to insist.

"If you really want to, then do it."

I had no strength, no desire, no will to stand and call my mother. We were quiet for a very long time.

What was I going to do? I couldn't just sit there. You shouldn't have raised the matter, I railed at myself. Look how out of hand it had gotten! What had I expected? Why did I raise it? Why was I so impulsive?. What had I achieved? The voices were screaming, mocking me. What was discussion, negotiation? This one had definitely failed.

I stood up, went into the house, into my parents' bedroom. I told my mother that my father and I wanted to talk to her. She was lying half sleep on the bed.

"Talk to me? What about?"

"Please come…"

"I'm so tired," she said. But she began to get up off the bed.

Chapter 15

I'D RETURNED TO THE movement. I wasn't sure what I meant by that, because I'd never really left it. But I'd also rediscovered my third ear: I was hearing lots about the country and its people. The movement felt different: there were many new comrades. Perhaps that's what I'd gone back to: to a movement that was now called the ruling party. At times it felt as if all South Africans were in the movement. Then something would happen, and I'd know I was wrong: not everyone was in the movement. It only felt that way because now everyone seemed to have always known there was no way South Africa could not be anything other than a nonracial, nonsexist and democratic nation.

But what was democracy? Where in the world did democracy exist? I didn't know of a single truly democratic country. Yet the world was calling on Africa to be democratic, and South Africa was grasping at it. The movement had been unshakable on this matter. Even before apartheid collapsed, the movement had stood firm on this, and alone. Now every party claimed to have stood for nonracialism, nonsexism and democracy. Change was like acid: quiet, subtle, erosive and permanent in its intent. We didn't notice it, but it was there. And with a lot of noise from everywhere about the change and the shifts it was manifesting, all at once what the movement had stood for had become real.

And then suddenly people seemed surprised that the country was this way. They had seemed to ask for change and not understand that it could not reply. The idea of a nonracial South Africa – the land, its wealth, languages and thoughts – had penetrated like the breeze into the empty spaces, where change resides because nature abides no vacuum; discomfort and expectation had taken anchor in the nation's psyche.

The land and the sky seemed silent in their beauty, sparkling according to the different light, shadow and darkness, accepting all because all will always happen, and all will be fine. It knows, we all know that we have to make good with what will be, good in thought and good in action. Light and shade come and go, the sky and landscape change character and mood like chameleons, for they are part and parcel of the changes and challenges that unfold as we spin on our axis. These are all a part of the universe, and as we move at times it seems there is no choice, no option: we must keep on going. Everything has its own momentum. Everything remains present, sharing what it has, never tiring of giving. As the conference in Polokwane approached, it almost felt like a pain, a deep, silent pain was settling in our being – we who called ourselves comrades.

Across the landscape, life plays out its roles. Ngaka once told me that if people could humble themselves before nature, they could humble themselves before each other. It was as we were putting finishing touches to my mission in Villiers. We were sitting on the floor of the rondavel, and he, in his beads and regalia, was in a reflective mood. He and I had buried the guns, and I'd finished making maps for about ten dead letter boxes. We both felt that my time in Villiers was running out. But he had this confidence, he kept saying he didn't foresee any problems. Dikeledi had taken two maps to the bases outside of South Africa; I'd given another two to a reconnaissance unit heading back to the rear, and two more were on the dashboard of the car I'd been using and had handed over to a roving unit. We'd created another dead letter box for the last two maps.

Ngaka and I had crisscrossed the land and felt familiar with it. It was impossible to describe his knowledge and his relationship with the land. But whoever had defined the term intellect had failed to include the likes of Ngaka. He had this air about him. He was so human, though he'd never been treated as such by his country or countrymen because he was black, a *ngaka*, a non-Christian, and was suspected of harnessing extraordinary powers of darkness from unknown depths. People therefore feared him, but also loved and respected him, and didn't know what to do with him. They waited and watched: that's when human beings are at their most dangerous. All of us waited, including some like him who knew us and our ways. However, they went on with what they had to do. Ngaka had this air. I wondered how many like him had been put on slave ships because they were regarded as savages and pagans. I also wondered why, taken away as they were, there'd never been a great uprising.

This passed through my mind many times as Ngaka and I crisscrossed the land in search of hiding places for weapons. As he chose these places, he taught me to dig them, prepare the holes, and return them to the landscape as if they'd never been tampered with; then prepare the place for those who would fetch the weapons. In all this Ngaka insisted that the landscape not be so altered that it couldn't return to its natural state. This experience made me deeply loyal to the movement, which, in its wisdom, had brought me to meet Ngaka.

Ngaka had discovered the relationship between humanity and nature. We were an integral part of the gold, diamonds, platinum, uranium and coal, he said. These minerals treated us as their own; we must treat them as a part of us. He said that the Boers were very human, that their battles for land, shelter, water and food were a human expression. But this could not be done at the expense of other human beings, because that started the spilling of blood, which could become a vicious cycle that lasted forever. "Do you know that Boers are Africans?" he would say out of the blue. He told me about their relationship with the Khoisan. That's why, he said, the Khoi spoke Afrikaans after they forgot their own languages.

Ngaka left me with many thoughts and questions. As I walked, worked, slept or lay awake, Ngaka's presence hovered over me. I felt how he read people, watched how he read situations. Many times I sat with him as he asked the bones about our work, about the country, about people we worked with.

I confess that all this kept me quiet, thoughtful. We had to find out ourselves by fighting apartheid what it was that made people forget that others were human like themselves; what prevented them from realising that their experiences with nature were the same as those of black people, and that we were one because all that we knew was learned from nature. Human beings can sometimes be so deaf and blind. He didn't know what could be done about this, he said. This was what nature in its wisdom had challenged humans to discover and use to improve their lives. It was late at night as we sat there in his rondavel. We had just come back from a mission that turned out to be our last.

⊗

Perhaps I'd become too used to the computer. As I tapped the keys and the screen told me all sorts of things, these past thoughts came flooding back. I was trying to find a place for them in the corridors of HQ, some way that they could penetrate the movement's network, be lived on the streets, paths and highways, and settle in the hearts of those who made up these networks. How was it possible?

A small pink house had been built for Ngaka next to his rondavel, but he'd had to fight for it. I was touched when he told me, and I went back to Villiers to see it. I felt that the new South Africa had given Ngaka a voice, that the land had overcome a deaf and blind spot. But I also wondered if it was only because he was a *ngaka*. Ngaka's house was a simple structure. It was ordinary. Why should any human being have to lay down his life to acquire a simple four-roomed house, which he, in his creativity, then painted pink? He'd created three gardens: a kitchen garden, a flower garden and a medicinal herb garden. He also built a chicken shed, for as a *ngaka* he used lots of chickens. He hoped that one day he'd also have goats, sheep and cattle, which he also used a lot as a *ngaka*.

When I visited the Alexandra cemetery in search of the grave of my grandmother on my mother's side, I observed that great care had also been taken to extend the house of the cemetery keeper, who was now very old. Initially they'd wanted to demolish the old house, he told me. But he'd talked to them, and they'd agreed to find a way to marry the old and the new, and reinforce the old. I hoped my people were finding a way to humble themselves before humaneness, but also to take no nonsense from anyone.

Once the movement had been humane. This was the context of the likes of Ngaka, not as a *ngaka*, but as a man. It had taken lifetimes to build that understanding, and it could not be taken for granted. How had it become a culture? How had it become the norm for this nation to nurture its children and for its children to nurture the nation through their actions? It developed through generation after generation, over many centuries, just like the mountains that hover over the land. This culture evolved through centuries of watching, listening, feeling, hearing and understanding, just like these boulders that stare at us in silence. The language of nature, which became part of the fibre of generations here, had started with a song about the whispering land.

History glides on, as relentless as the stare of the sun and the moon that declare time to the empty sky, moving on regardless towards their infinite destiny. History is the movement of things and of life itself, harnessed by destiny but also shaped by the hands of people. Ngaka also said that promises are the seeds of revolution and rebellion. Although I didn't understand or question him, I quietly concluded that superstition was like mist, but that spirituality remained intact. Science thrived on generalisations. The beginning and end of life had nothing to do with the living. That which must begin and end was dictated by destiny. We were its subjects, life was its promise. That promise was a revolution, a rebellion.

But now, when I thought about the context in which he'd said this, I felt anxiety. The promise of life and existence and the universe was enshrined in the pages of the Bible. I quarrelled with Ngaka about this, because I thought he was becoming Christian. But the Bible, he said, was written by prophets in exile; now they had become ancestors.

Earlier we'd been exploring what the movement could do to make our country livable for all. Once, as we were digging a hole, Ngaka had suddenly stopped me. The little sapling in the soil where I was digging was a rare and important medicinal plant. He took my spade and threw it aside, then asked that we be quiet. He took off all his clothes, knelt on the ground and began to speak to the plant. He told it that many *dingaka* were looking for it. He asked it not to hide, not to punish the human race for having abused it. Humbling himself before it, he asked it to multiply and forever reproduce itself. Then he made a deep, wide circle around it, searched around and returned with a large boulder which he placed next to the plant.

By sunset, still naked, he had placed a ring of thorny branches around the plant. Then he apologised to me, took me by the hand and said we should go. As a *ngaka*, he said, he had taken an oath to look after the plants for the rest of his life. As he spoke, he seemed like a lesson in morality. As MK cadres he and I had taken an oath to defend the Freedom Charter. Was there a connection there, I wondered. Maybe I needed education to be certain, although they didn't teach such things at school. But why not? How could the world become a better place to live in if they didn't teach these lessons in husbandry? There should also be lessons in *ubuntu*. If you could care for a plant as Ngaka did because the plant improved the quality of life for people, we should also care for people. They should teach that development means the development of people, because it is people who develop things. They must teach this.

Ngaka told me it was correct for the movement to entrench nonracialism in South Africa. When he was initiated as a *ngaka* he was told to heal all people, including his enemies and those who disliked him; he was to discriminate against no one. The plants were us, in that they depended on us: on our thoughts and our hands and how we used them. They were food, they were medicine, they were poison. It is strange how people who are educated forget this. Ngaka and I talked a lot about this in his rondavel. Within a few days of my arrival in Villiers, Ngaka had already taught me that no day would pass without us entering this rondavel, his *ndumba*. His *ndumba* exposed me to a future that was as far away as a star glittering in the sky. Ngaka and I would talk and talk whenever we could slip away from Dikeledi and Mma Lerato. It was all so long ago now, it seemed like ancient history, a far and inaccessible time and reality, stored in the memory of the universe, promising one day to come out into the open.

❧

The underground of a movement is a network of spirits. You were invisible when you went underground, yet you had to be highly visible. You had to hide your intentions from treachery, from evil, but ensure that these intentions got transformed into reality, a reality that spoke out, walked and visibly penetrated every and anything to become the spirit of the masses, enmeshed in their hearts, hopes and needs, reflecting their interests.

Ngaka's major concern in those days, which I held onto with my life, was that we'd one day achieve peace, that it would emerge from the freedom we were fighting for, and that this freedom would be what we wanted it to be. We had to talk like that and it would be like that. He had a lot to say about how to make peace out of war. He would describe this negotiation between the two sides in English, Sesotho, isiZulu and at times in Afrikaans too. His favourite phrase in isiZulu was *u kugeza' imikhonto*. I had never imagined that people could actually go and wash their spears together in a river at the end of a war with each other. They would exchange the spears they'd used against each other, and then wash them: wash off the blood, the deaths, and let these be swept away by the flow of the river. It was this that helped adversaries to negotiate, in those days of *loowe* when they would enter into negotiations.

During the negotiations that led to the establishment of a new South Africa, there were difficult and spirited discussions in the movement once Mandela, later known as Madiba, announced the suspension of armed operations. It was a mental and spiritual struggle to accommodate the drastic changes happening at that time. When dilemmas took centre stage, Ngaka often ruled my mind. When I looked at Madiba's face in those days, on TV, at rallies and occasionally in the corridor at HQ, even as he smiled and waved to people,

I sensed a sternness, a firmness in him. It was before he introduced the Madiba shuffle. Later, when I was working at the pension desk at HQ, I battled another reality. I was surrounded by the faces of new comrades, and kept cancelling files of the elder comrades of Madiba's generation, who were passing on. Tambo had already passed, and at times I became afraid. You couldn't be at ease when fundamental change was happening before your eyes. It was like someone saying they'd become used to death. Death is drastic. It leaves an empty space that is undefined in place of the person who filled it. There's nothing anyone can do about it. And somewhere inside us we know that the empty space is permanent.

Change has too many unknowns. It manifested even in the new, enthusiastic comrades who strode the corridors of HQ. Maybe at times Madiba too, when he smiled and called out greetings to us in his warm voice, asked himself, who are these people? He called us by our first names, although I don't know how he came to know them – especially mine, as in those days I was mostly with Bra Shope.

When Madiba walked into Parliament for the first time, the Parliament of the Republic of South Africa, he broke away from the entourage and went over to the opposition leaders. As he was embracing them, I thought of Ngaka. Bra Shope and I were watching it unfold on TV. "May hope settle in our hearts," Bra Shope said.

I was later to tell him about Ngaka. In a sense, Bra Shope represented Ngaka's generation to me. But Ngaka spent his life far from white people, while Bra Shope interacted with whites on a daily basis. Ngaka once told me that there were white farmers who occasionally consulted him. He said there would be more in the future, which was why the movement's nonracialism was correct. The new generation of *dingaka* would have to track down white ancestors who had black heritage. Nonracialism, he said, was the washing of the spears. There would be white *dingaka*. He had seen them in his spiritual eye at times, in banks, in garages, in cars reading newspapers; he'd seen them everywhere, even if they were refusing the call. I thought about this a lot. I'd never thought about them before.

I'd seen many *dingaka* in Alexandra, and even attended their ceremonies as a child. All I remembered was that as children, we received sweets and cooldrinks during those ceremonies, while the old people ate and drank African beer. The *dingaka* played drums, sang, chanted and danced. My mother, a Mokgatla woman, wasn't always sure that I should attend those ceremonies, but my father somehow managed to get her to allow me.

"If they're playing and by chance these ceremonies happen, why shouldn't they watch? Let them watch, leave them." He'd shrug as if it were no big deal, but at the same time be nice to the old lady.

I'd never understood this two-faced quality in my father, but since I'd grown up I knew, I understood what was going on. Besides, most of my childhood friends, now fathers and husbands, knew that if you understood the art of the tongue, you also knew the art of action.

Now as I thought of my childhood friends, I realised I didn't know where they were. It was as if, while we were in exile during the struggle, something had gobbled them up. They were nowhere to be seen. Only Molefe and maybe one or two others from that time were still here. I couldn't imagine how I would get into contact with the rest of them again. The earth was so vast.

I didn't know how many people were members of the movement before and after Madiba. In spirit there were hundreds. But the movement didn't live by spirit alone, it lived also by participation. That was why it was a movement: it moved. Participation was totally engaging. It took us, once more, all over the country. Yet I had hardly met any of my childhood friends through this travelling across the landscape.

The movement seemed to live in townships and villages, and occasionally in boardrooms. But no, this wasn't true, the movement kept expanding into everything. I often found myself in former apartheid offices, talking about pensions with former apartheid officials. I wished at times that these officials would relax and begin to reveal what they were really thinking. I remained a terrorist in their minds, and we would be discussing how to rescue the lives of other terrorists, dead or living. I tried now and then to steer the discussion to the fact that we were all just human beings, but it was difficult for them, and at times for me, to continue. So, because we had a job to do, what else could we do? We shuffled papers, called out numbers and names, wrote reports, filled in forms. These were our instruments, along with computers and phones, desks and chairs.

Why did my mind note these things? Maybe this was what they'd called "involuntary action" in primary school science. Why was there involuntary action in a thinking body? And how did this link to politics? The movement had taught me not only to be a soldier, but also to think politically. Ngaka, I now realised, had been trying to make me link political thinking with spiritual thinking. But Marx had said that spirituality was whisky, or something similar. These things were very complex, but so was life. I had a feeling there was a lot I didn't know about life, about people, about their make-up. Maybe when spiritual and political life struggled and produced difficult and complex issues, life was further developed. I thought so. But then spiritual life addressed the matters of heaven or where the ancestors dwelt. It dealt with heavenly matters because heaven was spirituality. The earth, being of heaven, was also encompassed by heavenly matters, like us, and like spirituality. Was this what was called a continuum?

I didn't know how it had come about, but now I was on good terms with my parents once more, and full time with the movement again.

I was using both the camera and the computer. Perhaps it was time to think about a movie camera. How could I begin to search at my age? I thought it had to do with what was happening in the country, which was really about what was happening to people and their lives. There was something grim about dealing with pensions on a full-time basis. But I didn't want to become a professional soldier or a professional politician either. I wanted to live, to feel alive, to know – and do what? For there was the business of making a living, of paying for the house, the food and the children's upbringing. Maybe life was about this search, right until the end. And then you became an ancestor and dealt with the lives of those who were still living.

But I had jumped a lot of steps to arrive at being an ancestor! What was it that I was trying to feel the pulse of? My country? It had gone through major upheavals, unprecedented upheavals, it would seem.

The problem was that we who were involved might not realise this. A Ghanaian lady Bra Shope had introduced me to – one of many from different African countries now in South Africa – argued vehemently when I tried to understand our country's role in the African Renaissance. A Senegalese musician told Nkwame that Senghor had initiated the concept of the African Renaissance, and a Nigerian acquaintance mentioned a Nigerian leader who'd spoken of it in the fifties. We were at one of the embassies where all-African cuisine was on display.

I left the party thinking that it was good that Africans were now in dialogue with Africa as their platform. This was good for South Africa. South Africans, black and white, had a warped understanding of Africa. The Afrikaners of Africa were underground now. It was a network of spirits in dialogue within an illegal context. It behaved like a ghost: now you thought you saw it, then you didn't. It lived in the telephone wires, and outside of that insulation it wailed like the breeze.

But political liberation was not enough; there was more to life than that. So now a new struggle had begun. I wasn't sure if Ngaka was correct when he fought for a rondavel and accepted a small four-roomed house. What if we'd planned rondavels for the poor, instead of the little pink, green and yellow houses that spread across the land? Why had Africans created the rondavel? Rondavels had spread the length and breadth of Africa, they were African architecture. South Africa was part of the wider world now; hopefully it wouldn't learn the bad habits of that environment. It was things like this that made the masses who'd fought for freedom long for the past. This was also partly because change is demanding, difficult and painful. That's why at times the masses revolt against freedom. We see this in Africa all the time. Once when we said "the people", it was almost like saying God. But who are the people?

The thought was frightening. How could people be amorphous? Maybe then, the people were a spirit. If they were, then Marx had missed a very important fact. The spirit of a people cannot be whisky or opium. Religion was the opium of the people, it was true. But who or what were the people? I questioned this because now, after liberation, it was difficult to know who was part of the movement and who was not. Yet everyone made demands on it.

There were some South Africans doing everything to make South Africa work. Other voices were also occasionally heard, like some young Afrikaners who said that they didn't want the country of the past, but did want the country of the future. What made them say that? Did they want the same thing we did? I wondered because I had something to defend: something I'd fought for. If you're a fighter you have a suspicious streak that pops out now and then. It shows up and says, as the African Americans say: what's this, man The Afrikaners had also been fighters. They fought the Amazulu, the Batswana, the Basotho, the Khoi, the San and the British. In name they'd fought for freedom, but in essence they were fighting to become South Africans. But they sought their freedom through dehumanising blacks: that's where this white tribe had missed the point.

It was late in the day when the black tribes – the Batswana, Bapedi, Basotho, Amazulu, Amaswati, Amaxhosa, Vhavenda, Bashangana and Amandebele – discovered the idea of unity. By then they'd been defeated and the land all taken. They too had missed the point, and the stage was set. A bloody stage had been set for all South Africans.

Other voices said they were defending freedom on behalf of black people. What did that mean? I wouldn't want anyone speaking on my behalf. I wanted to be informed. I needed to be informed. Ngaka was correct. Religion should talk to *bongaka*. But I wanted to extend this. Initiation should talk to education; traditional leaders should talk to members of parliament; indigenous knowledge should talk to science; Sesotho to Afrikaans; African languages to English; extended family to the single-unit family; customary law to judicial law. All these and more needed to talk. And they had to talk now. That was what we'd meant when we fought for freedom.

In the song *Lolita*, Selaelo Selota sings "Why don't you learn these things from the sun?" I think he means that the sun talks to all of us daily; even to the moon; perhaps even the stars. In a sense, we have only each other to talk to, on earth and even afterwards. Archbishop Tutu in his robes should talk to Ngaka in his regalia. What would they say to each other? Come and see my cathedral; come and see my rondavel. That's a crossover, an *mpande*, for we speak to Jesus in the church, and to the ancestors in the *ndumba*. I hoped the archbishop wouldn't then ask, "What are ancestors?" I hoped he'd just listen. Ngaka could then sometimes ask the ancestors to talk to Jesus or God, as Tutu could ask the saints and angels to talk to God.

I hoped Ngaka wouldn't ask, "Who are the angels and saints?" Tutu would say that they were holy people. Nor should Ngaka then question whether they were African or European, because it was he who'd said that the ancestors are both black and white. The difficult thing for them to discuss would be where it all began. For Ngaka the beginning was the rock, followed by fire, then water, and then an explosion. The water ran away to become clouds and oceans and rivers. The fire became lightning, electricity, the sun, moon and stars. The rock became the earth and its landscapes. There was germination and vegetation, and there were reptiles, ants and other small animals.

The human race came out of the reeds near the rivers and wetlands. Then the relationship of the diviner and the creator towards all creation – that of wisdom and great love – was bestowed upon humans. They were to be merciful and to procreate along with the ants, reptiles, mammals and all living things. The chameleon then came to announce the phenomenon of death: all life of the flesh would also perish, and after death had come, those in the flesh would sometimes see and speak with those of the spirit who were no more, through dreams, visions and intuition. Tutu and Ngaka knew all this. There were thus the departed spirits to whom the church spoke annually, and there were the ancestors to whom indigenous knowledge spoke daily.

Then there would be a consolidated body of knowledge that could give the human race great silence and allow the living to be in contact with the powerful force linking the spirit with the creator's love. Let the human race be at peace with itself. Invisible routes were opening: highways for the human race to walk, with or without knowledge of nonracism, equality or power sharing. We must not be afraid to state this fact. Wherever people have gone they have started new things. When Tutu and Ngaka talked they should say calmly that this was a difference, that was a similarity; and the other was as yet undecided.

The purpose of this discussion would be to enable Africans to discuss religion and *bongaka* without fighting, to learn from each other, and to find ways to use this newfound knowledge to improve the quality of life. If they did this, their followers would begin to do so too. They had to learn from Madiba and Mtwana. As an MK cadre I knew many comrades who'd fought in Natal – Madiba's men fighting Mtwana's men, resulting in bloodshed and death. But Madiba and Mtwana began to talk: what were they fighting for? What were Africans fighting for? Why were Africans fighting Africans? Why should they fight now when they had lives to protect, a country to build and a future to look forward to?

Madiba also talked with De Klerk. One night, however, Madiba lost his cool on TV and talked harshly to De Klerk. Since then, De Klerk had written a book that we as South Africans should all read. The point was that in those days there was a lot of talking, and nobody thought it was a waste of time, until the massacre of Boipatong and the death of Hani. Then the movement said there could be talk but that the election date had to be set – for April 27th, 1994. But that was only possible because it had been preceded by talks, so that both sides knew each other, and mistrust had receded.

It was like an African-style marriage. There was a great deal of talking among the families. Because of *lobola,* meetings and talks took place, because two families were joining, not only on earth but even among the ancestors. There was lots of talking. And then the date would be set and the celebrations and ceremonies begin, the feasts with family and neighbours. But most importantly, a new family would be born with commitment, within the context of the extended family.

But that was long ago. Nomazwi didn't think much of all of this. Yet here I was, humbling myself before my father about this, allowing him to talk to me like I was a little boy. But I knew he had good intentions: I was his son.

"Otsile," my mother said, "listen carefully. I'm a Christian. I cannot allow myself to preside over my son's marriage, then over his divorce, and then his next marriage. Where would it end? Are there no feelings in this? Are we not creating relationships and friendships when we preside over marriage? What do you expect me to do?"

My father kept very quiet. I wasn't sure whether his expression was one of amusement or not. He was listening. My younger brother Matime was also with us. We were in the lounge at my parents' home, sitting on the sofas. My mother was a firebrand, a fighter. Her husband understood her as a woman. We understood her as our mother. Whenever she gave her backside a smack that sent her dress flying and said *"Dit sal die dag wees",* then, my God, there was trouble! Endless trouble. But I didn't want Teresa and myself to be excluded from my family. I had to find a way; it had been going on forever.

I had hinted to Teresa about the matter, always saying to her that she should help me speak to our ancestors, to bring reason to my family about us. She looked me straight in the eye then. I didn't know why it was my role to negotiate all this. But it wouldn't help to complain, I knew.

I had told Matime what Teresa said about a "young woman" for me, and that I couldn't make up my mind about it.

"Why did she say that?" he asked.

"She's going to be very busy, but she doesn't want to lose me, and she doesn't want me running around," I said.

"That's got nothing to do with me," he'd told me. "Don't involve me in it, especially when we talk to Mother and Father. Father won't have a problem, but Mother... Please, Otsile, don't you and Teresa go and complicate matters."

"Divorce is no good," my father said. "It's no good for anyone. You people divorce as if you're responding to a whistle in a soccer game! What's the matter? Why is this?"

"The world is changing..." my brother said.

"So!" my father interrupted. "Now you change partners like they're underpants!"

Before I could protest, my mother, even as she was seated, smacked her bottom, although her dress remained tucked beneath her. "*Dit sal die dag wees*! I won't help you change your underpants!"

"That's not what Matime's saying," I said softly to my father. "Please give him a chance to explain."

"Mma," my father asked politely. "Could we give Matime a chance to say something?"

"The roles of men and women are changing," Matime said. We need your help to cope with this." He sounded rather desperate. I wanted to laugh but dared not.

"Roles? What roles?" my father asked.

My mother was watching like a hawk, as if we might run away. Matime had a special relationship with my mother, while I was my father's son. That was why I'd asked Matime to come. My mother listened to him. My father would sort of listen to him but then check with me. Perhaps he didn't consider Matime enough of a man. He and my mother had fought viciously when Matime had to go to *koma*. Matime hid behind my mother, and my father had to take him by the scruff of his neck and drag him to Sekhukhune. Without saying so, I think my father was asserting his manhood and his culture as a Mopedi. Not surprisingly, it came out whenever his fiery wife became too much of a Mokgatla.

Then he would say, "You're married to a Molepo, remember? We paid *lobola* to the Bakgatla, so they have a place here, but they mustn't stifle the Molepo." As children, we'd know then that the line had been drawn. We'd back off when the leopard and the firebrand took centre stage. My father would walk out then, and my mother would go to the bedroom.

We would then quietly ensure that we did all our chores properly. When rocks fall, as the saying goes, the earth shakes and plants get hurt. Even if they hadn't resolved matters, they'd emerge from the bedroom presenting the impression that all was well. We'd know if it wasn't, because we knew them, but if they gave that impression, we'd pretend all was well. And once, I remember, my mother took us away after one of these stormy episodes.

My father had stayed alone at home for maybe a month then, after my mother smacked her dress. Finally my father sent some elders – our aunts and uncles I think – to fetch us. He never once came to see us. I remembered that, because I really missed him. When I'd said so to my mother, she never said a word. I decided then to keep my longing for my father private. But I was afraid I'd never see him again. My sister didn't seem to mind, but Matime and I talked about it quietly. I felt then that I had to look after Matime. He was little. I think that was when we became friends.

But since I'd returned from exile, my brother had handled me cautiously. There was a look of reserve in his eyes when we talked. He was a medical doctor, and his wife was a manager somewhere. So Matime knew what he was talking about. But my father and mother had no clue about the changing roles of men and women. Matime explained, and my father and mother listened. I was very happy that I had parents who weren't afraid to listen to their own children. The conversation began between Matime and my father, then switched to Matime and my mother.

"Do these women want to be men then?"

"No, they want rights."

"I have rights, but I don't compete with your father. Why do they want to compete?"

"We need to try to negotiate, so that they have power as well as us."

"I also have power," my mother insisted.

My father was smiling.

"I don't know what changes you're talking about," my mother said to Matime. "Nobody is powerless. It's how you use it that matters."

"Perhaps what I said about power isn't entirely correct. What I should say is that women are being liberated by law. And now that this is being expressed in real life, men aren't coping. I'm not saying women always handle matters as they should. For instance, if a woman has a car and a bank account, and she can buy a house and be independent, when she's married, she may ask herself why she needs this man. It's the wrong question, because although these things matter, their relationship should also be based on love, and the question should be, 'Do I still love this man?'"

"Is that why Otsile's divorced?" my mother asked.

"No. I'm just giving an example."

"But why did he divorce?"

They all looked at me.

"I don't know," I said.

"You don't know? What do you mean you don't know?"

"I mean I think I know, but I also don't know."

My mother clapped her hands in despair. "Miracles, ominous miracles! What are we supposed to do and say if the one with the issue doesn't know? So he could come tomorrow and say, 'I don't know why but I must divorce my wife, and I want to marry another one.' And we're supposed to say okay fine, do as you please?"

"No," I interrupted. "All I'm saying is that I didn't want to get divorced. But Nomazwi was clear that she wanted a divorce, and after that I couldn't do anything. I was just a spectator."

She looked at my father, who was listening and wringing his beard. He didn't look at her, nor at me or my brother. I didn't know what he was looking at. There was silence among us.

"Papa, you're quiet," my mother finally said to her husband. He brushed his hand over his white hair, and looked this way and that.

"What can I say?"

"Something. You're his father," she said, laughing.

"That's right, I am his father. I'm listening."

"But where does this divorce stop? I hear all the difficulties, but is divorce the only way?"

"Otsile told me that he didn't divorce Nomazwi. He asked me to help, but I couldn't, because his wife didn't want to hear of it. He's not lying, he told me that. I advised him to talk to Tolo."

"After the divorce, Nomazwi stopped phoning me," my mother said.

"I know," my father said.

"She told me Otsile had changed from when they were in exile," she said. "Money, child, late coming home. My feeling was that they weren't talking to each other."

"Otsile must have done something very wrong. Nomazwi's a well-brought-up woman," my father said.

"I agree," my mother said.

I tried to remember what the problem had been, and my mind reeled. Money, child, late coming home... All true, but was that why we'd divorced? Or because these things had driven us mute? I didn't know. It was complicated. Some of this was already happening between me and Teresa, I thought. What was I supposed to do?

"Whose child is this Teresa?" my mother asked. It was the first time she'd ever asked me this question. I told her. I told them about Nkoko, Nkgono, Teresa's mother and father, and Mantwa.

"Is Teresa the only child from her home?"

"No, she has a younger brother."

"Is he married?"

"No."

"If she's a lawyer, won't she have this power Matime is talking about?" she asked.

I thought I'd better not mention her being a *ngaka*. It would complicate things. I'd tell Tolo, but not them. I could tell my father, but not in this context.

"She will," Matime said.

"And then?" my mother asked.

My parents excused themselves and went to their bedroom to discuss the matter. I wondered what they would say. I imagined being a fly on the wall. I could feel that they were backing down.

Chapter 16

HERE I WAS AT MY flat now, and soon I'd managed to get inside. It felt a bit underhand, seedy, to use my skills in this way. My training had been intended to help me liberate the people, not to work against them as I was doing now. I rationalised by telling myself that I answered to myself and no one else.

Where did we, Lindiwe and I, go from here? She had the key to where I slept, and where I used to sleep, and she was entering my life and Teresa's.

The flat was serene. It was spacious because it was half empty. Lindiwe had fitted a large mirror in the bathroom: a floor to ceiling mirror that reflected the whole of me, standing there at the toilet, lifting the lid and relieving myself. Soap, towel, toothbrush, wash rag and packets of pads. Panties drying. A packet of multicoloured cotton wool. Toilet paper on the reel and spare rolls on the shelf. Men's and women's deodorant. Slippers neatly placed on the floormat, tiles fitted on the floor. The bathroom was tidier than a hospital, the latrine hissing. I touched a crimson Cutex toiletries bag, containing lemon-flavoured lip ice, a toothbrush, two types of deodorant, a small toothpaste tube, a brush and a comb. It must be for travelling, I thought.

I went to the bedroom. A queen-sized bed with an African-patterned duvet and matching pillows, small and large. A book on the side table under the bedside lamp, entitled *Racial Economy and Science* by somebody named

Harding. Next to it an envelope that must have been hand delivered: I recognised Teresa's handwriting. Before I settled down to read the contents, I took a quick look in the wardrobe. Neat. A colourful wrap, skirts, blouses, shirts, scarves, jackets – all women's clothes. I noticed a folded paper on the shelf: Lancet Laboratories. She'd taken an HIV test just two days ago. It was negative. I recalled Teresa urging me to test. I moved into the lounge. A piano, a music set, a small television set, calabashes, beautiful handwoven baskets, small and large, a coffee table with lecture notes on the writing pad. A leopard-shaped ashtray carved from stone, and some seashells.

I sat on one of the sofas, and began to read.

Dear Lindi

Love to you. May the ancestors preside over you and what we intend to do. Before I go further, I must say that I am a lucky person; I feel blessed and do not know how to thank you for my blessings. One day I will understand why your father Ongithwasisesilo (is that the correct spelling?) – but you know what I mean. And then I met you. You turned out to be the person I was searching for. We connected immediately, and I told you right away what was inside me. You humbled me the way you listened, the way you seemed totally unsurprised by what I told you about Otsile and me and you. I cannot recall whether you said yes or no. I recall that you said you were studying at Pretoria University, and that we would meet. The rest is history. You encouraged me to go for a test, and to urge Otsile to too. I agreed with you.

I just want to tell you that I love Otsile very much. And I love you very much. The rest I leave in the hands of our ancestors. I feel a great ease. The road is wide open for us to walk. I have never felt so at peace. I look forward to our discussions and I want you to know that I really cherish them. Otsile has begun to use *mpepa*, the smoke of the plant that cleanses and calms. Using it means that Otsile has accepted that *bongaka* is valuable. I am proud of him. I know he thinks a lot, and questions a lot without questioning me. I suspect he has decided to wait and watch. When he does that, he assumes, privately, the role of a guerilla, without showing it. He is a passionate person who strives to be honest. I hope he develops that. It is the only salvation. But I know he is very suspicious, although he hides it. He is searching at present for a way forward. As you and I know, he is a man. You know what I mean by that. I told him he must know that you are a woman and I am a woman. He did not ask what I meant. He just turned his large eyes on me. We will wait for him to ask. I know he will.

This letter is to acknowledge our union and our love, our reality and our striving. What more can I say? I wish I was a writer – I would write you a novel. I do hope that what I mean, if it is not in the words, is between the lines. At times I think I am in a dream. And then I discover that everything is real. And there you are!

Humbly and with love

Teresa

The flat became alive again. The purring fridge, the whistling toilet, the smell of *mpepo*, the sunshine making patterns on the red carpet. I put the letter back where I found it. I locked up and left.

So this was how far Teresa had gone in this matter. I recalled a conversation we'd once had.

"You understand that I'm not being a lawyer now," she'd said.

"Then what are you being?"

"I'm offering us an opportunity for friendship," she'd said.

"Is that so?"

"Yes, and since I'm younger than you, I'm also offering you my youth."

"What do older people have to offer, or have we expired?"

"You wouldn't be here with me if you'd expired. You're a seasoned man, and I relish the opportunity you give me to experience that which has seasoned you." She looked at me then, seeming to consider what she'd just said, and what I was.

"But how does this fit in with what you're saying and where we are now?"

"Don't sell the flat. I won't sell the house. We must decide if we're going to stay in the flat or the house. Keep your bank account and I'll keep mine, and then we can put a certain amount into the common account. Let's find a way so that, where possible, property, money and material things aren't in the equation of our love for each other. Our love should be free of that. Then love can set us free." Our eyes met then. "Otsile, I love you, you know. I really do," she said.

Something happened then, which forever after was to be our way of doing things. Anywhere and everywhere, if there was privacy, we would make love, if we so desired and the urge arose. I undressed her. I was kissing her. She looked at me as if stunned, but she was so silent, her eyes reading me like X-rays. Her bra, which she never wore again, fell off as I unhooked it. Her skirt fell to the floor as I unzipped it. I pulled off her shoes, and slid off her stockings till she was only in her blouse and panties. I lifted her to the arm of the sofa, and then laid her down, pulled her towards me and gently parted her legs. I was already inside her, and she on top of me. She readied herself, positioned herself, and I could feel her strong thighs as she began to squat, holding onto my shoulders. I didn't wait for her to move; I began the movement, and gradually I felt her become wet.

This was the movement of ages. We are born with it in our loins, our thighs and our spirit. It is a movement given us by the creator so we can exercise the power of creativity; but also so that we can embrace the gift of gifts to us from the creator. No one is taught this movement. She closed her eyes. Her nipples were hard now. She was tight around me. I could feel all of her around me. We moved, finding an agreeable rhythm. Slow. Deep. Head at the entrance. Deep. Slow. We found the rhythm. She held onto me, her hands around my neck. She was in total control. I was hard. I was inside her. I had to find the soft, comfortable roundness of the sofa arm. I was getting ready to give all, to give her everything she needed. We exploded together in the lounge that day. It was simultaneous. That day our love for each other was confirmed.

These thoughts were in my mind as I walked down the street from the flat. We had expressed our freedom to each other. That's what she told me days later. I too understood what had happened, though I hadn't been able to express it. Love thrived on freedom.

CR

I went to see Tolo. Sitting under a *morula* tree, I told him everything, including my going to the flat. I was intensely aware of the patched earth, the scorched landscape, the cattle, goats, sheep and chickens, the men, women and children going about. The sun was hellishly hot, and we were sweating as if in a downpour. There was no breeze. The sun seemed to stand still. Tolo was smoking his pipe, puffing and puffing. I could see he was listening intently. He kept looking at me when I wasn't looking at him. But I was completely at ease.

"And where is your son... Seabe, is it... do you support him... where do you work... what does Teresa do... what does Lindiwe do... where does she stay... does she have children... where are her parents... oh, she's Umndebele? We're related to the Amandebele. One of our generals long ago went to fight there, and brought back women and children. That's why there are two types of isiNdebele, one with a sePedi base, and the other with more isiZulu. They were great fighters, the Amandebele, fierce. Have you met Lindiwe's people... how did Teresa meet them... so she's a lawyer and a *ngaka*... what's her last name? There's a relationship between us and the Batswana. Did I tell you about Lepane... by the way, were you in MK? I hope Lepane will look very kindly on you..."

My uncle Tolo was faraway now. I waited for him to come back. I'd watched him absorb my answers to his string of questions, giving immediate answers and analysis. Other questions still ran through my mind. He'd grown thinner and older. His blue shirt had been washed a million times. His trousers, which were supposed to be dry-cleaned, had also been washed with soap and water millions of times, dried in the scorching sun and ironed and ironed and ironed. But my uncle was neat in his clothes. They gave him an elegance, a dignity that stuck to him like superglue. But poverty also hovered there, defining his life and the life of the people here. In that sense my uncle had succumbed to the whims of a humiliating life under a cruel system. In other ways, against the greatest odds, he'd held the faith. He'd held on to the faith of the Bagaga, Bakwana, Baetane, Batswana, Bapedi – the faith of the Africans – and survived. I was evidence of this faith. The fact that I still hopefully had a life to lead in South Africa, that I'd been raised rooted in my traditions, and had served in MK and fought for my people and my country, meant that the faith of my uncle's generation had held. We'd fought, and now we were living in what was called the new South Africa. We'd been victorious. We were now Africans.

Something in the way he sat – leaning forward on a chair he himself had made out of wood and hide and sinew from the leather of his cattle, all from the soil of this land – something in his old face told me that nothing could ever shake his faith. Only death could remove it from his eyes. I tried to search out what it was saying to me. But my uncle Tolo just sat there on his chair, puffing his pipe and pondering.

"Where will all these children and you stay... in town... where in town... is that so? Those were white areas. When your father and I first went to Jo'burg we stayed in Greenside. We had friends in Rosebank, Killarney, Yeoville and Observatory. In those days white people behaved like they'd gone mad. They used to put a needle and thread through our trouser pockets so we couldn't put our hands in our pockets – because if we did, we'd think we were white people. We never sat in the front seat in a *bakkie* or a car. On a *bakkie,* whether sunshine or rain, we stuck it out on the back while the silly white man would be alone in the front. In a car, they packed us in the boot with the tools and all, and then closed the boot. When we arrived we'd be wet with sweat. Anyway, where were we? Oh yes..."

He was half smiling, but still looking far away, a frown on his forehead. "Members of parliament have been here to the royal kraal many times. They call it custom and tradition, customary law meetings. But then, as the white people say, what's in a name?" He laughed. "You see, I know some English sayings, but I'm better in Afrikaans. You know, I don't know where the English learned this, but if you're not careful, you never know what they're saying. You hear their words, you understand the words; but because of the way they're said, the meaning eludes you. The Afrikaners believed in *skop, skiet en donner, ba tella*. But the truth is, neither had any regard for Africans. They didn't think we were human... I'm sorry, I keep deviating. Bear with me. Do you want more tea? You don't drink *bojalwa*? And do you smoke? Okay. I hope you don't mind, I'm trying to understand things. You know, you and I live in different times. I was saying that members of parliament come to the royal kraal often. I like it when they come. I get a sense of what our country's up to. I ask them lots of questions. Why aren't you in Parliament? I see. Well, as the Afrikaners say, *'n boer maak 'n plan*."

He was shaking his head. "I say *'n man maak 'n plan*. Why *'n boer maak 'n plan*? Do they want to give the impression that the Boers are the only ones who can make a plan? Forgive me. I hope you understand that I'm very happy you're here. In sePedi we say *tlogo ntsho e ruta tlogo tshweu*. That's how ancestors begin to live with the living – while they're still alive."

He chuckled. "No, seriously, what do you think about all this you've told me? I'll tell you something: none of it's new to me. But I'm trying to see if you understand that you live in new times from me. You can't say *botata* did this and so I'll also do it. We had a plan. Do you? I'm being unfair. I'm sure you've come here with a plan. I'm sure you're here to test your plan on me. What does your father say about this... what does your mother say... and your brother and sister... have you talked to your mother's brother about this matter?"

He laughed again. "Your mother's a lion. Your father, since I've known him, has been afraid of nothing. When he was proposing to your mother, I became aware of her lion streak. I asked him, will you manage? And his answer was *phokoj ego tshela e ditshetsana*! You know, your father was a rogue when he was young – I mean it in a very pleasant sense. No one could come between us. It was only your mother who did. She had to. She's a woman. And you know, love... love is terribly unpredictable. You must know that.

You're a man, that's what brought you here. You've travelled all across this land, coming here to the back of the moon because you're on heat with love." He laughed again.

The tea came. He was thoughtful as he poured the milk and stirred the sugar. Then he cleaned his pipe, peering through its nozzle, blowing it, pushing a feather into it, scraping it, and then filling it. Then he took his time lighting it for the umpteenth time, and began to puff again. He puffed and puffed, blowing clouds of smoke into the air. His tongue was tar black, his teeth crusted. He puffed and puffed. And he giggled.

"My view, my view is that – and I say this having listened to you only once, but carefully – my view is that you need to take this path carefully." He paused, watching me, his pipe in one hand and a cup of tea in the other, sighing heavily.

"I want us to think more about this," Tolo said. "Do you understand what I'm saying? It's very good that your father said you should come so you and I can talk and think this through." He thought a bit. "But you say he doesn't know about Lindiwe... Matime knows... your mother doesn't know... and your sister?" He laughed. "Oh, so this we keep between our cheeks... it's the shit that doesn't get shat... hmm... I agree, I agree... you're right, but *when* it gets shat is very important!" We laughed.

He looked at me. "You're holding fire in your bare hands, heh? When you have time, when you can make it, I want to see Teresa. You know, and I know you know, I can't plan too far into the future. It's a long way I've come; I'm very near to where I'm going." He looked away.

Then he looked me straight in the eye. "I want to meet Lindiwe, you hear me?" He laughed. There's a laugh among men that only men laugh. And there's a laugh among women that only women laugh. It's when they talk about the other sex. Just as each knows the laugh, what causes it remains a mystery to the other. We looked away, avoided each other's eyes.

"We can't take this matter further between us alone. How do you want me to handle it now... no, no, that's not a problem... Kgathi is not a problem... you're right, he will, he has to." He chuckled. "Mma Otsile, what a woman. But you see, she's the only woman who can handle your father!" He laughed again.

"Tell your father that I've met with Malome in Mafikeng." He was rubbing his hands now, pipe in mouth. "He took me to Lepane's grave. My view is that the old man must be left to rest there. There's been a lot of talk here, *ga* Kgoshi Sekhukhune, that we must fetch his remains. I don't think we should. For now I'm in the minority. But I support my view by saying that he's not among strangers where he's lying now. Lepane is directly related to Tau. He's not among strangers at all. We must talk about how to look after Lepane's grave: us and them. If we can come together on that, our people will agree. We are one. Please tell your father this. Tell him also that you and I have talked. Tell him I said he must come and see me. I'm not a young man. I'm old. He mustn't take his time in coming. Do you hear me?"

I asked if I could take a picture of him. If it was for Seabe, Teresa, Mantwa and Lindiwe, he said, it was okay.

"Why not for me?" I asked.

He laughed. "Did I exclude you? Oh, but you'll have it anyway. What do you actually do with these photos? Last time you were here you took lots, even of sheep and cattle and chickens and stones. What for?"

"As a record for future generations. Portraits of us as a people, for posterity."

I realised as I took his picture, that my uncle was very, very old. Only he and these rocks knew his age. They didn't measure age in years. They measured it in terms of the tragedies and events they'd experienced: the plagues, the wars, the droughts.

I'd touched the poverty of his life and his family; his many wives and his many children, and the poverty of this, the community from whence I came. I'd touched their sorrow, their absolute humiliation. I knew their courage, which wasn't and never could be mine. I guessed at their pain. I knew the movement was doing everything against formidable odds and vitriolic opposition, against all expectations, racing, racing, racing to do something about this abject human condition that the world knows didn't happen on its own, and certainly, I hoped, couldn't have fallen from heaven. It had come from hell, but wasn't hell supposed to be after death? Why all this? Who could repair Tolo's life, and how? I had to find a way.

"You know, Uncle Tolo," I said, "I love you dearly. I've been through so many thoughts and feelings since I've been here. And I have many questions. But I have few answers."

BOOK THREE

BOOK THREE

After the end
When we have to begin again
Our footsteps go backwards
They must
To the long-gone past.

Chapter 17

I'D RECEIVED AN e-mail from Dimakatso. Musa had died in a car accident. And she and Sarah were coming to South Africa. Dimakatso has been invited by a South African dance group, and Sarah was coming to find out about indigenous knowledge, and whether her university could twin with one here. She'd been e-mailing the University of Transkei. Dimakatso and Sarah also wanted to visit Bra Shope's grave.

Sarah, Dimakatso and I were just emerging from a cave, Dimakatso in front of me and Sarah behind. We'd been on the road through the Eastern Cape for what seemed like months. This was the last leg of our journey. Soon we'd meet up with Teresa and Lindiwe. I had the same feeling of deep sadness as when we'd left Bra Shope's grave. Sarah and Dimakatso had wept then, uncontrollably. Many times when I'd visited Bra Shope's grave – alone, or with Teresa or Seabe and Mantwa, or Lindiwe, or all together – I'd left laughing, because I'd felt that wherever Bra Shope was, he was laughing at our sad faces. He had lived his life, I felt, and that was why he'd suddenly let it go.

But when I visited his grave with Sarah and Dimakatso, their pain was too deep. They left me with a deep sense of loss. Maybe they were also crying for themselves. And perhaps also for Musa. And maybe for the severed link that Bra Shope had made for them, a link with a past they didn't know or understand. Or for a future, which, while pregnant with promise, was also packed with unknowns. For Bra Shope's death was a confirmation of the unknown: of unknown ghosts, and of unknowns in their own lives about which I could only guess. Sarah, I felt, knew other things that we would never know, things that were very private, from a time that had been silenced by sheer, naked cruelty, which even the gods seemed to have had a hand in.

The cave from which we were now emerging was in the Drakensberg. We had just experienced a journey through its rock paintings. It was said that this site had been protected for centuries by a huge boulder that had fallen, but miraculously hadn't harmed the paintings. By falling it had actually created a shelter for them, shading them from the sun, wind and rain, and from being roughed up, both by animals that might have leaned or scratched against them when brushing past, and from humans who might not have recognised their significance if they'd found them earlier.

We walked silently in single file, and then stopped. We said nothing; we couldn't after seeing those paintings. We were from the same generation, each from farflung places on distant continents, and each still carrying the terrors of our history and the brutality of fate and destiny. Our silence was the voice of our apprehension.

I also sensed, as we walked on again, that we didn't know each other, yet were on a serious journey together. There were too many unknowns among us. But we'd come this far, and in another sense we really did know each other. As we walked there among these paintings – these delicate paintings on that rough rocky surface – our shared history was a culture of sharp and protracted confrontation that now bound us together. It was asking us if, given everything, we had yet learned how to be human. Asking if, from all we'd seen, heard and experienced beneath the blue sky, we realised that these were actually opportunities given to us by destiny, generation after generation, to help us to find our humanity, to extract dreams from our nightmares, so that we could forge a common dream together.

We could still have turned back. And yet there was no way to turn back. We had to make our journey. Sometimes it's like that. You see the options, yet you're pulled by things you don't know or understand, and you respond to the pull. You understand then that there are no coincidences. Like eventual death or constant change, opportunity is inherent in the universe. In a sense, the three of us were bound by Bra Shope. Whatever we could claim, we were destined always to refer to Bra Shope. Why? I stopped and looked at them then.

Sarah, a yellow top over her long black dress, took a step past me, without looking at me, her hair glittering in the sun, flowing almost to below her behind. Dimakatso, stepping lightly in flat black sandals and a long, white pleated skirt, was wiping her eyes with a snow-white handkerchief, avoiding eye contact. The sun shone overhead in a clear sky. The heat was gentle with a thin, light breeze. We walked on, carefully and silently in single file, with Dimakatso ahead and me now behind them both, going down the mountain slope. I felt Bra Shope as a fourth being among us.

Then Sarah spoke. "Bra Shope wants us to be here together. I wonder why."

Dimakatso looked back at Sarah, neither questioning nor acknowledging what she'd said, but searching for the answer. Then she looked at me. There was a long pause. Then we walked on.

I understood these rock paintings that had been here for thousands of years. Perhaps they'd been read correctly or incorrectly; perhaps they hadn't been read at all. Things in this part of the world have always been interpreted by foreign languages and cultures, unwashed by the rains of the indigenous sky; cultures burnt under the sun of a different sky; not baked in these landscapes, nor formed by the winds of this land; cultures whose history not only contradicted ours, but was hostile and violent towards it.

"All things await us," they whispered. We must learn how to listen.

The sun had dropped lower in the sky. It would return for the umpteenth time, after the moon and the stars, to light up the cave once more. The distance and the vastness of the sun, the breadth of the blue sky, the expanse of the breeze, the valleys and mountains went on and on, dotted with boulders and embraced by the friendly, sprawling greenness. There was a silence here; a silence so profound, so alive, so infinite, unbroken for over thousands of years! What did this silence say, what had it seen? In the presence of all this, the spirit and being of my ancestors – expressed through the delicacy of these paintings, as fragile as life itself – made me feel so minute, witness to the ages and the things they had known.

The figures in the rock paintings were stark and neat, these people three thousand years ago on the journey of life, doing their daily chores just like us, just as bewildered by the possibilities of the human mind. Yet the Bushmen, all those centuries ago, had rejected the idea of homogeneity with the words *!ke e: /xarra //ke*: unity in diversity. They were admonishing the coming of the global village.

Who had these Bushmen been? And what did the word Bushmen mean? Who coined this name, and why? A decision had been taken to decimate them. But Sarah knew, Dimakatso knew and I knew that they were there in the blood in our veins, flowing forever. They lived in us. They had taken sanctuary in the flesh, blood and spirit of the human race.

Women know the pain of giving birth. Afterwards, they are able to bear all kinds of pain and still walk and work in silence. All those who are no longer white know this too. I had always wondered how a human skin could be white. I'd seen blue-black skin: Dimakatso wore it. But white, what was white skin? What did it mean to have a white skin?

We walked away. I didn't know what Dimakatso and Sarah were thinking and feeling. For days we never talked about this experience, only about cars, food, petrol, time, and about who was going where when. But something had changed among us. And when Teresa asked us all into her rondavel to speak to the ancestors, Dimakatso and Sarah wept and wept, Sarah shaking like a tree in a violent storm.

Bushmen? I kept thinking, picturing the rock paintings again and again. And as we entered Teresa's *ndumba* the paintings seemed to be praying, eternally praying through the stark figures, the colours and movement on the rough rock, forever dancing, forever playful.

I still thought all these things, and believed them. So be it. Even the elongated shadows of the images on the rocks, which fell behind or in front of those figures, seemed watchful as they carried the tools of life on their backs, in their hands, on their heads; as they danced in silence in the breeze that was now a part of us too. In the *ndumba* Teresa's urgent voice was interceding with the ancestors. I looked searchingly at Sarah and Dimakatso, whose deep pain was pouring out uncontrollably through their tears, and their endless sobbing made me wonder.

Lindiwe was kneeling between them. Her quietness was contagious. She kept the rhythm, kept pace with Teresa's voice through a rhythmic clapping of the hands, almost urging Teresa on. Sarah and Dimakatso were also clapping in rhythm with her.

I focused. I clicked. "What now, my brother?" I asked Bra Shope.

And all was quiet. Except for Teresa's voice and the

sound of their clapping hands…

"Now, as a people, we are preparing for Polokwane. Oh ancestors, let this name not be a prophecy. Luthuli, Tambo, Sisulu, Kotane, Mabhida, Sobukwe, Biko…" Teresa paused, "… counsel our leaders, give them wisdom, save our country."

Mongane Wally Serote, Durban, July 2010